The delicious sensation of Guy's kiss lasted perhaps half an hour for Cressida.

It was replaced with the sinking realization that she had been very foolish indeed. It would have taken only the simplest of gestures to turn away his lips, but now she had added the knowledge of what it was like to be kissed by Guy Thurlow to her existing attraction of him. Worse, she had shown herself to be more than willing to succumb to his embraces.

And what can he conclude from that? she thought with an internal squirm of embarrassment. *That you are willing to be his mistress? Or simply that you are a fast young woman eager to do more than simply flirt?*

What would Guy do now? Offer her carte blanche to be his mistress or continue to snatch kisses and perhaps expect more?

Neither was possible for her, she knew that. She would no more throw away her reputation than Guy would force her. And besides, there was no knowing whether being even closer to him would trigger some recollection, some hint that made him recognize his runaway bride.

Author Note

Sometimes I know just where an idea for a story comes from—a place, a character, a fleeting what-if thought. But I have to confess, with Cressida and Guy, I have no idea what put them into my head.

All I had was a bride fleeing down the church aisle and a handsome young officer left at the altar, which had me wondering why on earth anyone would run away from him. So I wrote this book in order to find out and discovered two characters I grew to like, and to worry about, a lot.

I hope you enjoy discovering Guy and Cressida's journey to their happy-ever-after as much as I enjoyed writing it.

LOUISE ALLEN

The Earl's
Mysterious Lady

HARLEQUIN
HISTORICAL

HARLEQUIN®
HISTORICAL™

Recycling programs
for this product may
not exist in your area.

ISBN-13: 978-1-335-72329-1

The Earl's Mysterious Lady

Copyright © 2022 by Melanie Hilton

For questions and comments about the quality of this book,
please contact us at CustomerService@Harlequin.com.

Harlequin Enterprises ULC
22 Adelaide St. West, 41st Floor
Toronto, Ontario M5H 4E3, Canada
www.Harlequin.com

Printed in U.S.A.

Louise Allen has been immersing herself in history for as long as she can remember, finding that landscapes and places evoke powerful images of the past. Venice, Burgundy and the Greek islands are favorites. Louise lives on the Norfolk coast and spends her spare time gardening, researching family history or traveling. Please visit Louise's website, www.louiseallenregency.com, her blog, www.janeaustenslondon.com, or find her on Twitter @louiseregency and on Facebook.

Books by Louise Allen

Harlequin Historical

Marrying His Cinderella Countess
The Earl's Practical Marriage
A Lady in Need of an Heir
Convenient Christmas Brides
"The Viscount's Yuletide Betrothal"
Contracted as His Countess
The Duke's Counterfeit Wife
The Earl's Mysterious Lady

Liberated Ladies

Least Likely to Marry a Duke
The Earl's Marriage Bargain
A Marquis in Want of a Wife
The Earl's Reluctant Proposal
A Proposal to Risk Their Friendship

Visit the Author Profile page
at Harlequin.com for more titles.

To AJH, as always.
Thanks for getting me through a
year that's been hard for all of us.

Chapter One

St Margaret's Church, Stowe Easton,
Hampshire—July 1809

The bride was late.

Unmoved, Captain Guy Thurlow, Earl of Easton, continued his study of the memorial plaque to Alderman Thaddeus Wilmslow who had died in 1673, a credit to the town of Stowe Easton and a model of domestic virtue.

Brides were always late, apparently. It was their last opportunity to demonstrate independence before they became wives and he was quite prepared to tolerate this traditional gesture. He intended to be a benevolent husband. After all, how difficult could it be?

The Honourable Miss Viola FitzWalden had been reared to be the wife of an aristocrat. As far as he could tell after three formal and stilted meetings, she appeared to be dutiful and without any irritating idiosyncrasies. It went without saying that she had no vices. She was even tolerably pretty, although at only seventeen years of age she still had to grow into her looks and out of youthful plumpness. An expensive lady's maid would soon deal with the deplorable eyebrows and the unflattering mass of ringlets.

By the time he inherited, she would make an entirely suitable Marchioness of Thornborough. Her late father, the Viscount FitzWalden, might have been a nonentity in public life, but he had a duke for a cousin, as well as relationships to most of the members of the Cabinet. Even better, his daughter came to the marriage with a dowry that included the manor of Bishop's Fulling, land that the ancestors of the Marquess of Thornborough had coveted over many generations.

There was the family black sheep, of course, but Guy had dealt with that, making it clear to his betrothed that her uncle, the *dis*honourable Mr Charles FitzWalden, would never cross any threshold of his. She had agreed without hesitation.

Beside him Captain Arthur Graham, his best man, stirred, the gilt buttons and gold lace on his dress uniform catching the sunlight from the east window as he moved. 'She's here.'

Of course she was. Guy could hear the stir at the back of the church quite clearly, despite the size of the place. The wedding should have been in the chapel at Easton Court, of course, but that, along with the rest of the ancient family estate, was in disrepair. But however much the Marquess preferred the modern conveniences of Thornborough Chase, the family seat built by his own father, he was enough of a traditionalist to want his son and heir married fifty miles away where

Alberic de Turloe, follower of the Conqueror, had received the lands that began the family's rise.

Easton Court had been tidied up sufficiently to hold the wedding breakfast in the great hall, but the chapel roof was decidedly unsafe. The parish church allowed a far larger number of guests to attend, even if it meant that everyone was exposed to the gaze of the local population, who had seen nothing quite as splendid since the day that George II's carriage broke a shaft in the High Street.

The organist broke into something that managed to mingle solemnity with joyfulness and Guy listened until the ripple of sound from the congregation told him that his bride was about halfway down the aisle. Then he turned and found it no hardship to smile.

The gown of primrose silk was fashionable, tasteful and disguised any imperfections in the bride's figure. The drifting veil of ivory gauze was modest, but gave glimpses of dark brown hair, the pale oval of her face, the glimmer of pearls. Blue eyes or grey? He tried to recall.

Voila was supported by her elder brother, Cedric, the Viscount: dull and harmless in Guy's estimation. He delivered his sister to her position at the altar rail and stepped aside so that Viola could hand her bouquet of yellow roses and myrtle to one of her attendants.

Her hands shook, just a little, Guy noted. Bridal nerves, presumably. That was only to be expected from a well-bred virgin. The wedding night was certain to be a little tense, of course, but he had every hope that Viola would prove to be as responsive as any husband could wish for, given time. With good fortune—and suitable application on his part—she might even be with child by the time his month's leave was up and he returned to the Peninsula.

That security for the title would please his father, although Guy had no intention of getting himself killed. He had the Thurlow luck, his colonel said: bullets whistled past his ears, shot ploughed into the ground just where his horse had stood moments before, cavalry lances did no more than rip holes in his sleeve. He, Arthur and their tight-knit group of friends called themselves The Indestructibles and they were having a very good war.

A waft of perfume rose to his nostrils, the scent of the roses mingling with something warmer and more herbal from his bride's skin. He glanced down at her pale hands and felt his body stir pleasurably.

The Vicar cleared his throat. 'Dearly beloved, we are gathered together...'

'...can show any just cause why they may not be lawfully joined together let him now speak, or else hereafter for ever hold his peace.'

He really is the most dreadful old poser, Guy thought as the Vicar scanned the pews, milking the moment for maximum dramatic effect. The congregation obliged by producing a ripple of little gasps and nervous laughter. Guy smiled faintly. They would be appalled if someone actually leapt to their feet with a cry of, 'I am his true wife!' or, 'That woman is not who she seems!'

Silence fell. The Vicar took a deep breath, ready to launch into the rest of the service.

'No,' said a faint voice beside him. Then, louder, 'No! I cannot marry him.'

The bride flung back her veil, sent Guy one desperate look of appeal and fled.

She ran down the aisle, her little kid shoes making hardly any sound on the stones. The congregation rose raggedly to its feet and her brother spun around, calling her name, but Viola FitzWalden did not pause. For one moment she was framed in the west doorway against blue sky and the darkness of the churchyard yew trees, and then she had vanished.

Captain Guy Thurlow, Earl of Easton, was left standing on the altar steps, a jilted bridegroom.

Chapter Two

Stowe Easton, Hampshire—July 6th, 1814

'Looks like they've got a spanking new sign, Colonel. Knew you were coming, did they?'

The town's handsome name-board was resplendent with the Thornborough crest of a raven holding a lightning bolt. Guy, who had reined in the bays just short of it, held the restive pair steady. '*My Lord*, Griggs,' he reminded his former batman, now valet. 'We're not in the army now. And, no, they had no idea I would be passing through the town.'

And neither had he, not until a month ago when his father, more irritable than usual, thanks to the latest batch of dressmakers' bills incurred by his second wife, had announced that it was time his heir set up his own country establishment and stopped cluttering up Thornborough Chase.

Guy, well used to his father after twenty-eight years of uncomfortable experience, did not make the error of pointing out that inhabiting a suite of six rooms in a thirty-bedroom mansion could hardly be called 'cluttering'. Nor did he draw his sire's attention to the fact that since selling out of the army he had spent much of his time in his London chambers in Albany, nor that he owned a Leicestershire hunting lodge, but merely responded, 'Sir?'

'You'll be wanting to marry soon, set up your nursery before you're thirty. I want to see my grandsons before I die.'

As his father was a hale and hearty fifty-eight, it seemed to Guy that he had ample time to gratify this desire. 'John has two sons,' he pointed out mildly.

'If it was not for your brother and his offspring I'd have had you out of the army long before now,' the Marquess grunted. 'Should never have let you join up in the first place. Leading forlorn hopes, getting half-frozen in the Pyrenees, insisting on staying in right up to that damned Corsican's abdication! It's a miracle you survived, let alone in one piece.' He shifted in his big chair. '*The Indestructibles?* Pah. All of them dead or missing parts, even you.'

Guy had folded his right hand over his left, covering the shortened little finger and the start of the long scar that ran up his forearm, a legacy from Badajoz, and told himself not to retort. Five friends dead, Arthur without his left arm—he would not think of it. Instead he said, 'I do not find myself tempted by marriage just now.'

'Still brooding over that business with the Fitz-Walden girl, are you? Bad business that, but no need to fret over it. No blame attached to you.'

'I am well aware of that, sir.'

'Yes, yes.' The Marquess waved an impatient hand. 'Don't get on your high horse with me. I mean that public opinion attached no blame, nor shame. The foolish chit ruined herself and everyone rightly said you were well out of it. What if she'd bolted after the knot was tied, eh?'

'Quite. A fortunate escape indeed. I had intended looking for a bride in the next year or so.' It was the truth. He should start his family before his nephews were old enough to overhear suggestions that their father might eventually inherit.

'In that case you should have no objection to what I propose. You will oblige me by bringing Easton Court back to what it should be. I have had disturbing reports about the state of the Great Hall ceiling.'

Guy had gazed thoughtfully at the mass of plans under his father's right hand: he'd been giving this serious thought, it seemed. 'And the cost, sir?'

'Whatever it takes. It should not be allowed to fall into ruin and my heir must have a suitable country seat. Get the farmland and the tenancies sorted out and it will pay back the investment. Good land, thereabouts.'

Guy might have protested that a good steward could do the work as well as he could, but after almost seven years in the army he was restless. What he wanted, exactly, he was not certain, but he did know that sinking into the indolent life of a man about town was not it.

Restoring Easton Court would be an interesting challenge. But when he had agreed, he had not considered that the nearest town of any size was Stowe Easton, the place where he had last been seen striding out of the parish church without his bride, leaving the wedding guests and half the town to gasp and speculate. They were probably still gossiping about it to that day—there cannot have been a bigger scandal for years.

Guy clicked his tongue at the horses and the curricle moved on smoothly past the sign. A man did not serve under Wellington to be routed by a gaggle of gossiping shopkeepers, or by the actions of a feckless girl.

Beside him Arthur Graham shifted in his seat. 'Five years, almost to the day,' he remarked. 'Place hasn't changed much that I can see. Pretty little town, I thought at the time.'

Arthur had many good points. Tact was not one of them, but then, Guy told himself, his old friend and comrade would make an admirable steward and that was what counted.

The main street wound its way up a slight hill and then around the churchyard that sat on a raised hillock. It gave the impression that it had been there for ever and the town could accommodate itself to it and that might well be true: Guy remembered a tutor of his rhapsodising about the reused Roman tiles and stones in the church tower.

'Handsome building that, My Lord,' Griggs remarked.

Guy grunted, keeping his attention on the horses and the sharp bend ahead where the street levelled out into the market place. Ahead was the Raven's Nest, the chief inn in the town. He was aware that he was focusing on that and carefully ignoring the lychgate to the churchyard.

Coward, he thought. *You can't keep avoiding this. Or the town.*

On an impulse he swung the curricle through into the yard of the inn. 'Get them to check the pair, would you, Arthur? It's another five miles yet and I thought Firefly stumbled on the hill. Have yourself a pint of ale, stretch your legs. I'm going to the church.'

He jumped down, thrust the reins at Griggs and strode out of the yard before Arthur could express an opinion on the improbability of Guy attending church at any time, except on a Sunday.

He entered through the south porch because the great west door was firmly closed, doubtless unlocked only for services. The building was larger than he recalled, made to seem even more so by the clear glass in the windows and a freshly applied coat of whitewash. On his wedding day the old oak of the box pews had been draped in swags of greenery and roses— now there were ranks of gleaming modern bench seats. Their polish scented the air with beeswax, almost overcoming the ecclesiastical smell of damp and dusty prayer books.

His boot heels clicked loudly on the stone slabs of the aisle, unlike those pattering, running footsteps of his fleeing bride. Despite the changes, two great box pews still stood at the very front. The one on the right belonged to Thurlow Court, that on the left to some old local family whose name he could not recall. Clearly the Vicar's refurbishment had stopped short of asking to demolish those.

Guy stopped at the altar steps where two large vases had been filled with evergreens, but no flowers. Possibly a funeral was expected. Then he saw that sacking had been spread out, topped with a bucket, shears and a pile of discarded cuttings, so presumably the arrangement was still in progress. It was, now he looked more carefully, very pleasing already. Instead of the usual lumpen mass of laurel, this was composed of a variety of foliage arranged with an eye for variation and careful shaping. The parish was blessed with a floral artist, it seemed.

But he was not here to admire flower arrangements, but to confront uncomfortable memories. On impulse Guy turned to his right and went through an ornate stone screen into what he guessed was once the Lady Chapel. He would sit for five minutes or so, lay the ghosts of his place to rest once and for all.

It was cool and the light fell in pleasing patterns across old stonework and glittered off well-polished brass. He closed his eyes, felt himself begin to drift. It had been a long drive, following a poor night in an inn with a lumpy mattress in what the landlord swore was the best bedchamber. Worse, he had shared with Arthur, who snored.

The sound of a heavy door closing, the tread of soft footfalls, almost seemed part of a dream at first, but he was not quite asleep. Someone was walking up the aisle and he had no intention of having to make polite conversation with whoever it was. It would be just his luck if it proved to be some local spinster full of enthusiasm for ecclesiastical architecture and ready to pour out information for a good half-hour. Guy opened his eyes, sat up straighter and looked through the battered stonework that encased the tomb of some long-dead cleric.

It was certainly a woman, one carrying a sheaf of flowers in her arms. She walked straight to the altar steps and laid them down, then knelt, vanishing from his sight except for the crown of her fashionable poke bonnet. The flower arranger had returned. How long would it take her to complete her task?

Not long, it seemed. After perhaps five minutes she stood again, stepped back and surveyed her work, looking from one vase to the other, giving Guy a glimpse of her face.

Young, but not a girl. Attractive, but not a beauty, he judged from what he could see of her features beneath the bonnet. An oval, calm countenance; eyes that were blue or grey, slightly tilted; a glimpse of dark brown hair; a full, lush mouth giving colour to her face and sending a jolt of sensual awareness through him. No, not a beauty, but she had a certain something. *Quality.*

The woman gave a decided little nod, as though approving her arrangements, and bent again, gathering together her tools. Then she straightened and turned fully, her movements graceful, allowing him to appreciate a tall, slender figure. Her gaze met his across the cold stone of the tomb and she stopped abruptly, eyes widening, those warm pink lips parting on a gasp of surprise.

'Excuse me, ma'am. I did not wish to startle you.' He stood and bowed slightly.

'No, it is I who should apologise. I have disturbed your private contemplation.' A clear voice, normally confident, he guessed, now slightly husky with nerves.

A gentlewoman might well be disconcerted by an encounter with a complete stranger in such a secluded location.

'I was resting, that was all,' he said. 'And admiring your handsome church. It must be ancient,' he added, hoping to set her at her ease.

She smiled, seeming a little less uncertain now they had both apologised. 'Very old, yes. Well, I have finished the flowers. I must be off. The sexton will clear up for me—' She broke off, conscious perhaps that she was talking too much out of nervousness.

Guy stayed where he was, not wanting to fluster her but, when she descended the steps to the nave, he walked down the side aisle to the porch door, giving her plenty of space, but ready to open it for her should it prove stiff.

That heavy, ancient oak surrendered to her touch, but he caught up with her in the porch as she wrestled with the outer screen door that kept out birds and straying dogs. The metal fastening seemed loose and difficult to manoeuvre.

'Allow me.'

'No, it is all right. One simply needs to know the knack of it.' The lady kept her face averted as she struggled with the latch and, when he put his hand out to try to help, she went as still as a young animal in the wheat when the hawk swoops overhead. 'I can manage, sir,' she said breathlessly, as footsteps crunched on the gravel outside. 'Oh, Vicar! You are just in time to help us with this wretched catch.'

'Tsk, tsk.' The man on the other side doffed his hat to them, revealing a pink, amiable-looking face and

bushy side-whiskers. 'Good day, my dear. And…er…
sir. I must remind Abel Dickens to repair this. I did
ask him last week, but a sexton has many duties, I fear.
Now, just allow me, I believe I have the trick of it.'

'Thank you so much.' She slipped through as soon
as the door opened wide enough. 'This gentleman is
interested in the history of the church, Mr Truscott,
and I am sure you can satisfy his curiosity far better
than I. Do excuse me.'

And she was gone, leaving Guy trapped in the porch
with no option but to make polite conversation. Whatever the circumstances, one could not shove a vicar
aside and appear to be pursuing one of his female parishioners through the churchyard. Not that he had any
desire to follow her of course…

'Cressida?' Marjorie stood in the drawing room
door, one hand holding a quill that dripped ink on the
fur of the white cat draped over her shoulder like a
faintly pulsating stole. 'My goodness, you startled me.
I was just writing to Cousin Harriet. The poor dear is
in such a taking—Frazer has been ordered back to his
ship and the baby is due at any moment.'

'I'm sorry,' Cressida apologised breathlessly to her
cousin and to Jane, the housemaid, who had come running at the sound of the front door slamming. 'Marjorie, you are dripping on Percy.' Somehow she couldn't
find space for thinking about Marjorie's young cousin
on her mother's side.

'Drat.' Marjorie looked around as though expecting a pen wiper to materialise, shrugged and passed
the cat to the housemaid. 'Can you see what you can

do with Percy, Jane? I fear licking it off would not be good for him.'

'Yes, ma'am.' Cat and maid eyed each other warily. 'Perhaps it will wipe clean.'

'If we hear screams, we must go and help,' Marjorie remarked, returning to the drawing room. 'Whatever have you been doing, dear? Anyone would think you have been running.'

Cressida dropped her bonnet on one chair, her reticule on another and collapsed inelegantly on the sofa. 'I have. All the way from the church. Guy Thurlow was there.'

Her cousin, usually hard to surprise, stared, her large brown eyes wide. 'Not the Earl of Easton?'

'The very same. He saw me, but he did not recognise me, thank goodness. Not unless he is a superlative actor,' she said with a frown, then gave herself a little shake. 'No. I managed to set Mr Truscott on him and made my escape. I don't think he can have seen which way I went.'

'Goodness,' Marjorie said faintly. 'What is he doing here? We haven't seen any of the family in Stowe Easton since—'

'Since the wedding that did not happen. Presumably he is just passing through, although why he went into the church, I cannot imagine.' She shivered. 'Is it really possible he did not know me?'

The older woman looked at her critically. 'You have changed a great deal, you know. After all, it is five years since he last saw you.'

'Almost to the day.'

'Indeed. You lost that rather endearing plumpness,

which has changed the shape of your face, as well as your figure, and I would swear you have grown two inches. And the way that you arrange your hair in that simple style is so much more elegant. And, of course, you have such refined eyebrows now,' Marjorie added, teasing.

'At the cost of much painful plucking,' Cressida conceded ruefully. 'And I suppose he took very little notice of me then. It was all arranged by our families. We only met a few times and I was probably looking at my feet and mumbling shyly.'

'The Earl never did find where you went afterwards, did he?' Marjorie asked.

'He did not. The fact that we were in possession of an eccentric great-uncle in the wilds of Devon seems to have escaped his notice, although perhaps he was not that anxious to catch up with me then. After all, he cannot have been pining for me.' She smiled wryly. 'I did wonder whether I would be sued for breach of promise, but I am sure any gentleman would think such a thing beneath his dignity.'

Marjorie got up to put her pen down beside her writing desk on the table in the window. 'No sign of a tall, handsome, vengeful aristocrat outside,' she said, tweaking the curtains to peer out. 'He cannot have recognised you.'

'You thought him handsome? I suppose he is well enough looking. More so now than when we were be-trothed—then he was scarcely twenty-three. Now life appears to have hardened him.' Cressida felt a shiver run through her at the way those broad shoulders had loomed over her in the shadows of the porch. He had taken care not to appear encroaching, let alone threatening, she realised, but even so, he was very…male. He had seemed to take up most of the space and much of the air.

'That will be army life—it would harden anyone, I imagine,' Marjorie said. 'Anyway, you are quite safe. After all, we have lived together for a year now without anyone realising who you are.'

Marjorie had been among the relatives who had attended Great-Uncle Rufus's funeral in Devon. When she discovered that her younger cousin now had nowhere to live, except with her brother and his family, she offered to share her home in Stowe Easton.

'Despite the scandal?' Cressida had asked.

'Goodness, yes. My standing in the town is, I flatter myself, good enough to counter any scandal.'

Miss Viola FitzWalden was not willing to take the risk. Her full name was Viola Louise Cressida and her grandmother had been Lady Amelia Williams so, when she arrived in Stowe Easton to live, she became Cressida Williams. Her brother, relieved, she suspected, not to have to house his disgraced sister, agreed it was the most sensible thing to do and addressed letters to her accordingly. She had exasperated him beyond measure by refusing to tell him why she had refused to marry the Earl, but distance allowed them to at least maintain an amiable correspondence.

'You must have had a good reason to flee from the marriage,' Marjorie had said when they discussed their new arrangement. 'Do not fear I will be nagging at you to tell me what it was. And you need not worry that

I'll expect you to settle down and be an old maid like me. It suits me, but it won't suit you, I'll be bound.'

If Marjorie, in her forties, lived the life of a typical old maid, then Cressida could see the attraction. Her cousin was at the centre of everything that happened in the town, it seemed. Charitable works, ladies' socials, church affairs, concerts and fêtes, sewing circles and outings: they all involved Marjorie in one way or another and Cressida was swept along with her. She soon knew everyone in Stowe Easton and it seemed sometimes that everyone knew her.

That gave Cressida many acquaintances and some good friends, and all of them would be appalled if they discovered that Miss Cressida Williams was actually Miss Viola FitzWalden, the young lady from Northamptonshire who had caused such a to-do when she had jilted Lord Easton at the altar all that time ago. But the risk of recognition, she was confident, was small. Her family was unknown in these parts and nobody had seen anything of her then beyond a white-faced girl in a veil bundling her trailing skirts into a carriage and shouting at the driver to, '*Go*. Now!'

Marjorie had liked what she had seen of the little market town when she had come for Cressida's wedding and had moved there a few months later on the death of her mother, Cressida's aunt. Her surname was Pomfret, so there was no connection to be made to Viola FitzWalden there either.

'I suppose the Earl has always wanted to know why you baulked, in case it is something about him that was at fault. He must ask himself if it might happen again, because he is certain to wish to marry sooner or later,'

Marjorie mused now. 'Oh, dear. I promised I would not pry and now here I am, speculating.'

'Well, it was most definitely nothing wrong with Lord Easton. I was quite prepared to marry him.' Prepared, but not eager. Seventeen-year-old Viola had been in no hurry to marry anyone and certainly not someone she scarcely knew, a man who was all self-confidence and shiny boots and sharp spurs. 'It was something I found out, very late. Almost too late. And it is not my secret to tell,' she added firmly. *I can't imagine it ever will be.*

'Then we must put him out of our minds, although I do not think that venturing into the town today would be wise. If he stopped in order to change horses at the Raven's Nest, he may well decide to take luncheon there.' Marjorie sat down at the table and picked up her pen, then put it down again, a frown between her strong dark brows. 'He can't have been going to Easton Court, can he?'

'Surely not. The Thurlow family abandoned the place to a caretaker years ago. Why should any of them want to go there now?'

'It still has its charms, so you say,' Marjorie said absently, her concentration back on rereading what she had written so far. 'You want it.'

'I do covet the grounds,' Cressida admitted. 'It is the most beautiful place I have ever seen.'

Her cousin chuckled. 'But you are a gardener unlike any I have ever encountered. You enjoy weeds and disorder.'

'I do not! I like a little managed informality with wild flowers and grasses, that is all. I approve of the

Romantic. And speaking of weeds, I shall go and speak firmly to those in the rose beds in the back garden after luncheon. Whichever way Lord Easton leaves the town, he cannot see me there.'

It was a sensible way to spend an enforced afternoon at home and working in the garden was usually guaranteed to take her thoughts far from anything disturbing or unpleasant. But, as Cressida buttered bread to accompany her cold ham with Marjorie's tomato pickle, she felt uneasily that the magic would not work that day.

When she had imagined her feelings if she was ever confronted by Guy Thurlow again, she had thought of alarm, fear of his anger, dread of scandal. There were all those feelings now, but there was also something strange and unexpected, a desire to cross swords with the man, to puncture that arrogant male certainty that what he wanted, he would have.

He had no right to demand anything of her now. She was free of him and glad of it. Or she should be. Cressida might still be a respectable young lady, an old maid in training, some would say, but she could still recognise the shiver of sensation, the thread of excitement, that underlay the fear and the need to stand up to Guy Thurlow. It was physical attraction. Desire.

Chapter Three

The lake at Easton Court had once been a muddy hollow turned by three springs into a bog Then, more than fifty years ago, Lancelot 'Capability' Brown had worked his landscaping magic on the park and built a dam, and now two of the springs bubbled up in the lake bed itself and the third emerged on the hillside to the west and wove its way through the parkland as a brook. Eventually it became a shallow stream, running over pebbles, before it emerged from under a well-placed slab of smooth stone and flowed into the lake.

The park was almost five miles from Stowe Easton by any decent road but, by taking tracks and then cutting through the deserted parkland, it was possible to reach the lake after a mile.

The day after the encounter in the church Cressida set out for the park. The weather was hot and the uncut grass uneven enough to make the low stone slab a very pleasant place to perch when she reached it. The burble of water beneath was cooling, and the view of the lake and woodlands spread out on the far side restful.

Cressida took off her shoes and stockings, gathered up her skirts and sat down, feet dangling. The water came up to her ankles, cool and refreshing, and she splashed a little, secure in the knowledge that she was quite alone except for a herd of fallow deer grazing in the shade of a clump of oaks a little to her left. There was an ancient caretaker up at the Court and a tenant farmer and his workers at the Home Farm, but no one ever seemed to come here.

The flow of the water, bird song and the rustling made by the browsing animals were the only sounds.

Hard work weeding the rose beds, followed by an evening stroll with Marjorie and supper with neighbours, had guaranteed sleep the night before, but it had done nothing to prevent dreams of a steady grey gaze watching her. She had woken with a sense of foreboding and the wisps of those dreams fading into unease before she could catch hold of them.

'There are shadows under your eyes,' Marjorie had remarked over breakfast. 'Why not take your watercolours and something for luncheon and escape to the park? I am spending the day with the Ladies' Quilting Circle—we have almost finished the bedspread we are making for Dr Symonds to commemorate his work for the town and, as he is retiring at the end of the month, we need to make a final push to complete it.'

That gave Cressida the excuse to escape with a clear conscience, and the rather disloyal thought in passing that the crusty little doctor might not be entirely delighted at receiving an elaborate and very feminine quilt.

Now she put her hands behind her on the warm

stone and leaned back, Villager hat discarded, her face turned up to the sun, and let the magic of the place wash over her. A great landscape park needed constant care and adjustment as it matured, but here the work had been neglected and nature was taking its course in a way that would have Capability Brown stamping on his wig if he was alive to see it. Despite that, it was beautiful in her eyes.

A pheasant rocketed upwards, screeching its alarm, and a twig snapped. The deer must be coming closer. Perhaps, if she sat very still, one would come right down and drink nearby.

Someone cleared their throat.

It was so close behind her, so unexpected, that Cressida started, lost her balance, flailed wildly and ended up in the stream, up to her knees in water. 'What? Who?' She turned, grasping the edge of the rock for balance as her bare feet shifted painfully on the little pebbles. '*You?* What on earth are *you* doing here?'

The Earl of Easton stood, staring down at her from the stone, booted feet planted squarely. His stance forced her to look up, past a disconcerting expanse of breeches-clad thigh, waistcoat and neckcloth to his face. He raised his eyebrows, very much the aristocrat. 'This property is mine,' he said. 'I believe I should be asking you what business *you* have here, madam.'

Cressida's soaked skirts clung to her legs, the force of the water pushing at them, unbalancing her so that she had to more tightly grab hold of the edge of the slab bridge. 'I am here because you crept up behind me and startled me so much that I fell in,' she said.

'I meant in my park, not in the stream, as you very

well know.' Guy Thurlow bent, held out both hands and, when she reached up instinctively, took her by the wrists and swung her up on to the slab in front of him.

'I do hope you have not hurt your back,' Cressida exclaimed, without thinking. Possibly not the most tactful thing to say to a man, but she was not exactly a frail waif and—

His grip tightened and she found herself flattened against his chest, which was heaving, although not, she feared, with exertion.

Cressida swallowed. The impression she had in the church of how large he was, how solid, was no illusion, she realised now she was plastered to him, her nose bumping on the gold pin in his neckcloth. She managed a gasp of protest, which was an added humiliation.

'Oh, for goodness' sake,' he muttered. 'There is no need to stand there squeaking and shivering. I am not a man given to assaulting females, even trespassers on my land.'

Cressida looked up into his face. 'I am not shivering because I am afraid of you,' she said, indignant now.

The grey eyes staring into hers seemed to darken as the pupils widened. His lips curved slightly and, with a jolt, she realised he thought she wanted this parody of an embrace, that she wanted to be kissed.

As the dark head bent towards her, she snapped, 'I am shivering because my feet are frozen and I am draped in wet skirts and, if you would only let me go, I could do something about it.'

The Earl released her so abruptly that she almost stepped back into the stream. Cressida snatched up her shoes, stockings and hat and walked to where she had left her basket in the shade of a bush. It was difficult to do with that much dignity because of the soaking wet muslin clinging to her bare calves.

There was a tree stump that made an excellent seat and this was a favourite picnic spot of hers. Now, as she wrung out water from her skirts, she felt all her enjoyment in the place would be ruined for ever. It was not helped by the fact that she knew she was in the wrong. She was trespassing. She had been out in a public place—however deserted—in a shocking state of undress. She had jilted this man at the altar steps with no explanation, even if he hadn't realised it yet. And if he recognised her then she would be in the most appalling situation.

Guy Thurlow produced a large handkerchief and offered it. 'It is quite clean.'

Of course it is. He probably carries half a dozen immaculate linen squares as a matter of course.

That thought was petty and so was the faint feeling of satisfaction that his glossy boots were now smeared with river weed from her skirts.

None of this is his fault, Cressida reminded herself.

'Thank you, but I have a napkin in here.' She delved into the picnic basket and pulled out a folded ging-ham square.

He moved to the nearest tree and set his back against it, his eyes scanning the park as if on the alert for more trespassers.

And he has the tact to turn away while I put on my stockings, she thought, keeping a wary eye on the broad shoulders while she tugged at the knitted cotton, which stuck to her damp skin. Really, she could do without adding any more virtues to his account.

With her shoes laced again Cressida stood, picked up the basket and cleared her throat. 'I will leave you in peace, My Lord.'

The Earl turned his head 'What is in that basket?'

'My watercolours. A picnic.'

He gestured towards the stump. 'You appear set for the day. Please, sit. Do make yourself comfortable.'

'Thank you.' This was awkward, but it would seem strange if she refused and left now, after he had made the offer. Cressida shook out the napkin that had been wrapped around the food and set out two apples, a wedge of cheese, a buttered bread roll and a chicken wing. Further delving produced a flask of lemonade, a plate and a beaker. She reached for the chicken and took a bite. Delicious. Cook could always produce a perfect roast fowl. 'There is enough for two, if you do not object to drinking from the bottle and having no plate.'

At which point she looked up and found the Earl regarding her with the narrow-eyed expression of a man who has just discovered his butler swigging the best port.

She swallowed, appetite vanished. 'Oh. You were being sarcastic.' Cressida began carefully placing the picnic back in the basket, reminding herself once again of all the reasons why she was in the wrong.

'No, merely taken aback. I am not used to young ladies of such an independent disposition. Do continue your meal.' He sat down on the other side of her napkin tablecloth. His valet, she mused, would be displeased when she saw how he was treating his immaculate buckskins.

'Why do you come here, to the park?' Lord Easton asked, reaching for an apple.

'Because it is beautiful and I covet it,' she said, startled into honesty, and cut into the cheese to cover her reaction.

'Beautiful?' He gazed around him again, as though unable to recognise what she meant. 'It is a wilderness. And what do you covet it for? What would a single lady do with *this*?' His gesture encompassed the lake, scummy with weed; the straggling margins of the woodland; the herd of deer; the rolling acres; the glimpse of lichen-stained columns showing where the little Temple of the Winds on the hilltop had been swallowed up by encroaching scrub.

It seemed to her that he regarded it with something more than incomprehension, almost as a man might gaze at the rookeries of London, assessing their dangers before plunging into the narrow, foul alleyways.

'I would love to restore it, bring it back to what it should be—a great landscape approaching its prime. It is maturing, just as Capability Brown envisaged it would, although perhaps it will not reach perfection for another hundred years. But it needs keeping in hand as it grows towards his finished vision, just like a person who must have their hair cut, manicure their nails and take regular baths if they are not to appear like an unkempt hermit. Instead, it has been simply left to go its own way and this is the result.'

The Earl stared at her, clearly taken aback by her enthusiasm. She should moderate her tone, she knew, because it was positively ill bred to gush about one's interests and opinions, but it was hard to suppress what she felt.

'Gardens and landscapes are a passion of mine. It would not take so very much work to dredge the lake, cut back the scrubby growth, reveal the eye-catchers. And it would create employment for local people, which would be very welcome, don't you think?'

'Passion indeed,' he drawled. There was something in his intent look, the droop of his eyelids over that penetrating grey gaze that sent the colour up under her skin. He was flirting with her, she realised. At least, she thought he was; she was hardly experienced in such things. Cressida put down the cheese knife, all appetite for food gone, lost in the realisation that she wished she knew how to flirt back. *Madness.*

'It all seems so overgrown,' he said, his expression changing in a blink to one of practical enquiry. 'It will be necessary to call in some expert to deal with it— Repton, perhaps.'

'If you wish to part with a great deal of money and still have to employ men to do the actual labour, yes. Perhaps Mr Repton would give you a miniature frigate to float on the lake so that the top masts could be seen from the south terrace, creating the illusion that the sea is just over the hill.'

'Ridiculous!'

'I thought so, when I read about such schemes. You could add a hermitage in the Gothic style, or a ruined castle, I suppose. Mr Repton has designs for those, I am certain, My Lord.'

'Call me Easton,' he said abruptly. 'Although doubt-less I should seek a formal introduction. A suitable matron to perform that office appears a trifle lacking, however, unless that anxious-looking duck might do.'

An unladylike snort escaped her, part amusement, part sheer nerves. 'Miss Williams. Cressida Williams.'

'Are you from a local family, Miss Williams?'

'No. I came here from Devon, where I lived with my great-uncle, to join my cousin who moved to Stowe Easton a little while ago.' It was best to keep to the truth as far as possible and she was certain he had no idea his bride had fled to Devon from the church.

Speaking of family reminded her of something he had said when she had been too agitated to take in the implications. 'You said I was trespassing on your land. Does that mean that the Marquess...? That you have inherited it?'

'My father is in the best of health, I am happy to say. He has presented me with Easton Court to be my country seat. It comes with the challenge of making it fit to live in.' He did not sound exactly delighted by the prospect.

'I am glad the Court will be occupied again,' Cressida said politely. 'It will do a great deal of good for the town to have the business and the opportunities for work, especially as I imagine there will be a significant restoration required. And I am sure the Vicar, now he has made your acquaintance, will not be backward in listing the many ways in which your support will be valuable in the parish. He has only held the living for a few years and is very active in making improvements.'

'I am sure he will already be drawing up a list. To divert him from his lecture on the antiquities of the church yesterday I informed him that I would be taking up residence.'

This was becoming too relaxed, almost friendly. She could not risk staying long in his company in case something she said, some fleeting memory, identified her to him. Cressida began to pack away her picnic. 'I must go, My... Lord Easton.'

'I thought you had come here to sketch.'

'The light is wrong now.' A lie. She couldn't meet his quizzical gaze, but Lord Easton surely realised she was making an excuse. Presumably he thought she was shy, a country miss overawed by an aristocrat. Instead she looked down, saw the bread roll lying beside the basket where she had missed it and tore in into pieces, then threw them into the lake where fish immediately rose to investigate. She brushed her hands, rose to her feet and bent to lift the basket.

'It looks as though I can at least expect a catch, should I turn angler, although whether the local poachers have left anything worth catching is another matter.'

'We are well stocked with rivers in the district, so I do not think you need fear that your fisheries will be pillaged. Good day, Lord Easton.'

'Good day, Miss Williams. I thank you for your advice.'

Cressida dipped her head in acknowledgment, despite not knowing whether that had been sarcasm or not, and turned to climb the slope back towards the track, keeping her pace steady, swinging the basket idly as though she had not a care in the world, when all she wanted was to cast it aside and run.

Run where? she asked herself. The serpent had invaded her Eden.

Guy stood watching Cressida Williams as she walked away from him. Tall, graceful…unusual. A grown woman and a devilishly attractive one, although no connoisseur would call her exactly beautiful. An original, and respectable, he reminded himself, recalling her blushes and sudden awkwardness when he had flirted a little. He was not here to set himself up with a mistress and certainly not to seduce respectable local ladies.

He turned away and tossed a stick into the lake, startling the ducks into noisy flight. Although possibly Miss Williams was not so respectable if she wandered the countryside unescorted, treated his park as though it were her own and lectured him so confidently on its maintenance and beauties?

He was beginning to wonder at himself. He should have escorted her back to the house, sent her home in the third-best carriage and made it politely, but firmly, clear that this was private land.

That would have been correct, but instead he had allowed himself to enjoy the shiver of awareness Miss Williams's closeness aroused in him. And that was ridiculous. She was far less lovely than any of his London flirts, far less sophisticated, and yet something about her intrigued him. Attracted him. And those ridiculous feelings had somehow made him prolong the encounter. *Fool.*

He kicked a tussock of rank grass and looked again at the landscape around him. *Beautiful*, she had said. He had spent too much time at war, in country where every overgrown copse, every acre of scrubland, could conceal an enemy. Now he found this dishevelled parkland unsettling, even though he knew that to feel that here, in England, on his own land, was to surrender to an illusion as false as his youthful belief in his own invincibility had been.

Guy began to walk back to the house, made himself ignore the feeling at the nape of his neck that he was in some sniper's sights and tried to see what lay beneath the neglect. What could Cressida Williams sense that he could not?

Gradually he found himself seeing with different eyes. The shades of green, so varied, soothed. The shapes of the land and of the plantations were harmonious. The glimpses of small buildings in white marble gave the impression of an antique land that went on for ever. By the time the house came into view, and he was walking through what should have been a meadow sweeping up to the ha-ha, Guy found his thoughts had become more coherent.

Arthur was leaning against a great oak tree to one side of the roughly cut sloping lawn. He straightened up when he saw Guy and walked down to meet him, his gait slightly uneven, as though his body had still not become balanced after the loss of his arm.

'I was about to send out search parties. That's wild country out there.'

'I know. At first I found myself eyeing every thicket and hollow as though they might contain snipers.' Guy noticed Arthur's quick nod of understanding. It would be a while before either of them fully accepted that they were no longer in the army, at war. 'But I met no French infantry. I did encounter what I suspect might be the *genius loci.*'

'The spirit of the place?' Arthur ventured after a moment's silent translation. Latin had never been his strong subject.

'The guardian spirit at that. I should not regard this as an overgrown wilderness to be tamed, it seems, but a thing of beauty that requires gently ordering.'

'Have you been drinking?'

'Not a drop has touched my lips today.'

'Then I can only assume that she is a fascinating spirit.'

'How did you know it was a female spirit?'

Arthur merely grinned.

'Intriguing, certainly,' Guy admitted as they reached the terrace.

Chapter Four

The one mile back to Stowe Easton might have been ten and her sensible leather half-boots felt as though they were iron-shod clogs. Cressida emerged from the lane beside the Raven's Nest Inn and sank down on the nearest bench, not caring that it was hardly the location for a lady to be sitting.

The pot boy came out, stared, then approached to ask if he could fetch her anything.

A pint of best ale, was a tempting response. Men appeared to be greatly revived by the stuff. But ladies did not drink ale, nor anything else, in the market square. Cressida thanked him, got up and walked as far as the lychgate into the churchyard where she could sit on one of the benches under its tiled roof, catch her breath and attempt to think coherently.

Her first instinct was to pack her bags and flee the town, but as the only place she could run to was her brother's house—and that contained Dorinda, his wife and mother of his five lively children—that was not a tempting prospect. Dorinda considered that sisters-in-law who threw away excellent marriages, scandalised society and discommoded their brothers were doomed to be old maids. And old maids were destined to be useful aunts. Cressida was quite fond of her nieces and nephews, but not at close quarters for long periods, let alone permanently. If she was reduced to being a domestic drudge, then she would hire herself out as a companion and at least earn a wage for her trouble.

Leaving Marjorie would upset her cousin, who had said only the other day how much she valued Cressida's company, and abandoning her was not a fair return for her unstinting kindness.

She rested her head against one of the worn oak pillars and watched the gentle bustle of town life. A small girl was petting a kitten rather too vigorously and received a scratch that sent her howling to her mother who was buying vegetables from Ernest Potter's barrow. Two lads, sure to be truants from the Dame school, were playing among the tombstones. Three ladies—she recognised them from Marjorie's quilting circle—were walking abreast across the square, heads together, deep in gossip. The distant flourish of a horn warned of the approach of the west-bound stage coach.

She liked it here in Stowe Easton with its friendly inhabitants. She enjoyed the comfortable routine of small-town life enlivened by its little dramas. She loved Marjorie and she felt at home in the little house with its cheerful servants. Why should a man force her to abandon it all?

He could not, she decided. Lord Easton had shown no sign of recognising her and if seeing her at the altar steps had not jarred his memory, then surely nothing would. They were never going to encounter each other in any other situation that might call to mind a shy debutante, dressed in white frills that did not suit her, and hardly able to whisper the correct social responses to a very formal wooing.

She was safe unless she lost her nerve. The important thing was not to panic, not to behave as though there was any secret, not to be flustered if she encountered him again.

Marjorie, when she returned with her basket of patchwork scraps over her arm, was flushed with triumph at the completion of the presentation quilt and it was quite half an hour, and several cups of tea, before she finished her detailed description of it and enquired about Cressida's day.

When the tale had been recounted, without mention of the unsettling effect Guy Thurlow had on Cressida's heart rate, Marjorie bit her lip, deep in thought. 'You are certain he did not know you?'

'I am sure,' Cressida said, convinced of it herself now. 'I have been considering, and the only place we are likely to encounter him is at church where we can simply keep well clear of him. Nobody would expect him to pay us any attention, after all.'

'He will attend church here?' Marjorie had the air of a woman distracted by the thought that her Sunday-best bonnet was a season out of date for an encounter with an earl.

'This is the nearest place of worship until the chapel at the Court is repaired, and the reason our wedding was to be in the church here was because the chapel was in such poor condition.'

'He may have brought a chaplain with him and hold household prayers, I suppose,' her cousin suggested.

'I doubt it.' She could not envisage Guy Thurlow with a cleric in his household. 'Perhaps he will not attend church,' she suggested hopefully.

'Surely not. If he is to take up residence here, then it is his duty to set an example. I imagine that the Vicar will ask him to read one of the lessons at Matins every Sunday.'

Cressida thought it highly unlikely that the Earl would agree, but she nodded agreement and selected another scone from the plate. It was true that food did not solve one's problems, but scones with jam certainly made them easier to bear.

The next day was Friday and, by the time Marjorie and Cressida began their shopping, the town was abuzz with the news that the Earl of Easton was taking up residence at Easton Court and would be putting it into repair.

They did not hear a single voice dissenting from the universal delight at the news. Even old Mrs Fortingbrass, a widow who was determined to think the worst of everyone she encountered, had to concede that His Lordship's name never appeared in the scandal sheets—not that she read them, but one heard such things—nor in any undesirable context in the more respectable newspapers. There would be no wild parties with gambling and riotous behaviour and young bucks carrying on with lightskirts imported from London, she declared.

Cressida, who had reached the stage of thinking she would scream if she heard the Earl mentioned one more time, could not help giggling at this pronouncement, overheard in Mr Millington's haberdashery.

'Oh, Mrs Fortingbrass, what is a lightskirt?' she asked, all wide-eyed innocence, and earned herself a sharp tap on the ankle from her cousin who was buying an ell of green ribbon and some artificial cherries to refresh her Sunday bonnet.

'What immodest young females become,' the widow informed her, casting a critical eye over Cressida's new walking dress.

By Sunday Cressida had convinced herself that Guy Thurlow would not be at church. Aristocratic bachelors, in the absence of wives to insist upon it, had things they would much prefer to be doing on a sunny July morning than listening to a rather dull sermon and the wheezing of the decrepit organ that accompanied the choir.

She was therefore relaxed enough to be amused at Marjorie's preening and allowed herself to be persuaded into wearing her rose-pink sprig muslin with the Brussels lace at the neck and the two flounces at the hem, as well as her best bonnet. If she had thought the Earl would be present then she would have resisted 'dressing up', she told herself: it gave him too much importance.

'There, I knew he wouldn't come,' she whispered as they took their places. They were six rows back from the grand Easton Court box pew with its oak panelling and prominent coat of arms. The walls were high, but it would be possible to see the top of the head of any tall adult sitting within it.

The Vicar had finally succeeded in replacing most of the ramshackle box pews with open seating and the ladies of the parish had embroidered hassocks and long cushions in wool work to add colour and comfort, but nobody would have dreamt of disturbing the Easton Court pew. Nor that of Sir Gregory Armstrong on the other side, Cressida thought with a smile as the aged baronet tottered down the aisle, supported on one side by his valet and on the other by his housekeeper.

The organ gave an anticipatory wheeze, the congregation shuffled itself into order and then the verger hurried towards the altar steps. Someone of importance had arrived. Cressida kept her gaze fixed on the back of the pew in front of her, although the rustle of Sunday-best gowns betrayed the fact that some of the congregation could not resist turning to stare.

The click of heels on the stone flags got louder, then passed her as the verger led two gentlemen to the right-hand pew and opened the door for them. It was, of course, Lord Easton. Cressida had a glimpse of sober, excellent tailoring, the gleam of a tall hat in one gloved hand, and then he was inside the pew.

Marjorie gave her a discreet nudge. 'Who is that with him?' she murmured.

'I have no idea. Did you notice his arm? An army friend, no doubt. The house is in a terrible state, they say,' Cressida whispered back. 'No place to invite guests, one would think. But perhaps two military bachelors do not mind making do.'

The organ music swelled and they all rose to their feet, everyone's attention on the Vicar and on the top of a well-groomed dark head, which was all that was visible of the intriguing new arrival. His shorter companion's blond hair was hardly visible at all.

To Cressida's amazement the verger opened the pew door to allow Lord Easton to make his way to the lectern to read the first lesson. Afterwards she would have been unable to say what it had been, although it was read in a clear, emotionless voice that must have carried to the very back of the church.

The verger opened and closed the pew door again, then strode off down the aisle, his long silver-topped *virge* clenched in his fist like a weapon, off to deal with an outbreak of scuffling in the gallery.

'Those wretched apprentices from the brewery,' Marjorie whispered. 'Mr Yelland insists they attend church. Very proper, I am sure, but then he provides no effective supervision.'

The disturbance dealt with, the service proceeded smoothly to its conclusion. Mr Truscott made his way down the aisle to take up his position at the west door to take his leave of the parishioners, followed by Lord Easton, Sir Gregory and his supporters, and then the occupants of each row of pews in turn.

Cressida dawdled over gathering up prayer book and reticule, allowing most of the congregation to file out before her. With any luck Lord Easton would have shaken hands and be on his way to his carriage by the time she and Marjorie reached the door.

She was wrong. His Lordship was still at the Vicar's side, although their conversation was constantly being interrupted by exiting parishioners. His blond friend stood silent at his side.

'...repair or replacement?'

'I fear it is beyond repair. Good day, Mrs Whitlow, Mr Whitlow, Miss Miranda. We had an organ-builder from Oxford to look at it. Mice in the bellows, woodworm in the pedals. Thank you for offering to help with the flowers next Sunday, Mrs Matcham. He was appalled at the state of it.'

'With your permission, I will send for the man who restored the organ at Thornborough, for the Marquess.'

The sound of hobnail boots clattered in the gallery over their heads.

'That would be most kind, My Lord. Jobson, will you please deal with those boys in the gallery? A trial to one's patience, apprentices, I fear. Ah, Mrs Kirststead. And how is poor Kirststead's leg? Better? Excellent. Now—'

He broke off as four youths came running down the steep stairs from the gallery, Jobson, the verger, in pursuit. 'Come back here, you young devils! Pet mice in church! I've never heard the like of it!'

There were screams from several ladies near the steps. 'Mice!'

The boys dodged away from Jobson's outstretched hand and a large matron stepped back suddenly to avoid them. She cannoned into Marjorie, sending her sprawling on the unforgiving flagstones.

'Ow!'

'Miss Pomfret, are you hurt?' the Vicar cried as

Cressida fell to her knees beside her cousin. The apprentices, verger in pursuit, vanished through the wide-open doors.

For a moment Marjorie seemed uncertain whether she was hurt or not, but at Cressida's urging she moved her limbs easily enough. 'I am a little shaken, that is all.' She would certainly have bruises where she had landed so hard, but Cressida was not going to enquire about those in mixed company.

'Even so, you should be examined by your doctor, just in case.' Lord Easton knelt on the other side of her. 'Allow me to take you to your home in my carriage, ma'am.'

'Ah, yes,' Mr Truscott said brightly. 'You met Miss Pomfret's companion the other day, did you not, when I had the pleasure of showing Your Lordship our church's finer features? You must allow me to make the introductions. Miss Williams, Miss Pomfret—Lord Easton. Lord Easton—Miss Williams and her cousin, Miss Pomfret. The ladies are pillars of our local community,' Mr Truscott added.

'We cannot allow pillars of the community to be tumbled,' Lord Easton said. There was a decided gleam of amusement in the grey eyes, despite his serious tone.

Cressida found herself surprised by the hint of humour, but it did not make her any more eager to prolong the encounter. 'I... Thank you, sir. But my cousin seems merely shaken. I am sure when she stands up and—'

'Would you be so good as to take my hat, Arthur?' Before Cressida could react, Lord Easton scooped Marjorie up in his arms and got to his feet.

In a disconcerting echo of the incident by the stream Cressida found herself saying, 'But your back!' Marjorie merely made a sound somewhere between a squeak and a gasp.

'I can assure you Miss Pomfret is not such a burden as to damage my spine,' he said as he turned to the door. Under his breath she thought she heard him mutter, 'Your effect on my sanity is another matter.'

'Put me down, *please*,' Marjorie whispered, quite as conscious as Cressida of the interesting spectacle they must be creating.

'Certainly.' He continued down the path to the lychgate. 'Griggs, the door!'

A wiry, middle-aged man swung down from the back of the smart barouche that was drawn up ready, its hood lowered.

The Earl stepped up into the vehicle, deposited Marjorie on the forward-facing seat and stepped down again to hand Cressida up beside her. 'If you would be so good as to give my man the name and direction of your medical man, he will fetch him to you, Miss Pomfret. For the lady, Griggs. A fall on a hard surface.'

'No, there is no need,' Marjorie said firmly, recovering her composure a little. 'Nothing is broken—look.' She held up her gloved hands, wiggled her fingers and kicked at her skirts. 'I will be a little sore, that is all. And I am perfectly capable of walking home,' she protested as the Earl and his companion took the seats opposite them and the vehicle moved off.

Now they were actually in the carriage there seemed no point in protesting. 'We live down Church Hill, My Lord.' Cressida waited while he called to the driver, then turned to her cousin. 'Marjorie, it is best to take care after such a shock and the force of the fall. You do not want to risk feeling faint halfway down the hill, now do you?' She was pleased that her voice betrayed no hint of just how awkward this situation was.

'Ladies, allow me to introduce my good friend and steward, Mr Graham,' Lord Easton said. 'Arthur—Miss Pomfret and Miss Williams.'

Within moments they had stopped by the front door. Like all the linked stone-built houses that lined the gently sloping street, theirs had no front garden, merely a narrow paved strip, edged with a wrought-iron fence on either side of the front door. Roses grew in tubs beside the step, but there was no hint of the garden that lay behind.

The groom jumped down from the box to open the carriage door and let down the step. Lord Easton descended. 'Are you able to manage, Miss Pomfret?'

'Certainly,' Marjorie said. She stepped down, placing her uninjured hand in his. The groom helped Cressida and, as she reached the pavement, Jane opened the front door, blinking a little at the magnificence of the equipage.

'Thank you, Lord Easton. We are much obliged.' Cressida bobbed a curtsy and turned to go in.

'You will join us and take tea, Lord Easton? Mr Graham?' Marjorie said before she reached the threshold.

'Thank you. But surely you should be resting, Miss Pomfret?'

'Not at all. I am quite revived.'

Cressida turned to stare at Marjorie who was positively sweeping the Earl before her into the house. As she drew level with Cressida she gave her a tight smile, ignoring Cressida mouthing, *What on earth are you doing?*

She had thought Marjorie would be as anxious to be free of the man as she was and yet now she was inviting him into their home.

'Refreshments in the garden room, Jane, if you please.' Marjorie ushered the gentlemen down the hall to the door into the room at the back which led out into a conservatory that ran the width of the house.

'But this is delightful.' Lord Easton stopped halfway to the doors which stood open on to the terrace. 'I had no idea you had such a large plot of land behind the house.'

'It is not so very large.' Marjorie came to his side and pointed. 'You see that line of trees? Those belong to the garden behind. The illusion of space is entirely due to dear Cressida's talent.'

Cressida almost groaned aloud. Marjorie was intensely proud of her horticultural skills and never failed to show off their garden to visitors. Despite the danger, the thought of an aristocrat's admiration was obviously too much for her. She could imagine Marjorie at her next social gathering—'Dear Cressida's talents were much praised by the Earl of Easton. He was particularly pleased with the rose garden,' she would say.

It seemed that he was. 'Might I go out? Your roses are magnificent.'

'Yes, of course,' Cressida said, catching hold of Marjorie's arm before she could follow the gentlemen through the doors. 'What are you thinking of?' she whispered urgently.

'If he has not recognised you by now, he never will,' Marjorie whispered back. 'We could hardly accept a ride in his carriage and not offer hospitality. It would appear most peculiar and rude.' She gave Cressida a little push towards the garden. 'Go on, we cannot leave them out there alone and I would not be able to answer his questions.'

'He won't have any,' Cressida retorted. 'He's not interested in gardening.' But she stepped out on to the terrace. Marjorie was right: now the gentlemen were in, they could not abandon their guests. She offered Mr Graham a seat in the arbour, then turned to find the Earl was already across the lawn, bending over a white rose, his nose almost buried in its depths.

He straightened as she came closer and she caught her breath as his attention focused on her. She had known him to be a handsome man, but here, hatless in the sunshine, soberly clad for a Sunday and standing tall and broad-shouldered against the sensual lushness of the blossoming roses, he was almost too masculine, too virile.

This was such a dangerous game to be playing, although, in reality, it was no game. She was finding herself attracted to the most impossible man. Even if Guy Easton could ever find it in himself to forgive her, there would still be the insuperable obstacle that had sent her fleeing from the church.

She was not the woman he had thought she was. She was not even her father's daughter.

Chapter Five

'You must tell me who your gardener is,' Guy said when Miss Williams hesitated halfway to the rose beds. Was she feeling awkward after their encounter in the park? He sought for innocuous conversation to put her at her ease, although it was hard to think of anything except how striking she looked, her bonnet discarded, her face still a little pale from the shock of her cousin's accident, the sun bringing out deep chestnut highlights in her hair. 'The combination of your eye for design and taste and his skill has produced the most harmonious result.'

She blinked at him as though confused, then said, 'Ted Darrell does the heavy work for me—the trees and hedges, scything the grass, moving stones or deep digging. He helps with many of the gardens in the town.' She seemed to recover her poise and with it a smile. 'You will be wildly unpopular if you poach him for the Court.'

'I must remember that,' he said. 'I have no desire to fall foul of every garden-proud lady in Stowe Easton.

But surely you cannot mean that you do everything else? Pruning, weeding, planting? There must be more than that, even, I imagine. I am sadly ignorant of the art.'

'Yes, I do it all and enjoy it. Besides, we could not afford to keep a gardener employed full-time, but Ted once a week for half the year is possible.'

She spoke lightly, but Guy could tell she was serious. Two spinsters would have to watch the pennies, he assumed, if they were to keep up this pleasant house and employ a servant or two.

'Then I admire the result even more.' He turned back to the rose, cupping his fingers around the bloom to capture the soft fragrance. 'This is very lovely. What is its name? I would like some for the garden at the Court when it is finally restored.' He shot her a wry smile. 'When Arthur has found me a gardener and staff, that is.'

'I do not know its name,' she confessed, lured closer, as he had hoped. 'It is an old variety, I think. We found it in the garden here and I planned the rose borders around it. Your gardener—when you find one—could take cuttings.'

'Thank you. *Aah.*' He had pulled his hand back carelessly and the rose had punished him for his lack of attention with a thorn in the index finger of his right hand. Guy held it away from him as the blood welled. 'I will just wrap my handkerchief around it.'

'No. Let me look.' Miss Williams took his hand without ceremony and bent over it. 'There is still a thorn in there.' She took the handkerchief that he had pulled from his pocket and dabbed carefully. 'I think my nails are long enough to pull it out, if you can keep very still.'

Guy stood and looked down at her bent head. Her nose must be almost touching his hand, he thought, amused. Then a waft of scent, sun-warmed from her skin, drifted up to him, mingling with the perfume of the roses all around them, and he closed his eyes, lost for the moment in the sensual pleasure of a summer's day, the closeness of a lovely woman and an elusive thread of memory. Then, like thistledown in the breeze, it was gone, leaving a strangely uneasy feeling behind it.

'There.'

He came to himself with a start to find Miss Williams wrapping his handkerchief firmly around his finger.

'Come inside and I will find a less bulky bandage for you and we will drop this into cold water before the stain sets.'

Guy lifted the pad away. 'No need. Now the thorn is out it has stopped bleeding.'

The maid came out on to the terrace with a laden tray and Miss Williams stepped away, their closeness broken.

'Put it on the table there, Jane,' Miss Pomfret directed the servant. 'Gentlemen, do take a seat. Cressida will pour, if you will excuse me. A crisis in the kitchen involving the cat and the joint for today's dinner. Cook is beside herself.' She limped out, urging the maid before her.

'Oh, dear.' Miss Williams pulled a wry face. 'Percy is a terror if anyone leaves the pantry door open. Last week it was a basket of crayfish, fresh from the river. And they were alive in a nest of wet waterweed. Percy was nipped and so was Cook, and Jane was the only person brave enough to retrieve them all.'

She took one of the wrought-iron seats set out under a pergola and arranged cups in front of her. 'Tea or coffee, My Lord? Mr Graham?'

'Tea, thank you. And I thought I had asked you to call me Easton,' Guy said, sitting down opposite her.

Arthur, always slightly awkward in the company of ladies, murmured that he, too, would like tea.

'That seems a presumptuous degree of informality.' Her concentration appeared to be all on the arc of hot tea as she poured. The scent of bergamot rose in a swirl of steam.

'How can it be, if I have requested you to use it?' He watched as she filled the other cup in silence.

'I suppose not. But I am not of your rank, My… Easton.'

'You are a gentlewoman. I am a gentleman. This is not the Court at St James's Palace, Miss Williams.' He took the cup and saucer she passed him, declined sugar but accepted a slice of lemon. 'Cressida is an unusual name. Charming.'

'Shakespeare,' Arthur said, then blushed. 'The only thing to read when I was recovering from this.' He jerked his head towards his left shoulder. 'I was stuck in bed at my uncle's house near Dover for close on two weeks when I first arrived back in England because I wasn't fit to travel further. He's a rural dean, you know, so the bookshelves held nothing but sermons, clerical directories and the *Collected Works of Shakespeare*.'

Cressida had the tact not to comment on the injury. 'Oh, Papa was not literary,' she said with a chuckle. 'I was named for a rather wealthy godmother, presumably in the hopes of a legacy. She died last year and left it all to an obscure religious sect.'

'It is too pretty not to use. I shall call you Miss Cressida,' Guy said.

She offered him a plate of tempting biscuits, studded with fruit. 'Do try one, they are Cook's specialities. Miss Cressida would be incorrect. I have no sisters, so I am Miss Williams.'

'Yes, but Miss Williams sounds like a rather severe Welsh schoolmistress, don't you think?' Guy took a biscuit and bit into it, wondering if their cook had a relative he could lure into the kitchens at Easton Court. 'I shall pretend Miss Pomfret is your elder sister so, if anyone remarks upon it, I will confess my error.' He brushed crumbs from his sober church-going waistcoat and smiled at Cressida.

I am flirting, which is not wise with ineligible young ladies who are far too respectable for anything but matrimony. On the other hand, she seems perfectly sensible and unlikely to take it for anything but flirtation.

An attractive woman made his rural exile seem more interesting, although he must take care, he cautioned himself. The aim of restoring the Court was to make a home to bring a bride to and he must raise no expectations in Cressida's mind, nor that of the residents of Stowe Easton.

'I suppose I cannot prevent you,' Cressida said, but there was a hint of amusement in her voice as she said it. It was strangely at odds with the serious, almost watchful, expression in her eyes.

Arthur, either being tactful or, more likely, mesmerised by the biscuits he was steadily demolishing, was taking no notice of them.

Very lovely blue eyes, Guy thought, smiling at her over the rim of his tea cup. And just what was she watching for from under those elegantly arched eyebrows?

At that moment, just in time to save him from risking further indiscretion, Miss Pomfret emerged from the house, a large white cat trapped firmly under one arm. 'I have rescued Percy from Cook's wrath,' she announced. 'The lamb is quite unfit to eat, but I have convinced Cook that the gammon joint will do perfectly well instead.' She beamed at him. 'Has our lovely garden inspired you with any ideas for the Court, My Lord?'

'Please, call me Easton, Miss Pomfret. It has certainly reminded me that I am without any garden staff beyond a labourer who apparently scythes down the worst of it. Arthur, you must advertise for a head gardener and he can appoint under-gardeners at his discretion. Perhaps you would advise us on what I should look for in such a man, Miss Cressida? All I can recall of the head gardener at Thornborough Chase is a fierce dislike of small boys and a complexion resembling well-tanned leather.'

Arthur swallowed the last mouthful of biscuit. 'I have done so. Advertised, that is. Before we left London, because no gardeners were listed in the staff ledgers. And I have a list of requirements from the head gardener at home, although I am sure Miss Williams's advice would be most helpful.'

'Excellent, I should have known you would have it in hand,' Guy said, mentally kicking himself. He was so used to Arthur being an invalid that he had forgotten how capable an officer he had been, one who deserved to have risen above the rank of captain. But a younger son, one whose father lavished all the attention and available funds on his heir, could not afford to buy the promotions that Guy could finance so easily.

Nine months at home being fussed over by his mother and sisters, and being told firmly by his father and older brother that of course he would be too handicapped by his injury to act as their steward, had left Arthur demoralised and even more than usually quiet. He did not need Guy implying that he was not capable of doing the job without the intervention of some chance-met local spinster.

And that clumsiness was a direct result of him enjoying flirting with Cressida Williams, which he had no business doing.

Guy finished his tea, checked that Arthur had, too, and rose to his feet. 'Thank you for your hospitality, ladies. I hope you suffer no ill effects from your fall, Miss Pomfret. Thank you for removing the thorn, Miss Cressida.'

He saw Miss Pomfret's eyebrows rise, but she neither corrected him, nor appeared too shocked at the familiarity.

Back in the barouche he said, 'I apologise, Arthur.'

'Whatever for?'

'Assuming you had not already set about finding a

garden staff. Or, to be honest, forgetting that I had a steward and not simply a friend.'

'Think nothing of it. After all, Miss Williams has a knowledge and an enthusiasm for the subject I cannot possibly match. Besides,' he added with what was perilously close to a smirk, 'I am nothing like as pretty.'

'Miss Williams is not pretty,' Guy said. 'She is handsome.'

'And alluring.' Arthur was most definitely teasing now. 'Pretty enough to flirt with, anyway, even if you had to impale yourself on a rosebush in the process to lure her into a tête-à-tête.'

'That was an accident. But you are right, I was flirting and I should not. She is a respectable lady.'

'And no match for an earl.'

'True.' Guy looked at his friend, eyes narrowed with sudden suspicion. Cressida would be a perfectly acceptable match for Arthur. Despising the stab of something akin to jealousy he found a change of subject. 'There is still the park to consider.'

'You will need a permanent staff of groundsmen,' Arthur said. 'There is the lake and the waterways to be dealt with, then the woodlands and the herd of deer, the fences and walls…'

'And there is no point in starting the men to work before we know what needs doing. I do not wish to change the structure of the park, so there is no need to employ someone like Repton, Cressida informs me, but it needs a lot of work.'

'I agree. A park keeper is needed eventually, of course, once it is set to rights. I do wonder…' Arthur trailed off.

'Pull yourself together, Mr Graham, and report! What do you wonder?'

'Whether Miss Williams would tour the park with me to point out what is required. From what you said the other day, she does know it well and has an affinity for the place.'

'I am sure she would, if only to stop me making decisions of which she would not approve—she clearly thinks I am incapable of appreciating the place and I suppose she is right.'

'I will call on Monday,' Arthur said. 'I can enquire about Miss Pomfret's health following the fall and offer to drive Miss Williams around the park in the gig—I can manage that one-handed now. Would she require a chaperon, do you think?'

'Not in an open carriage, no.' The little stab of jealousy was more like a sabre cut now. 'We will both call, because I would like to see what she proposes. I wonder if she can ride?'

Was that a look of chagrin that passed over his friend's face? Or were all the biscuits Arthur had eaten giving him a twinge of indigestion? Guy trod firmly on his conscience. The presence of both of them would mean that no particularity would be attached to Arthur's presence, because, after all, he did not want his friend rushing into an ill-considered attachment.

'It is a miracle I have not gone off into a swoon,' Cressida said. 'Honestly, Marjorie, what were you thinking, inviting them in? My pulse was racing the entire time they were here.'

'I told you why I asked them in,' her cousin said

calmly. 'And, if your pulse was racing, I would suggest it is because you are not as indifferent to Lord Easton as you would have me believe.'

'I never said I disliked the man, simply that I cannot marry him and it would be hideously embarrassing and socially ruinous if he were to discover who I am,' Cressida said, keeping a tight rein on her temper. She took a deep breath and told herself that Marjorie was quite correct: not to have offered hospitality would have been ill mannered. Still, it was tempting to tease her a little. 'Mr Graham is a very pleasant gentleman, is he not? I do admire his determination to earn his living despite the loss of his arm. I seem to recall he is a younger son, but of a very good family, so I am certain he could have been supported comfortably by them if he chose.'

Marjorie tutted. 'You are not going to catch me that way. You know as well as I do that Lord Easton's friend is as ineligible for you as he is. There is no way in which you could pursue more than an acquaintanceship with him without having to reveal your real name.'

'That is very true,' Cressida agreed. Mr Graham did indeed seem to be a nice man, if rather shy, but she had no desire whatsoever to pursue a flirtation with him.

Guy Thurlow, however, was a serious temptation, the very definition of forbidden fruit. It was fortunate that church was the only place their paths would cross. If one could not resist sinful temptation in a church, where could one?

Monday morning brought the usual crop of letters from friends and family, two bills—'The butcher has charged us twice for mutton again. I cannot decide whether he is foolish or thinks that we are!'—and a hand-delivered note from Easton Court.

Lord Easton presents his compliments to Miss Pomfret and Miss Cressida and thanks them for their hospitality yesterday. Mr Graham joins him in hoping that Miss Pomfret has suffered no lasting injury from her fall.

Having discussed the state of the park with Mr Graham, Lord Easton ventures to enquire if Miss Cressida would consider advising them on what work would be necessary to restore it to perfect condition.

Lord Easton appreciates that this would involve Miss Cressida in both time and the exercise of her extensive knowledge and trusts that the offer of compensation for such inconvenience would be accepted in the spirit in which it was offered.

'Fifty guineas! Marjorie, he is offering me fifty guineas in compensation for being driven about the park in an open carriage accompanied by himself and Mr Graham and advising them what must be done over the next few weeks. Fifty guineas. My goodness.'

Marjorie made a sound of protest. 'But, Cressida dear—'

'He says he will provide me with a carriage large enough to accommodate a maid as chaperon—or yourself if you are interested—but that in an open vehicle, in the country, I may not feel that to be necessary. Or, if I care to ride, he would provide a well-mannered mare for me.'

She dropped the letter on the table and stared at it as though unwilling to believe it was real. 'With fifty guineas we could afford to employ Ted Darrell to clear that patch of brambles and tree seedlings at the top of the garden and terrace it. We could have a gravel walk and a gazebo with a view down to the river. We could—'

'But employment, for money, and from a gentleman, too, is most…most unconventional. What will people think?'

'Who needs to know money is involved? Besides, nobody would think twice if he offered me money to be a companion to his aged grandmother or to be governess to his daughters, if he had any,' Cressida argued. 'Marjorie, it is the place I have been aching to restore. I thought it was impossible, just a daydream, but now I can help make it happen.'

'And you can never enjoy it,' her cousin pointed out. 'Once the gentlemen know what needs to be done, that will be all they will require. And once the work is complete it will be what it always was, a private park, and you cannot risk wandering there again.'

'I will know that it is restored, that will be enough.' That was not how she felt now, but she would have to make it so.

'It is not as though we need the money,' Marjorie persisted, as though Cressida had not spoken.

That was true. Marjorie had a small inheritance from her parents, enough for her to have bought the house and to keep herself well dressed and to employ the servants. Cressida had a very respectable allowance from her brother from which she paid her share of household expenses and all her personal needs, as well as the wages of their part-time gardener. But spending on an extravagant garden project was beyond her means.

'We have proved that Lord Easton does not recognise me, even close to,' Cressida ventured. 'I will be very careful not to say anything which might prompt his memories of me, which must be vague indeed after all this time. The park will be lovely again and your garden will be the envy of the town. Think how you will enjoy entertaining in it.'

'Yes,' Marjorie admitted. 'I would. Oh, dear. I am not your guardian—you must do as you think best. I only wish Lord Easton was not quite so attractive.'

'Guy Thurlow is not going to break my heart, never fear,' Cressida declared firmly.

Disturb my dreams, yes. If only... No. Regrets are futile. I made the right decision, the only decision, on my wedding day and it is still right.

Chapter Six

The final letter in the pile threw everything into disarray.

'Who on earth can this be from?' Marjorie peered at the wrapper. 'The handwriting looks almost illiterate.'

'You could open it,' Cressida suggested, but Marjorie was already breaking the seal.

'Oh! Oh, my goodness. Poor dear Harriet went into labour almost the moment the door closed behind Frazer and she gave birth to twins! Her maid wrote this. It is two boys. The maid sounds perfectly distracted and the doctor says Harriet must not stir from her bed and the nurse they employed has had to be dismissed because she drinks. I must go to her at once.'

'Wouldn't her mother be more appropriate?'

'My Aunt Daphne takes after her brother, my father. She has no sympathy for illness or weakness. Poor Harriet needs nursing and supporting, not bracing instructions to pull herself together.' She was on her feet as she spoke, reaching for the bell pull.

'I will hire Jem Tyler's chaise and driver. Jane must

come with me, I fear, because I will be a night on the road, but you will be perfectly comfortable with Cook, will you not?' She darted over to the bookshelves. 'Now where is the copy of *Dr Phillpott's Family Medical Advisor*? It will be so helpful, I am certain. Oh, Jane, there you are. We must pack and be off at once to Mrs Wilmott.

'Cressida, dear, could you go and secure the chaise from Tyler?'

Despite her anxiety Marjorie, complete with Dr Phillpott's weighty tome, was in the chaise only two hours later.

'You will be all right, won't you, Cressida dear?' she said, leaning out of the chaise window as the vehicle set off. 'You must go to the Misses Bartrum if you have any anxieties. Oh! And you will not go to the park with His Lordship, will you, dear? Not until I get back. Now promise me.'

Cressida waved and smiled and said nothing. After all, she would have had to shout her reply and that would be most unladylike.

The groom driving the gig that collected her the next day was smartly turned out and very respectful. 'His Lordship said he thought it would be more comfortable for you if he and Mr Graham met you at the park. I am Bates. Is your maid joining you, Miss Williams?'

It was thoughtful to send the groom, because even the most genteel of neighbours would gossip, and they had already had to deal with interested enquiries about the arrival of Lord Easton's carriage on the Sunday morning, to say nothing of Marjorie's hasty departure on Monday.

Cressida nodded acknowledgement of the point. 'No, I do not feel the need for a maid today.' Although the gig was large enough for three, she noted, appreciating Lord Easton's thoughtfulness. In any case, with Jane gone, that only left Cook who would not take kindly to being dragged from her kitchen and made to bump about the countryside.

Lord Easton met them at the main entrance to the park, his handsome bay hack a contrast to Mr Graham's ugly strawberry roan. Judging by its response to the slightest touch of its rider's hand or heels, and the scars that marked its hide, it was Mr Graham's old cavalry mount.

'I have a notebook,' Cressida told them after greetings had been exchanged. 'I will jot things down as we encounter them and then order them more logically later so that we can form a plan of action.'

Although ill mended, the main carriage drives through the park had at least been cleared of encroaching undergrowth, so they reached the lake easily enough and dismounted to view the dam at the end. It should have had a picturesque little waterfall where it drained to a stream—now there was a tumble of rocks with willow saplings growing amid them and masses of reeds.

'Even I can see that needs repairs,' Lord Easton remarked. 'That large breach there has lowered the level of the lake.'

'And the lake should be dredged in any case,' Mr Graham said, withdrawing his booted foot rapidly as he approached the water. 'It has become merely bog around the edges.'

'We could get a better view from the Temple of the Winds, up there.' Cressida pointed to where a glimmer of white through the trees betrayed the position of a little building in the Greek style. 'It used to be more visible, but those sycamore seedlings have grown up so quickly.'

They had to leave the horses with the groom about halfway up the hill when the track petered out into a mere footpath and, by the time they reached the temple, even the men were breathing heavily, more from fighting through the undergrowth to clear a path for Cressida than the actual slope.

'Now this is charming,' Easton said, standing back, hands on narrow hips, to admire the building.

'It needs a stonemason to survey it and to organise repairs and clean all the moss and staining off,' Mr Graham said critically, walking around it.

'And all these sycamores must be rooted out.' Cressida scribbled notes. 'And some furniture ordered, perhaps. It would make a delightful spot for picnics. The tracks must be cleared and repaired first, though, otherwise the stonemasons will not be able to get here.'

'There is another building down there,' Lord Easton said from somewhere above them and Cressida swung around, trying to work out where he was. Halfway up a tree, she discovered, hiding a smile. Sometimes grown men could not resist behaving like little boys, although there was nothing boyish about the figure standing so fearlessly on a branch with one hand bracing him against the trunk.

'What kind of building is it?'

'I can just see the roof below us, but that is all. It must be right on the water's edge, so a boathouse, I assume.'

'Shall we go there next?' Cressida suggested. 'That looks like the remains of a track over there which must lead downhill.'

'I had best go and fetch the gig and the horses,' Mr Graham offered. 'Then we can see if we can find a way along the lake edge to the boathouse and meet you there. If we can't get through, then I will walk.'

Cressida and Easton picked their way down the slope in silence. It was easier than climbing up, although occasionally they each had to catch hold of a tree to stop themselves careering down the slope.

'Almost there.' He pointed to a moss-covered tiled roof overhanging the water's edge and then they were on the shoreline, a narrow strip of shingle and weedy mud.

'It is quite large,' Cressida said, studying the wooden building. 'I'm surprised I've never noticed it before, although it does blend in with the trees very well.'

'Perhaps I have a small fleet inside,' Easton said, making his way to the landward end. 'Someone thought it worth putting a chain and lock on the door.' He gave it an experimental tug and it came away in his hand, the staples pulling clean out of rotting uprights.

He dragged the double doors open with an effort through piled-up leaf mould and looked in. 'Yes, there is definitely a fleet—look. Rowing boats large and small, and a punt and what I think might be a little sailing skiff. Although it has a tarpaulin over it, so I cannot be certain.'

He vanished inside.

Typical man, Cressida thought with a wry smile. *With all the things that have to be done before the lake is in a fit state for anything, he wants to spend time on the boats.*

Even so, she was intrigued. A little sailing skiff darting about on the water would make a picturesque touch and would be delightful on a hot day, or for fishing. Not that she would ever see it, of course.

'The building needs a lot of work,' she said dubiously, looking around her as she stepped inside. The boathouse was a large wooden shed built out over the water. There was a platform forming a dock just inside the doors and a walkway around the two sides. The front, which opened on to the lake, had slatted double doors that created bars of sunlight on the scummy water. The little windows in the sides were thick with cobwebs, but the holes and cracks in the structure were letting in far more light than they ever had.

'I will make a note that it needs extensive work, but it is hardly a priority, surely?' She made her way around the walkway on the right-hand side as she spoke, prodding at the walls as she did so. 'I suspect it will need completely rebuilding.'

Easton was on the opposite side. He shielded his eyes from the dazzle from the doors as he looked across. 'I think you should go back, Cressida. Those supporting timbers do not look sound to me.'

'It feels steady enough,' Cressida said. As she spoke the boards beneath her feet gave a sudden lurch. 'Oh… No, it isn't.' She jumped across the gap that appeared, landed awkwardly and the whole walkway creaked and tipped sideways, pitching her into the water. 'Guy!'

There was a fleeting, irrational second in mid-air when she thought, *I shouldn't have called him that—* and then she hit the water.

It was cold. That was the first shock as she flailed her arms, trying to get upright, trying to find the bottom with her feet. She couldn't swim, but surely it wasn't deep here?

Then her left foot snagged on something, jerking her under. Disorientated, weighed down by her skirts, she struggled, then her head hit something hard, she saw stars, gulped for air and found her mouth full of thick, disgusting water as the world went black.

It was a nightmare, one of those where you run until your heart is cracking, but your feet are deep in mud and the unseen monster behind you is breathing hotly on your neck.

He couldn't dive, there were the old boats in his way, so all he could do was run, with the rotting boards giving way under his feet with every stride. It took perhaps five seconds to reach clear water and by then he was too aware of the hidden dangers below the surface to risk plunging in recklessly. He would be no use to Cressida if he impaled himself on some sunken spar.

Guy, she had called as she plunged into the water, the water he had led her to, so intrigued by the boats that he hadn't taken a thought for her safety. There was no sign of her now, only an ominous silence as ripples like little waves slapped against wood and he struggled out of coat and boots and lowered himself into the water.

It might be July, but in the cover of the boathouse the black water struck cold. Under his stockinged feet he could feel wood and slime and jagged objects. Rotting boats, perhaps, or branches swept in during winter storms. Guy made himself wade slowly, feeling all around him, despite the urge to rush and flail about.

'Easton?' That was Arthur outside.

'In here. Take care, everything is rotten,' he shouted. 'Cressida has fallen in.'

Where was she? There couldn't be some kind of current, could there? Something that could have carried her out and under the doors? Horror tales of giant eels, of predatory pike, flashed though his imagination and were pushed aside. *Focus.*

Then, just as he was beginning to feel real fear, his outstretched hand touched fabric. As he hauled on it, he touched an arm, still warm, but so very unresponsive. Cressida's body came as far as he pulled, her face just above the water, then resisted.

'Something's holding her back,' he called to Arthur. 'I need to dive, but she'll slip below the surface again.'

'Here. There's rope, coiled on the wall. I think it is sound. Put it around her and I'll try to keep her head clear of the water.'

It was not the best throw. Arthur had to hold the rope and toss it to him, all with one hand, but it landed near enough. After what seemed like an hour struggling to get it around Cressida's shoulders, Guy managed it, Arthur pulled on the slack and Cressida's face was clear of the surface.

She isn't breathing, Guy thought as he dived, then made himself concentrate on getting her free.

Her foot was jammed in the crook of a branch, he found as he fumbled in the darkness. The wood was still solid, wouldn't break. Her ankle was jammed. He wrenched at the half-boot she wore, dragged it off and it made just enough room to free the foot.

'Pull!' he ordered as he broke surface again, half-blinded by foul, muddy water, his arms full of water-logged fabric, limp woman.

Afterwards he had no idea how they got her out. When he was thinking straight again they were in the open air behind the boathouse and he was holding Cressida by the shoulders as she coughed and retched to rid herself of the foul water.

Arthur came running back along the track with Bates, the groom, at his heels carrying the rug from the gig.

'Cressida?' Guy turned her so she lay back propped in his arms and wiped her face as best he could with his hand, ruffling her immaculately groomed eyebrows, smearing mud across pale cheeks.

She looked absurdly young and strangely familiar, like a memory from long ago. Then she opened her eyes, struggled to sit and the elusive wisp of familiarity vanished. 'Lie still.'

'Guy? I…I mean, Easton. What happened?'

'The rotten staging gave way, you fell in and trapped your foot.'

She moved it experimentally and winced. 'You pulled me out.'

'Arthur helped. Now, if you feel well enough to move, then Bates and I will make a carrying seat with our hands and take you back to the gig.'

Somehow they got her supported between them, but Cressida had lapsed into a daze by then, limp and unresponsive. How one slight young woman could be so unwieldy, he had no idea, but her sodden clothing did not help as they hauled her into the gig. Guy climbed up and took her in his arms, his horse followed Arthur's hack and Bates drove as fast as the uneven tracks allowed back to the Court.

Arthur had employed as his new housekeeper a woman who seemed not only highly experienced at her business—transforming the Court would be no job for a beginner—and also intelligent and calm.

Mrs Grainger's reaction when Guy strode, soaking wet, across the threshold with his arms full of unconscious woman, fully justified his decision.

'Upstairs to the damask bedchamber, My Lord.' She tugged at the bell pull. 'I'll send for the doctor. Milly—run up and get towels spread on the bed. Hurry, girl. Tell Griggs he'll need a hot bath for His Lordship and hot water sent up to the damask room.'

'Where am I?' Cressida asked as someone lifted her shoulders and began to wrap something around her head. Her mouth tasted foul, her ankle throbbed, her chest ached and, when she managed to open her eyes, she seemed to be draped loosely in towels. 'Where are my clothes?'

'You are at Easton Court, Miss Williams,' a reassuringly female voice said. 'The maids and I undressed you and we've sponged you down as well as we can, but we can't wash your hair yet, so that's wrapped up.'

'What happened?' She had been up at the Temple of the Winds. How had she become sick and...*damp*?

'You fell in the lake at the boathouse, Miss Williams. His Lordship got you out, but you were half-drowned and you have hurt your ankle. The doctor will be here soon, I've no doubt, and he'll tell us whether you can get up and have a bath.'

Cressida managed a weak smile. Trust another woman to know that what she wanted more than anything was to be clean again. The memory of the scum on the muddy water made her shudder.

'Are you cold, Miss Williams? Maud, fetch some blankets.'

'No, I feel... I would like a drink.'

'Hot chocolate, that'll be the thing. It is on its way. Now, you just close your eyes and rest, try to sleep.'

Cressida must have dozed, because the next thing she was aware of was dear old Dr Symonds telling her firmly to sit up and tell him where it hurt. When she looked at him, she saw a handsome stranger standing just behind.

'My chest and my throat and my right ankle,' she said, half-distracted by the other man.

'Yes, you may blink, Miss Williams. After my gnarled old face our new physician will be quite a shock, I imagine. This is Dr James Crozier who arrived yesterday to take over my practice. Crozier, I can tell you that Miss Williams is usually far too sensible to find herself in such a pickle. Now, Dr Crozier will examine your ankle and I'll take a look at the rest of you.'

Having a tall, blond, good-looking young man examine her bare leg was embarrassing, but being poked and pummelled by the old doctor was sufficiently distracting.

'Drink as much as you like of water or tea. Cough as much as you can to clear your lungs. What say you about the ankle, Crozier?'

'It is badly skinned and bruised and sprained, but nothing is broken. I would suggest a good soak in warm water to make certain it is clean and then Mrs Grainger can bandage it up with a salve I will leave her. You should rest it as much as possible and not put any weight on it for several days, Miss Williams.'

'But may I take a bath?' she asked, feeling that, just then, it was all she wanted.

'Certainly. But with help, we do not want you fainting.'

It was truly wonderful how much more human she felt once she was clean, and dressed in one of Mrs Grainger's nightgowns and sitting up in bed with a stool over her bad ankle to keep the bedclothes off it. She would send home with a list for Cook to pack up the clothing she needed and then she could leave. The thought of her own bed was alluring, but she supposed she'd have to use the couch in her cousin's drawing room until she could put weight on her ankle and manage the stairs. If only she didn't feel so peculiar, as though she was about to come down with a nasty cold.

It was the effect of swallowing all that water, of course, and then bringing it back up again. Her throat was sore, her ribs ached, that was all that was wrong with her. And there was the shock, of course.

'Your hair is almost dry now, Miss Williams.' Maud, the maid who had been rubbing it energetically for almost half an hour, tossed down the towel and ran the brush through Cressida's hair. 'We'll just leave it loose on your shoulders for a little while and then I will plait it for you. Oh, and His Lordship asks, may he visit you?'

'Yes, of course.' It was ridiculous to feel self-conscious about being in bed. The housekeeper's modest flannel nightgown and shawl could not have been more decent and Mrs Grainger herself took a seat in the corner, clearly intent on preserving the proprieties.

'How are you, Miss Cressida?' Guy Thurlow did not look at all like a man who had been immersed in a lake only hours before.

'Much better. And I must thank you most sincerely for saving my life, Lord Easton. I would have drowned if you had not been there.'

'You would not have been in the slightest danger if it had not been for my negligence,' he said, his mouth grim. 'Now we are in a position to give Miss Pomfret reassuring news I will drive over there and invite her to spend the night here, which I am sure would be a comfort to you both. Then, if you feel well enough to attempt it, I can take you both home tomorrow in my carriage.'

'My cousin is away from home, visiting a relative who is sorely in need of her at the moment. But I would be most grateful to be taken home by carriage, just as soon as my gown is dry. Or perhaps I might borrow something from one of the maids, or send home for something?'

Guy came to the foot of the bed and regarded her though narrowed eyes. 'And who does that leave at home, Cressida? I assume Miss Pomfret took her maid with her.'

'There's Cook,' Cressida said, managing a smile despite the unpleasant sensation that her teeth wanted to chatter like a bird-scaring rattle.

'One female servant, one who is not used to looking after a lady, and you unable to put your foot to the ground? I think not. You must remain here.'

'It would be most imp-proper.' What was the matter with her?

'Are you suggesting that Mrs Grainger is not a perfectly respectable chaperon?' he asked, with a quizzical glance at the housekeeper.

'No. No, of course not.' If she could only think straight… 'That isn't what I th-think.'

'Might I suggest you call at the Vicarage, My Lord?' Mrs Grainger said. 'You could explain the situation to Mrs Truscott and ask her advice.'

'I do not want to be any tr-trouble.' Now the room was swirling around in a most disconcerting manner with Guy's face the only fixed point in the centre of her vision. 'I think I am going to faint. But I never…'

Chapter Seven

'I never faint,' Cressida said, with as much emphasis as she could manage. The tall figure leaning over her was blurred and somehow wrong. 'You aren't Guy,' she protested.

'I am Dr James Crozier, Miss Williams. And you have a fever. Now drink this.'

Someone behind her lifted the pillows until she was almost sitting. A glass pressed against her lips and she instinctively opened them.

'Ugh!' It was disgusting.

'Swallow,' Dr Crozier said. 'You can lower her again now, Mrs Grainger.'

'I want to go home.' That was the one clear thought in her head. That and wanting to say it to Guy, not this autocrat of a doctor who made her drink revolting medicine.

'You are going nowhere, Miss Williams, not until your fever lowers and, even then, not for at least a week. Try to sleep now.'

* * *

Guy stood outside the door, which was just ajar, and listened intently. Cressida was being just as difficult as might be expected, he thought with a smile. And she had expected to see him. Or perhaps had wanted to see him. That was flattering and disconcerting, both at the same time, because he wanted to see her and the degree of anxiety he was feeling about her was beginning to worry him.

Flirting with Cressida Williams was one thing. Falling for her was quite another and letting it be seen was dangerous. Even Arthur, who was delicately negotiating their new relationship of employee to employer, friend and junior officer to senior, had ventured the occasional slyly teasing remark about her.

When he had called on her the day before, he had half hoped, half feared that the Vicar's wife would tell him to bring Cressida to her house to be nursed, but the youngest Truscott, ten-year-old Paul, had just succumbed to the measles. Mrs Truscott, distracted though sympathetic, was clearly in no state to accept another invalid into the house. Nor did she suggest any other lady in the town. 'I am certain nobody could consider Mrs Grainger anything but the most respectable of chaperons, My Lord, but the delicacy of your scruples do you credit.'

So that was that. He had a bedridden houseguest; the maids were all far more eager to wait upon a young lady than they were to tackle the grime of ages in the house and his new French chef was spending more time concocting tempting trifles for the invalid than substantial meals for two hungry men. And he wanted nothing more than to sit by Cressida's bedside and talk to her, or hold her hand or read aloud or whatever would bring the sparkle back into those deep blue eyes. He must be feverish himself.

Crozier came out and raised one eyebrow at the sight of Guy.

Insolent devil.

'How is she, Doctor?'

'Very weak, but coherent. What she caught from that stagnant lake, I have no idea. I did fear at first that it might be cholera, but mercifully it does not appear to be that. I have told Mrs Grainger to continue with light, sustaining foods and plenty of water. Miss Williams needs fresh air and complete rest. I am sure you would prefer to be free of your involuntary guest, but I would not wish her to be moved for at least a week, if then. I shall call daily.'

'Miss Williams is very welcome to stay for as long as necessary. You will oblige me by sending your account to me.'

There goes that damnable eyebrow again.

'Miss Williams was kind enough to be offering me advice on the landscaping of the park. You may not be aware that she is a most accomplished horticulturalist.' Damn the man for forcing him into making excuses.

And she is not my mistress, whatever your suspicious mind thinks.

'Certainly, Lord Easton.'

Griggs, a pair of Guy's boots in his hand, came around the corner and observed the doctor's retreating back. 'Handsome, isn't he, My Lord? He'll have the devil of a job fighting off the ladies, I'll be bound.'

'And I'm having the devil of a job turning a batman into a halfway decent valet,' Guy retorted as he tapped on the bedchamber door.

It was opened by his housekeeper.

'Is Miss Williams strong enough to receive a visitor? I wondered if she would like me to read to her.'

'She may not be able to concentrate, My Lord. But it may help her to drift off to sleep.'

That was not quite the reaction to his voice that he was hoping for, but Guy told himself firmly that if sleep was the best thing for Cressida, then that was what he would help her find.

As he entered the room the pale-faced figure on the bed opened her eyes and blinked at him. 'Guy? My Lord, I should say.' Her voice was a thread, but at least she was coherent.

'Guy. How are you—or are you heartily weary of people asking you that?'

'I feel like a cushion that has had all the stuffing shaken out of it,' Cressida admitted with the ghost of her old smile.

'I came to see if there is anything I can do. Perhaps you would like me to read to you? Mrs Grainger suggested that would send you to sleep.'

Cressida gave the ghost of a chuckle. 'That would be very kind. Mrs Grainger found some old copies of journals in the library. There may be something in one of those that would not be too much of a bore for you to read.'

Guy inspected the pile of bound periodicals. He had glanced once into the library, shuddered at the ranks of dusty, cobweb-covered tomes and hadn't ventured back since.

One volume bound in brown calfskin shed a very dead spider when he opened it. *La Belle Assemblée or Bell's Court and Fashionable Magazine, Addressed Particularly to the Ladies, Vol. III, 1807,* the title page announced between a pair of Egyptian-style figures on columns and over a sphinx with improbably large, round breasts.

'Let me see what delights this holds.' He thumbed though. 'I can offer you a biographical sketch of the Queen of Prussia, a curious account of two elephants, culinary researches or perhaps a description of the city of Vienna and the manners of its inhabitants.'

'Difficult to choose,' Cressida said. 'I think Vienna, followed, should I still be awake, by the elephants. I do not feel very interested in food at the moment and the Queen of Prussia lacks appeal for me, I fear.'

Out of the corner of his eye Guy noticed his housekeeper settle herself in the far corner of the room and take a piece of linen from a workbasket. All very proper.

'Very well, Vienna it is.' He turned to the correct page and glanced at Cressida. Her eyes were closed, her dark lashes fanned out on her cheeks. She looked very vulnerable and something in his chest seemed to twist. Compassion, perhaps, or guilt, he told himself and began to read.

'Vienna has for many ages been considered as in some measure the capital of the Roman empire...'

'Literature does not flourish in this city. Whatever title the Germans have to the appellation of a learned nation, the inhabitants of Vienna and the north of Germany can have no share in the honour.'

What on earth?

She could not quite summon the energy to open her eyes but, surely, she must be very ill and hallucinating if someone, in Guy's voice, was slandering the Germans, a perfectly well-educated nation as far as she knew.

'Guy?' She reached out a hand and it was taken immediately in a warm, firm grasp.

'I am here.'

'Oh.' She did look then, but it seemed the lack of energy had moved to her hand. She ought to withdraw it, but it somehow remained in his. 'Whatever are you reading?'

'You told me to read about Vienna,' he protested, holding up a book. He laid it down and, with his free hand, began to page through it. 'I could read about the antiquities of the Strand, or principles of tuning instruments or the importance of soups, if you like. The item on elephants appears to be missing.'

'You are teasing me. Whoever can be interested in those topics?' The expression in his eyes when he glanced up from the magazine was certainly amused and—surely she was imagining it?—tender.

'I am not.' That was mock indignant. 'It says quite clearly on the title page that this journal is addressed particularly to the ladies.'

'I am obviously not the kind of lady the publisher had in mind. How lowering.'

'I think you are perhaps a unique kind of lady,' Guy said, so softly that she thought for a moment that her ears deceived her. She saw Mrs Grainger glance up from her sewing on the other side of the room. She could not have heard the words, but something in their tone must have reached her.

'Guy—'

'Yes?' He released her hand and closed the volume.

'How long have I been here?'

'This is the third day since the accident. I wrote to Miss Pomfret the day afterwards when it was clear that you would be staying here for a time. Your cook gave us the address of her relative, but I have received a reply today saying that she is unable to leave as the lady is very unwell and so also is one of her new infants. Miss Pomfret expressed every confidence in your care—I had mentioned Mrs Grainger and also the frequent attendance of Dr Crozier. She sends you her love.'

It was hard to concentrate, but Cressida made herself think of the implications of Marjorie's letter. Harriet was clearly in need of support, but surely that would not have stopped her, at the very least, sending Jane back, let alone bombarding the Vicar's wife and the other worthy ladies of the town with demands that they rush to Cressida's aid. The sneaking suspicion that Marjorie was matchmaking could not be banished.

She would not succeed, obviously. Guy was merely being a good neighbour and showing concern that she had almost drowned while assisting him. He might flirt, but then he probably flirted with any young lady who came into his orbit. He was an attractive man, after all.

A very attractive man.

And even in the event that he completely lost all sense of what was due to the heir to a marquess and fell for a lady who was, apparently, merely of the middling sort socially, then she would refuse him. She could do nothing else. To tell him the truth of who she was and why she had been unable to marry him all that time ago was completely impossible. It was not her secret to tell and the shame of it would fall not only on her, but upon Mama.

Her mother might no longer be living, but the thought of scandal touching her name made Cressida shudder. Beside which her young nieces, Cressida's cousins, were making their come-outs and their prospects would be blighted by any connection with such a scandal. It had taken long enough for the talk to die down after Cressida's flight from the altar steps.

And then there was her brother and his family— five young children who would grow up with people whispering, *Oh, but you have heard about their grandmother, didn't you know...*

The tight feeling in her chest would not go away. Cressida tried to cough, but that was difficult when lying flat on her back.

'Could I sit up?' she asked, trying not to sound as plaintive as she felt. 'It feels so strange having to look at the world from this position.'

'Even if the world consists of a rather shabby and ill-furnished bedchamber? I can well recall that such surroundings make you feel even weaker than you actually are.'

'When were you confined to your bed?'

He held up his left hand where the top of his little

finger was missing to the first joint and a pale scar ran across the back of his hand. She had noticed it before, but it had clearly healed well and did not appear to cause Guy difficulties.

'It doesn't look very dramatic,' he said, 'and compared to Arthur's arm, of course it isn't, but that slash laid my arm open from wrist to shoulder and put me on my back for a few days.'

'The pair of you had bad luck.'

Guy grimaced. 'Not as bad as some of our comrades. We lost several good friends. War is not the exciting adventure we all thought when we were green young men. The Indestructibles, we called ourselves. That was asking for trouble, of course, and the Fates heard us and duly punished us for our presumption.' His shrug dismissed the subject and he looked around. 'It seems Mrs Grainger has deserted us. Some domestic crisis, no doubt. I did not notice her leave.'

Neither did I, but then, I was trying not to stare into a pair of intent grey eyes.

The door had been left open, of course. 'Never mind, I can lie here and wait until she returns.'

'No, I am sure I can manage.' He shifted to sit on the edge of the bed and leaned over to pull the two pillows from the other side towards him. 'Can you sit up?'

'I... No.' It was her weakness, not his proximity, that was to blame, Cressida told herself.

Guy bent low. 'Put your arms around my neck and clasp your hands together. I will pull you up and push the pillows behind you at the same time. It will only take a moment.'

His shoulders felt broad and firm as she lifted her

arms. His hair was surprisingly soft as her fingers fumbled to link behind his neck.

'Ready?' His face was close to hers and she could feel his breath on her cheek.

Cressida closed her eyes. 'Yes.'

Guy sat back, pulling her up as he did so, one arm coming round her back to support her. 'Hold tight.' He sounded strangely breathless. Surely she wasn't *that* heavy?

He shifted position slightly, stretching to pull the pillows across with his free hand until she felt their soft bulk behind her.

'They are a trifle twisted, but we can straighten them up in a moment.'

She opened her eyes again and found herself almost nose to nose with him, his eyes dark and intent on hers.

'Cressida?'

A question she knew the answer to. Cressida swayed forward the half-inch that was necessary to bring her lips against his and sighed as she met the warmth and yielding softness. She had kissed this man before long ago, or, rather, she had been kissed—the respectful, passionless and formal press of lips to cheek that seemed necessary to seal a wedding contract.

There was no formality here, no want of passion either: she could tell that for all her lack of experience. Despite the absence of demand from either his mouth or his encircling arm, this man wanted her, wanted considerably more than this gentle exploration, the briefest touch of tongue against the seam of her lips. She answered instinctively by opening to him, allowing the tip of her own tongue to touch his.

Heat, moistness, the taste of coffee and man, a shiver of awareness that tingled from mouth to belly and, shockingly, to her nipples that hardened, protected only by the chaste flannel nightgown from the pressure of his chest against her.

He must have taken her slight movement for rejection, Cressida realised, as she found herself lying limply against the stacked pillows. Guy was back on the chair. They stared at each other, silent, then, as he opened his mouth to speak, the door opened wide and the housekeeper entered in her discreet, soft-footed, way.

'Oh, you are awake and sitting up, Miss Williams. Now that *is* a good sign. I had not realised you had the strength to raise yourself.'

'Yes, it was a surprise to me, too,' Cressida said. 'Clearly Lord Easton's reading has had an invigorating effect. I do feel much better like this,' she added, conscious of an urge to chatter as though to distract Mrs Grainger's attention from whatever it was crackling in the air between herself and Guy. Surely it must be visible?

'I do hope that my presence was not…unhelpful,' Guy said, his expression impossible to interpret.

'Indeed not. And, after all, I could always have asked you to leave. Or pretended to fall asleep,' she added, a sudden wicked urge to tease him coming over her. Where had that bubble of happiness come from? It was impossible, rash, utterly unwise—but, oh, she felt so reckless suddenly.

It was worth the indiscretion to see the expression on Guy's face. People did not tell earls that they might ignore their unwanted company by falling asleep and women most certainly did not allow slumber to over-take them in Guy's arms, she was certain of that.

For a second she glimpsed the aristocrat affronted, then his sense of humour got the better of him and he laughed out loud. 'That would certainly have given me a hint that my, er, *efforts* were unwelcome, Cressida.'

'No, they were not,' she admitted honestly. 'But perhaps unwise, given my condition.' The word was ambiguous, but she saw him take it as she meant it: not a reference to her health, but her social standing.

Mrs Grainger, gathering up her sewing basket, ap-peared to take no notice of the exchange. 'Dr Crozier will be returning tomorrow morning, Miss Williams,' she said as she straightened up. 'Such a pleasant young man, I thought, and so very handsome.'

'Everybody appears to be of that opinion,' Guy said. 'Even my valet remarked upon it. What is your view, Cressida?'

'Exceedingly handsome. And very masterful—I declare I would be quite afraid to disobey him and not to get better when he ordered it would certainly be rank ingratitude.'

Guy made a sound remarkably like a growl and stood up. 'I will leave you to dream of flirting with your doctor then, Cressida. They do say that good-looking doctors and clergymen attract much admira-tion from the susceptible ladies of any parish. It must be quite a burden to them.'

The door closed behind him and Cressida found the housekeeper regarding her with something very close to a smirk. 'Oh, dear! There is nothing a handsome man dislikes as much as ladies praising another Adonis, is there?' Mrs Grainger said.

Chapter Eight

Guy found Arthur Graham in the library. One of the large tables had been cleared and dusted and he had several very large maps spread out, a stack of notes by his side and a pencil tucked behind his ear.

'I have located all the estate maps at last,' he said, straightening up from a close examination of something in the middle of one of the plans. 'They were on the map stand in here. No wonder these were not in the estate office when I searched—just look at the size of them.'

They were certainly large enough to create wall hangings, or possibly a tablecloth for the table in the Great Dining Hall, Guy thought. As opposed to the Chinese Dining Room, the Small Dining Room or the Breakfast Room. He was still discovering rooms and there seemed to be at least four for any given purpose. They were all equally spider-infested and dusty.

'These are charming, as well as useful,' Arthur said, resuming his scrutiny. 'See the little drawings of deer in the park and the figures by the house? I think this one must be the oldest, Elizabethan, perhaps. What do you think?'

When Guy greeted this enthusiasm with a grunt, Arthur pushed the map away. 'You are worried. I should have asked how Miss Williams is feeling, not rattled on about maps.'

'She is sitting up and taking notice, especially of that damned doctor.' Guy pulled a different map towards him and tried to focus on identifying features.

'Crozier? A very handsome fellow, is he not? Quite enough to rouse any frail lady from her sickbed,' Arthur added with a snort of laughter that made the pencil fall from its perch.

'I do not find that amusing, Arthur. Miss Williams is too much a lady to be so vulgar as to harbour unseemly thoughts of her doctor,' Guy said, sounding ludicrously pompous to his own ears.

'I beg your pardon, Easton. You are quite correct, that was an inappropriate observation.'

Guy waved the apology away. 'No, forgive my sour temper. I am out of sorts and tired of hearing my household lavish admiration on Crozier for his looks, as though they add value to his worth as a medical practitioner. Doctors appear to have exalted opinions of their own skill, regardless of the number of patients they kill with their expensive cures.

'Not that Cressida appears to be in any danger,' he added when a look of concern crossed Arthur's face. 'She is far from well, but there is a distinct recovery. Even I can tell that.'

And kissing a sick woman was inexcusable, he told himself. *Not that Cressida had been unwilling,* he argued with his own conscience. That pointed out, sharply enough, that raising expectations in the breast of any female was ungentlemanly and could well lead to serious repercussions. Taking a woman in his arms and kissing her was the very definition of raising expectations unless she knew him for an out-and-out rake.

'A very pleasant young lady, I think,' Arthur observed after a moment, his attention apparently fixed on a field in the far corner of a tattered map.

'Yes.'

'And well read.'

'Indeed.' Where was his friend leading now?

'Doctor Crozier would make a very suitable husband for Miss Williams, I would have thought.'

The anger that flashed through Guy was almost painful. Long army discipline kept him from snarling back at Arthur, but it was a close-run thing before discretion got the better of him.

They looked at each other for a long moment. Guy scowled and Arthur stared back steadily.

Guy knew his expression, or perhaps his lack of words, must have betrayed him. Arthur, with more courage than tact or discretion, said, 'The Marquess would be strongly opposed to such an unequal match, of course.'

'I cannot imagine what my father would have to do with the matrimonial affairs of a country town doctor,' Guy snapped, wilfully misunderstanding his friend who was not, he thought grimly, going to remain his estate manager very long at this rate.

'I was not referring to Crozier,' Arthur said mildly,

surprising Guy by neither taking the hint, nor being intimidated into silence. 'She is a delightful young lady and clearly well bred. So surely the Marquess would come round in time, whatever his initial reservations?' He frowned, retrieved the pencil he had been making notes with and began to suck the end thoughtfully. 'She reminds me of someone, but I cannot for the life of me think who.'

'She reminds *me* that my duty to my father, and to my name, is to marry well to enhance our standing and to protect our inheritance. And stop chewing that confounded pencil like a schoolboy,' Guy said irritably. He sat down, the anger ebbing in the face of such determined frankness. 'You know as well as I do what that means: good breeding, significant connections and a good settlement, preferably in land.

'I cannot deny that I find Cressida attractive.'

That is an understatement, his conscience remarked. Guy ignored it and attempted to sound as though he was making a reasoned, detached, assessment. 'She has the manners and the attitude of a lady, but she lacks everything else that would make her acceptable. I do not even know who her parents are, for goodness sake.'

'Find out,' Arthur said, staring at Guy as though he had said something profoundly stupid. 'You are leaping to assumptions. She may have excellent breeding and connections, but be of a minor family line. Her father may be an East Indies nabob rolling in money he is too mean to distribute until his death. Her godfather might be a duke, ready and willing to shower benefits upon her husband if he approves of him.'

'You should be writing fiction,' Guy retorted, although he could not help feeling a stir of hope. And then a stab of surprise. What was he thinking of, speaking as though he wished to propose marriage to Cressida Williams?

Yes, he was attracted to her, it would be strange if he was not. She was a handsome young woman with an interesting personality, intelligence, humour and courage. He had enjoyed that first careful kiss very much indeed and the memory of the sensation of her body against his lingered, demanding more. But that was not love, was it? And that would be the only possible excuse for marrying with so little regard to the conventions. Whatever love was…

And what had love to do with anything anyway? Passionate attachment would be the only excuse for him contemplating such a misalliance, but the heir to a marquess did not marry for sentiment.

'I do not deny that I find Cressida very appealing. I like her and find her interesting,' he said carefully. 'But I am here restoring this house and this estate so that I have a fitting home to bring a bride to and I will find that bride in London during the coming Season. That is the prudent, logical way to approach finding a suitable wife for a man in my position.'

'It did not work very well the last time, did it though?' Arthur ventured, looking wary, as though he expected a paperweight to be thrown at his head for his daring.

'It did not.' Guy managed not to grit his teeth. 'But then I was foolish enough to allow a lady to be selected for me. I came home on leave and found a virtual *fait accompli*. I could hardly complain—the match was

one which appeared to be entirely suitable. But Viola
FitzWalden was too young, too shy and too lacking in
worldly wisdom and confidence I concluded, once I
could think through the matter calmly. The marriage
would have been a disaster.

'I do not intend to make a mistake this time. This
time I will select my bride with great care and make
certain I know her well. She will be exactly according
to my requirements. And willing, of course.'

'I hardly think that any lady of sense on the Marriage Mart would find an offer of marriage to the Marquess of Thornborough's eldest son unacceptable.'

'Miss FitzWalden did,' Guy pointed out drily. 'Presumably you would say she was lacking sense.'

'You never did discover the reason, did you?' Arthur asked. 'Her brother appeared to be as surprised
and baffled as we were.'

'I never felt the need to investigate,' Guy said. Then
added with a burst of honesty, 'What if the problem
had lain with me? I do not think, at the time, that my
amour propre would have stood the blow.'

'And now?'

'You are suggesting that I probe into Viola's reasons, because now I am more mature and can cope
with discovering what made me so unacceptable then?'

'Exactly,' Arthur said.

He tossed aside the mangled pencil as though sig-
nalling a change of subject and pointed to the table.
'That is the most recent map of the estate. I will copy
it on to canvas so I can hang it on the wall in the estate office. I had no idea that the experience of drawing campaign sketch maps would come in so useful.

Then, when Miss Williams is recovered, I would like to go over it with her and mark up the works we had noted the other day.'

Guy, recognising wryly that he was probably surplus to requirements now that his estate manager had lectured him on his marital affairs and love life—or lack of—took himself off to begin a systematic survey of the interior of the house. He might as well depress himself thoroughly while he was at it. And it would keep him away from Cressida and the temptation to either make a complete fool of himself by wanting to make love to her again or launching into a humiliating and clumsy apology.

An apology there would have to be, but only when he had composed it carefully first.

The delicious sensation of Guy's kiss, and the exhilarating realisation that he was jealous of Dr Crozier, lasted perhaps half an hour for Cressida. It was replaced with the sinking realisation that she had been very foolish indeed. It would have taken only the simplest of gestures to have turned away his lips and she knew the man well enough by now to believe he would not have persisted.

So now she had added the knowledge of what it was like to be kissed by Guy Thurlow to her existing attraction. Worse, she had shown herself to be more than willing to succumb to his embraces.

And what can he conclude from that? she thought, with an internal squirm of embarrassment. *That you are willing to be his mistress? Or simply that you are a fast young woman eager to do more than simply flirt?*

What would Guy do now? Offer her a carte blanche to be his mistress or continue to snatch kisses and perhaps expect more?

Neither was possible for her, she knew that. She would no more throw away her reputation and risk all the perils of becoming a kept woman, or a casual lover, than Guy would force her. He had not thought about the logical consequences of that kiss any more than she had, she was certain. And besides, there was no knowing whether being even closer to him would trigger some recollection, some hint that might make him recognise his runaway bride.

So now what was she to do? Go home as soon as possible, that was quite clear. She had promised to advise on the restoration of the park, but there was no reason why she should not deal directly with Mr Graham.

The first thing was to get up, get dressed and be ready to leave to forestall any arguments from Mrs Grainger, let alone Guy.

Cressida threw back the covers, swung her legs over and sat up. The room swayed disconcertingly. After a minute she stood up, tottered two steps to the bedside chair and sat down with a thump. The room began to move again and her breakfast threatened to do so, too. Time to face reality—she was not capable of pulling on her own stockings, let alone getting dressed and demonstrating that she was quite well enough to be moving about and going home.

And if she did return to Church Hill, there was only Cook in the house and she was notoriously incapable when faced with illness, as had been proved on a number of occasions. A head cold was enough to prostrate her and, if either Cressida or Marjorie were unwell, she protested that she had *come all over faint*.

The Vicar's wife had a house full of the measles and she did not trust any of the other ladies of Stowe Easton not to put the worst possible construction on her flight from Easton Court. Unfortunately, their speculations would be all too close to the truth.

Cressida realised that she must stay here until either Marjorie came home or she was strong enough to manage on her own and that would no doubt mean having an embarrassingly frank discussion with Guy.

Cressida took a deep breath, staggered back to the bed, hauled the covers over her head and attempted to shut out the world.

'Miss Williams is well enough to sit up in the armchair now, I am glad to say,' Mrs Grainger reported at breakfast, two days after that imprudent kiss.

'Oh, excellent. I can take in the most recent estate map to show her,' Arthur said. 'I am sure she will find it fascinating. I will ask two of the footmen to carry up the trestle table to set it out on so she can see it easily.'

'There is something I must discuss with her first,' Guy said, mentally stiffening his sinews. 'Then the two of you can pore over the map to your hearts' content.' The day before his attempts to visit and deliver his carefully worded apology had been thwarted by his housekeeper, who said firmly that Miss Williams was suffering from a slight relapse and needed a day of undisturbed rest.

Cressida was, indeed, sitting up and wearing a loose gown that Guy recognised as a *robe de chambre*, although one considerably less frilly and provocative than similar garments worn by ladies of his past acquaintance. On the table beside her was an opened letter.

'Mrs Grainger sent one of the maids to collect some clothes for me,' she said with a smile. Guy suspected it was forced. 'Will you sit down?'

'No. Thank you. I came to apologise and that is best done standing at a distance.'

'In case I throw something at you?' There was an acid tinge to the smile now.

'In case I succumb to temptation again,' Guy said frankly. 'I should not have kissed you the other day. It would have been wrong of me even if you had been well and on your feet, let alone weak and in your bed.'

'I kissed you back.' Cressida sounded angry, although whether at him or herself, or both, he could not tell. 'I was not so weak that I was unable to say no— or box your ears, come to that. I wanted you to kiss me and I enjoyed being kissed by you, so the blame is equal. And the blame is not for the embrace, but for the fact, on both sides, that we knew perfectly well it could go no further.'

'We did?' Guy sat down on the nearest chair and tried to read Cressida's expression, because her dry tone gave him no clues. 'You have every reason to expect consequences.'

'An improper proposal?'

'A respectable one,' Guy said stiffly. 'You are a lady.'

'You are the heir to a marquess. I would have to be

deluded if I thought your intentions towards me included marriage, Lord Easton.'

'I had no *intentions*,' he retorted. 'I acted on instinct and attraction and I should have thought first. For which I apologise.'

'Accepted.' She looked away from him, out across the front lawn which was being scythed by three men, the synchronised swing of their bodies quite mesmerising.

'Perhaps it would be best, to avoid any further misunderstandings, if I assure you that I have no intention of marrying anyone, ever. Neither would I accept an irregular relationship from you or any other man. So, you may relax and not wake at two in the morning in a cold sweat, imagining yourself having to explain to the Marquess that you are entangled with a nobody who has ideas above her station.'

'But why? I mean, I am not so arrogant that I imagine you would want to marry me for myself and I acquit you entirely of scheming for a title, let alone envisaging an *affaire*, but why are you set on remaining single?'

'For an independently-minded woman of comfortable means spinsterhood seems to me to be a perfectly reasonable state.' She was still watching the scythe men.

'Should a woman of means find herself without offers of marriage, I can see that it is. But why assume that you will never encounter a man you would wish to marry?'

'What I wish has nothing to do with it. We must all live according to the situation we find ourselves in.' She looked back at him at last and smiled faintly.

Guy found himself staring at the twist of those soft lips. He knew now how they tasted, how they felt beneath the pressure of his.

'Would you be so kind as to ask Mrs Grainger to come and speak with me?' Cressida asked after the silence had stretched rather too far for comfort.

And that is me dismissed, Guy thought as he stood.

'Of course. I should have said that it is a pleasure to see you looking so much recovered.'

He rang for the housekeeper when he reached his study, passed on the message and then drew paper and inkwell towards him.

The Marquess of Thornborough employed a confidential enquiry agent in London and paid him a generous retainer to put the needs of the Thurlow family before those of any other clients. Time for William Brent to earn his money, Guy thought. He must focus on finding his bride and before he could do that he wanted to know what had happened to the last one.

I wish you to ascertain the whereabouts of the Honourable Viola FitzWalden, daughter of the third Viscount FitzWalden and sister of the present Viscount. You will not reveal your principal in this matter. The strictest confidentiality must be maintained.

He dipped his pen again to sign his name, then sat thinking for a moment while the ink dripped back into the container. Finally he added a final paragraph.

I also require to know the family and history

*of a Miss Cressida Williams, presently resid-
ing with her cousin, Miss Marjorie Pomfret, on
Church Hill, Stowe Easton. I believe Miss Williams had a great-uncle, now deceased, living
in Devon.*

Guy signed the letter, folded, addressed and sealed
it, then sat with it in his right hand, tapping it against
the palm of the left. He had no qualms about investigating the whereabouts of his errant bride—in fact, he
thought he should have done that much earlier, if only
out of concern for her welfare.

But did he have any right to pry into Cressida's past?
If she had said she was simply disinclined to marriage,
then he would have accepted that as a matter of personal preference. But her words had implied that circumstances had forced her into that position. If that
was the case, then there might be something he could
do to mend matters.

As a friend, of course, nothing more.

Chapter Nine

'Good morning, Mrs Grainger.' Cressida sat up straight and smiled. Her cheeks were tingling from the brisk pinching she had just given them to bring some colour back into her face and the encounter with Guy had stiffened her resolution. 'This morning's post brought another letter from my cousin.' She gestured towards the closely written sheets.

'It seems she is still needed by Mrs Wilmott, although the baby is gaining in strength, thank goodness. It occurs to me that, if you were to spare me one of the maids for a few days, I could return home. Not only would it be less of a burden on your household, but now I am able to leave my bed there is perhaps less justification in my remaining here.'

'Or so the good ladies of the town might think,' the housekeeper said with an understanding nod of her head. 'That does seem an excellent solution if you feel well enough to make the short journey, Miss Williams. Might I suggest that you have a bed made up downstairs for a few days?'

'That does seem sensible. Could you arrange for a maid and a carriage for me? I will write a note to Lord Easton—we have already spoken this morning.' If that left Mrs Grainger with the impression that Cressida had agreed with her employer that she would leave that day, then so much the better. She would write to Mr Graham as well. There was no reason why he should not call and discuss the work on the park, should he wish.

In the event she met the steward as the two footmen carrying her downstairs in a chair reached the hall.

'You are leaving us, Miss Williams?' He stood to one side, somewhat hampered by several large rolls of paper tucked under his arm. 'I was just about to visit you with these estate plans—and Capability Brown's scheme is with them.'

The footmen set down the chair with a bump and surreptitiously stretched what must be aching backs.

'What a wonderful discovery. I am going home now, Mr Graham. But perhaps you would like to call the day after tomorrow and bring them? We can go over our notes together. Would two o'clock suit?'

They agreed on that, the footmen hoisted the chair again and Cressida was delivered to the waiting carriage along with Maud, one of the maids, and her small amount of luggage.

She supposed she should have sent a message home to Cook first, which risked finding nothing in the house to eat beyond bread and cheese. She and Maud had to be fed, but the maid, or Cook, could always go out and buy something. But practicalities such as meals were not important now—as the carriage set off down the drive it felt ridiculously as though she was escaping, although not from Guy as much as from her own desires and folly.

Of course, she must finish the work she had undertaken to do for him, she thought as the carriage rattled across the market square. That was only right, especially as she should have refused the commission in the first place. But it would be quite safe, Cressida assured herself, clutching the hanging strap as the vehicle began to descend the hill. Mr Graham would visit her with the plans, they would refine their notes and that would be that.

There would be no need to meet Guy Thurlow again, which was a relief. She would send a polite, cool letter thanking him for his hospitality and passing especial thanks to Mrs Grainger and her maids, of course. And then she would write to Marjorie, telling her cousin that she was home and much recovered. Marjorie could then return to Stowe Easton if that was what she wanted, or, if she was really needed in Portsmouth and not merely trying to matchmake, then she could stay without worrying about Cressida.

'Here we are,' she said to Maud as they drew to a halt.

The groom jumped down to hand her out and offer his arm to the front door while Maud knocked.

Cook answered it, her head wrapped in a turban with twists of rag curlers peeking out. 'Oh, my lord, Miss Cressida! I was just turning out the larder and here you are and there's no beef tea in the house.'

'I do not need beef tea, Cook. Maud, this is Mrs

Butterworth, our cook. Cook, Maud is from Easton Court and has very kindly agreed to come here for a few days to help look after me until I am strong enough to manage by myself. Come in, Maud. Now, Cook, what do we have in the house to eat? Everything at the Court was delightful, of course, but I have missed your cooking.'

'You let her go?' Guy demanded. 'Without a word to me? What were you thinking of, Mrs Grainger?'

His housekeeper regarded him calmly from the other side of his desk, apparently neither intimidated by an annoyed employer, nor by the wide expanse of mahogany that separated them.

'Miss Williams expressed a desire to leave, My Lord, and said that she did not wish you to be disturbed. I am sure she has explained in her letter.' She nodded towards the folded paper now crumpled in Guy's hand. 'Maud has gone with her to stay as long as necessary and she is a most competent and sensible young woman.'

Guy opened his hand, allowing the note to fall to the desk. 'Of course, we could hardly keep Miss Williams against her will,' he said, lowering his voice by several degrees.

'Exactly so, My Lord.'

'I would have preferred the doctor to see her first, however.'

'I am sure Miss Williams will send for Dr Crozier if he is needed. She appears to be a most level-headed lady, if I may be so bold as to make the observation.'

Guy was fairly certain that Mrs Grainger would be

so bold as to make any observation she wished, when she wished it, but he merely inclined his head. 'Thank you, Mrs Grainger. The extra work carried out by you and your staff is much appreciated.'

'My Lord.' With a brief bob she turned and left, the keys dangling from her chatelaine jangling softly as she went.

Guy broke the seal on Cressida's letter with an angry jerk of his thumb. He should not have let himself lose his temper with his housekeeper and he knew it. His problem was a severe attack of indecision over the letter he had sent to Will Brent, the enquiry agent. It had been taken with the morning post—he knew because he had gone down to the hall to take it back to brood over and found the post box empty—but he was in two minds whether or not to write countermanding the order to investigate Cressida.

His errant bride was one thing, an unrelated young lady, quite another, his conscience told him. And yet… Something was wrong and he wanted to put it right for Cressida. Was this a case of good intentions balancing out a dubious action? He gave his conscience a prod and it as good as shrugged its shoulders.

Could he be like a clergyman or a lawyer and disregard anything he read in the report that he could not help with? Undecided, he pressed Cressida's letter flat on the desk.

My Lord,
Thank you so much for your care and hospital-
ity. I am sure I could not have been better looked
after and I would be glad if you would pass on

*my thanks again to Mrs Grainger and her maids
who were so very kind.*

*I will communicate with Mr Graham about
the notes that we made—please be assured that
I will finish the work you commissioned me to
carry out.*

With respectful regards,
Cressida Williams

'Respectful regards,' Guy muttered. 'That young
woman hasn't a respectful bone in her body, for all her
pretty manners.' Infuriatingly, it was one of the things
he liked about her. One of a long list that included intelligence, courage and a fine pair of blue eyes. And
a mouth that was warm and soft and innocently demanding under his.

He did not have to make a decision about his enquiries yet. After all, it would take quite a while for
Brent to carry out the work and, when the report arrived, he could always ignore the section relating to
Cressida if he decided by then it was the best thing to
do. His willpower would be capable of that, he was
almost certain. As an officer and a gentleman, he told
himself sternly, it had better be.

'I have arranged for us to call upon Miss Williams
this afternoon at two with the estate plans and all the
notes. I have managed to dry out all the pages of her
notebook and almost all of it is legible.' Arthur looked
across the breakfast table two days later. 'I quite forgot
to tell you yesterday,' he added, his frown anxious. 'I
do hope that is convenient?'

Guy returned his coffee cup to its saucer with some care. It was a very good Spode set. 'Cressida is expecting both of us?'

'Oh, yes. After all, she and I could hardly make decisions that are properly yours and I know you are anxious to start the work as soon as possible.'

The proper thing to do with temptation was to ignore it. But yielding to it was usually far more interesting and, besides, Guy wanted to be certain Cressida was recovering as she should. His conscience, which was carrying a number of bruises at the moment, was still sore from the knowledge that he had led her into that deathtrap of a boathouse and then failed to protect her once inside.

He was not certain whether seeing Cressida again would help with the enjoyable, but frustratingly vague, dreams that had been haunting his nights recently, or would make them worse by giving his imagination more to feed upon. He should say *no*, tell Arthur to go by himself.

'I am free this afternoon,' he said and opened the topmost of the stack of correspondence that Herring, his butler, had just placed by the side of his plate. Being a very good butler, one who knew to a nicety what was in his employer's best interests as opposed to what he might actually want, he had placed the missive from the Marquess of Thornborough on the summit of the pile.

Guy winced at the sight of both the frank on the wrapper and the thickness of best hot-pressed paper and looked at the second instead.

The wrapper revealed a further folded and sealed

sheet heavily inscribed *Confidential. For Lord Easton's eyes only.* Will Brent, the enquiry agent, was making his first report and it was not one packed with information either, to judge by the flimsiness of the enclosure.

> *My Lord,*
> *I regret to inform you that I am unable to proceed immediately with the investigations you require as Your Noble Parent directs me to travel to Liverpool to deal with a matter of some urgency.*
> *I will, naturally, treat your commission with the utmost priority upon the completion of Your Noble Parent's business.*
> *I beg to remain your respectful servant,*
> *Wm Brent*

Guy folded the sheet and tucked it into the breast of his coat. *My noble parent, indeed!* He told himself not to be impatient, that it was better to wait for Brent than to trust someone whose discretion was less certain, and slit open his father's letter.

Lord Thornborough wasted little time in enquiring about his heir's health, being certain that any bad news would have reached him with dispatch, nor did he ask about the progress with work at Easton Court, because once he made his wishes clear it would be inconceivable that they would not be carried out.

Instead, Guy found, when he flattened the pages out, his father had created a list of the young ladies he considered suitable as his future daughter-in-law. Guy ran a finger down the names, counting. Twenty-five.

Not, fortunately, arranged in order of preference, but each accompanied by his father's very frank opinions.

Handsome, good countenance, excellent connections; family runs to daughters, however, read one. *Would bring useful lands in Suffolk; inclined to corpulence*, said another.

Those were two of the less damningly frank appraisals.

Presumably this list was intended to encourage Guy in his efforts to bring the Court up to scratch in time for the next Season and allow him to put in place a strategy for wooing the lady who was his first choice on the list.

'Look at this.' He brandished the page at Arthur. 'My father appears to have forgotten that I am approaching twenty-eight years of age, have held responsible army command and am in full possession of my wits,' he remarked, tossing the list across the table and narrowly missing the marmalade dish.

Arthur peered at the first page and nodded. 'I know. Mine's just the same. Admittedly I came home rather the worse for wear, but they insisted on treating me as though I was a sickly child. I believe the problem is that they remember us when we went off to war as skinny seventeen-year-old ensigns and have seen very little of us since. Medals, battle honours and scars, never mind the fact we are both somewhat larger than we were then, cannot wipe that memory from them.'

'That is very true.' And, while he felt no urge to go against his father's wishes for the sake of rebellion, it was beginning to dawn on Guy that he might well do so for the sake of his own happiness.

The Thurlows had money, lands and resources beyond the imaginings of many people. They had status and respect. Why should those need bolstering by marriage into more money, more land and more lofty connections? It might do the bloodline some good to add a dash of healthy yeoman blood, he thought rebelliously.

But there were two problems, leaving aside the Marquess's wrath. He had, after all, faced charging French cavalry and even his father could not beat that for sound, fury and the appearance of lethal intent.

Firstly, he had no idea whether what he was feeling for Cressida was anything other than liking mixed with physical attraction. Both, of course, seasoned by a good pinch of pique that the lady concerned had flatly turned down any kind of relationship with him. Secondly, he had no idea whether Cressida could possibly feel anything for him that would overcome her declared intention to stay single.

There was only one way to answer both: spend more time in her company.

'Herring.'

'My Lord?'

'Have my curricle brought around at ten minutes to two.' The gig would be more practical for two men and several large rolls of paper, but a curricle was a vehicle to impress a lady with.

Cressida had spent the night in tolerable comfort in a truckle bed set up in the dining room. Now, as the clock struck a quarter to two, she was fully dressed, seated at the table in the drawing room and filling a sheet of paper with a neat list of headings.

Temple and other eye-catchers
Lake
Boathouse
Woodland
Ha-ha
Carriage drives
Vistas...

They would need putting into priority order when Mr Graham arrived, although her opinion was that the repairs to the ha-ha should be undertaken first. That would allow the parkland to be grazed properly by both sheep and deer without them getting into the ornamental grounds.

They could set the woodsmen to work at the same time, and start dredging the lake, she decided, then looked up at the sound of horses in the street outside.

They were very fine horses. Mr Graham must have Guy's complete confidence if he allowed him to drive his blood team. Then she saw who was holding the reins.

As the knock came Cressida realised she should ring for Maud, tell her to say she was not feeling well enough for visitors, but the bell pull was several steps away across the room and she could already hear the maid answering the front door. She had told Maud to expect a visitor, so she announced both men without asking Cressida first.

'Lord Easton, Mr Graham, ma'am.'

'Thank you. Do take a seat, gentlemen.' What else could she say? But it was clear that she had not kept her surprise from showing. Guy sent his steward a sharp glance and Mr Graham was managing to avoid his employer's eye in a manner she could only call suspicious, although he made a great show of fussing over the armful of rolled maps he carried.

'What a surprise, Lord Easton,' she said coolly.

'Not unwelcome, I trust?'

I should faint. Now, this minute. Slide to the floor in a graceful heap and then they will have to leave.

But she was too late for that now, she saw, as Mr Graham gestured towards the plans. Instead, she smiled faintly as though Guy's question had been meant as a joke. This was so dangerous, but oh, her foolish heart was reckless. She wanted him there, wanted to talk with him, look at him. She dared not consider what this longing meant, but while she was occupied there was no risk of brooding on it and discovering just how her emotions might be betraying her.

'Shall we move this table in front of your sofa, Miss Williams? Then I can spread out the most recent sheet.' Arthur Graham had his hand on one end of the low occasional table at the side of the room and, without waiting for her reply, Guy stood and took the other. Cressida found herself neatly trapped by the table in front of her and a gentleman on either side.

'Here is your notebook, Miss Williams.' Mr Graham handed her a stack of stained and crinkled pages. 'I had to remove the cover, but it is generally legible. And here are my notes. I will record our decisions as we go.'

Cressida pulled herself together with an effort and told them her conclusions so far. 'As to prioritising work,' she concluded, 'it all depends on how many resources you wish to commit, Lord Easton. And the labour force you can raise.'

The steward reported on the excellent response he had received from local craftsmen and the gratifying number of labourers who had come asking for work. 'The work on the ha-ha can begin at once and we have enough woodsmen to clear the carriage drives through the woods to the Temple of the Winds and the boat-house. That should be demolished immediately, before there are any more accidents.'

'I believe my friend Luston has had both a boat-house and a summer house built at his place in Wilt-shire,' Guy said, making her jump. He had been silent, listening to them. 'I will write and ask him who designed them.'

'We can also set labourers to dredging the lake and repairing the waterfall at the dam. I assume punts and some form of canvas scoops will be necessary,' Mr Graham said, scribbling notes. 'I will consult *Notes and Queries* and see if anyone has reported on such an operation.'

'There are more buildings in the woods, see?' Guy leant over the map, his sleeve brushing Cressida's hand as he moved.

She caught her breath at the touch and he turned his head at the soft sound, his grey gaze sharp and intent on her face. She knew her cheeks were growing warm, that she should look away, but her muscles did not want to obey. Somehow she managed to close her eyes and she sensed his attention turn from her, back to the map. She felt hot and flustered and a disturbing sensation was coiling itself deep in her belly, sending little flickers into the intimate core of her.

How was she going to endure this without betraying herself?

Chapter Ten

'More buildings?' Cressida said blankly. It occurred to her that nothing that the men had said for the past few minutes had registered with her at all. She supposed she must have contributed something reasonably coherent as neither man was staring at her.

'So there are! I hadn't noticed them.' Mr Graham was leaning forward, peering intently, apparently oblivious to the silent exchanges taking place beside him. 'Another temple here. What does it say? The Temple of the Moon, I think. And a shelter of some kind on this high ground here, marked the Arcade of the Spirits. I will order the rides cleared so we can inspect both of them.'

Cressida dug her thumbnails into her palms until the pain cleared her mind. 'This map is useful for discovering just where the saplings need to be cleared to open up the vistas. See, here and here, for example.' She leant forward in her turn, making no obvious effort to avoid touching Guy, but managing it none the less.

'I would suggest ordering seats. Perhaps classical

marble benches close to the temple buildings and rustic ones for the woodland and beside the lake. The deer and sheep will keep the grass in the open spaces clear, but I suggest you set scythe men to clear the low scrub and bracken first. Then—'

An hour, and a tea tray, later, Arthur sat back and began to gather up his notes. 'I have a plan of campaign now and quite a list of letters to write. If you will excuse me, Easton, I will begin to walk back to stretch my legs. If you catch up with me, I will ride the rest of the way with you, but if I reach the lane leading to the park first, then I may well cut across that way.'

He thrust his notes into a folder and bowed himself out with thanks to Cressida. The door clicked shut behind him. Guy was left with the strong suspicion that his steward was attempting to matchmake and he was not at all certain whether he was annoyed or pleased with the excuse to be alone with Cressida.

She might well ring for the maid, of course, or at least ask him to set the door open, but instead she sat silent, hands clasped in her lap. Was that trust, or indifference?

'Thank you,' he said. 'With Arthur's practical bent and energy and your understanding of how the landscape should look, I believe I have all I need to transform the park. I do not suppose you have an equal talent for interior design, have you? The house is in sad need of refurbishment.'

Cressida looked up. 'No, I do not. In any case, I believe you should simply see that the house is in full repair and clean, because your bride will want to arrange the interiors to suit her own taste. Not yours and most certainly not mine.' Having delivered that firm put-down she added abruptly, 'Do you suppose he believes that he is helping? I cannot believe Mr Graham means mischief.'

Guy almost said that he did not know what she was talking about and then closed his lips firmly on words that would simply make him seem foolish. 'Yes, I do think he is assisting in…something,' he admitted. 'He is not amusing himself at our expense. Arthur never had an unkind thought in his life, unless it concerned the French army.'

'Why did you come here today? That certainly is not helping in the slightest either, is it?'

In a strange way the fact that Cressida acknowledged that they had something between them, problem or not, was encouraging.

'I came because I allowed myself to believe Arthur when he said you were expecting us both,' Guy said frankly. They were still side by side on the sofa, their elbows almost touching. He got up and moved to a chair on the other side of the low table to give her space. 'In fact, I admit I wanted to speak with you and took the opportunity.'

'What can we possibly have to talk about?' Cressida asked. 'I thought I had made my position quite clear.'

It felt to Guy as though she had erected a large notice: *Trespassers Will Be Prosecuted*. There were probably mantraps in the undergrowth as well, judging by her rigid posture.

'Yes, you did. But what you told me was not the whole truth, was it?'

'How *dare* you? I am not a liar.'

That had brought a faint wash of colour up over her cheekbones, almost as though she had a guilty conscience. But, of course, it was simply indignation. He tried not to be drawn into the depths of her fierce blue gaze. Emotion deepened the colour of her eyes; he had noticed that when they had kissed.

'It was the truth, but not the whole truth,' Guy said steadily. 'I am attracted to you, like you. You feel something for me, do you not?'

'You flatter yourself, My Lord!' Yes, that was most definitely anger. The strange feeling of *déjà vu* he had experienced when he had been sitting beside her earlier and she had reacted like a shy debutante, all downcast eyes and nervously twisting fingers, had quite gone. This was no timid girl just out of the schoolroom.

'I thought we had established just now that you are not a liar,' he said, deliberately provoking.

The slight rose in Cressida's cheeks was an unmistakable blush now. 'What I might, or might not, feel for you is irrelevant. We discussed the difference in our rank, our situations.'

Guy answered that with a flick of his fingers. 'You speak as though you are a dairy maid or a cobbler's daughter. The Thurlows can very well withstand the addition of some healthy gentry blood. But I had not mentioned the word *marriage*, I believe.' Cressida opened her mouth, indignation writ clear on her face. 'And I am not now talking about any kind of irregular relationship.'

'Then what, exactly, *are* you talking about?' she retorted.

'I do not know,' he confessed. 'But there is something, is there not? And it seems perverse to ignore it, dismiss it. I would like to get to know you better, Cressida. And, no,' he added as her lips tightened, 'that was not a euphemism. I do not know what it is, but what if we were to find we shared some strong...connection? Isn't it worth finding out?'

'I have no idea what you might mean.'

He had thrown her into complete confusion, he could see. Probably into almost as much emotional turmoil as he had thrown himself, because he had not thought this through before speaking.

'Neither do I,' Guy admitted frankly. 'All I know is that what I feel for you is quite different from anything I have felt for any other woman. Perhaps we could begin with friendship?'

'Yes,' she said warily. 'But there it ends. I told you—'

'You told me that you do not ever wish to marry. Is there something that you fear? Has someone hurt you in the past? I want to help, Cressida.'

'You cannot.' She looked away and he saw her hands were moving again, twisting in her lap as though trying to escape. With a visible effort she stilled them. 'It is nothing in my experiences, nothing about marriage that I fear. It is not the result of a broken heart or ill treatment by a man. I— No, how can I tell you?'

There was so much pain in her voice that it brought him to his feet, then to the sofa beside her. 'Cressida, you can tell me anything. I would never betray your confidence.'

She turned abruptly towards him and instinct sent

his arms around her, gathered her close. 'I cannot,' she said, her voice muffled against his shirt front.

Guy managed to get two fingers under her chin and tipped up her face gently until he was looking into her eyes, full of confusion and, he realised, desire.

There only seemed one thing to do. He kissed her and she melted against him, warm and lithe, intensely female and sensual in her need. What that need was, his mind was too fogged with sensation to know. Did Cressida want to be comforted or to be made love to? Perhaps both.

The part of his brain that was working registered the fact that the light gown she was wearing had beneath it no corset, that only two or three sliding, fragile, layers of cloth were between his hands and the soft skin that was perfuming the air with a heady mix of warm, aroused female, a haunting perfume mingling with the innocent scent of freshly laundered linen.

Her hands were under his coat, pushing beneath to slide over the silk of his waistcoat, her fingers exploring between the buttons until he could feel the press of her nails through the thin shirt beneath.

It was as though someone had loosened shackles that had bound them, set their inhibitions free, and the sensation was heady, liberating, reckless.

Cressida's mouth was open to him, her tongue demanding as she gained confidence, began to discover what she wanted, what their bodies could do together She was lying back on the heaped cushions at the end of the sofa now, his weight over her, the junction of her thighs hot against his aroused body.

As he took the weight of her left breast in the palm

of his hand and ran his thumb over the nipple, taut under the muslin, Cressida gasped, arched towards him and, through the onslaught of sensation, the realisation hit him that he was making love to a virgin, on a sofa, in her front room. It was broad daylight. The curtains were open and the pavement not a few feet beyond them.

It had the effect of a bucket of icy water. Guy sat up, ran one hand through his hair, pulled his neckcloth straight with the other and took a deep breath.

Cressida, still tumbled—and that, he thought bitterly, was absolutely the correct word—against the cushions, blinked up at him. Then she turned her head sharply to look at the window with its view of the street outside. The mercifully empty street.

He braced himself for hysterics, reproaches or a slap. But this was Cressida. She stood up, straightened her skirts and went to the mirror over the fireplace to tidy her hair. 'I do not know about friendship,' she said. Her voice held a slight tremor. 'But there is certainly desire.'

'I—'

'Don't you dare apologise,' Cressida said fiercely as she turned to face Guy where he stood at the far end of the sofa. The abrupt end to that embrace had left her shaken and shaking, furious with herself. She should never have yielded and it was every bit as much her fault as his that this had even begun. 'That was mutual. Insane, but mutual. Very well, I see I must make myself clearer or we are both going to forget ourselves again.'

'I very much fear that you are right.'

'I have no personal objection to marriage. No fears either,' she said, quite truthfully. 'But my family circumstances make it impossible.'

'A batty relative?' Guy asked lightly. It seemed that he expected to be told of some embarrassing problem that had assumed gigantic importance to her family but which, to an outsider, was not so shocking. 'I have a great-uncle who believes he is the rightful heir to the throne of Norway.'

'No. Not insanity. And it is not my secret to tell in any case.' It affected her, of course, more than anyone, but she had a duty to others as well.

'I will not pry,' he said, almost with a wince she could not understand. A guilty feeling that he had already pressed her too hard, perhaps?

'I know you want to help,' she said, finding that she truly did believe it. 'Thank you.'

His smile was unexpectedly gentle. 'Friends, then? But friends who should take care never to be alone together, don't you think?'

'Yes, I would like to try.' She was affected by that smile, far more than she could believe possible, and turned away before he saw the glimmer of tears in her eyes.

Guy stood, turning to pick up the rolled plans. 'Good. Now I must go. I will let myself out.'

She heard him speaking to Maud in the hallway, heard the soft thud of the front door closing, felt the corresponding thump in her chest at his absence.

So that was what it was like to be in a man's arms, to feel his desire, his weight over you, to understand how deeply, urgently, your own body wanted to respond to his lovemaking. It was potent, dangerous. Enough to melt all traces of willpower.

Was that how her mother had felt when her own brother-in-law had taken her in his embrace, pressed kisses on her lips? Had Mama been overcome with desire, reckless to the point of committing adultery, conceiving a child, or had Charles forced himself on her? Was she, Cressida, the child of passion or rape, betrayal or assault?

The marriage had not been happy: even as a child she had understood that. From something her mother had once said the marriage had been one of suitability, rather than affection and love had not grown with familiarity. The kindest way she could describe her father's character as a husband was neglectful and indifferent.

He was very charming, her wicked Uncle Charles, everyone said so, even as they shook their heads over his sins. Had Mama been charmed, too?

He also led a charmed life, somehow never succumbing to an enraged husband's bullet in a duel, or being beaten to a pulp by furious gamblers discovering he had fuzzed the cards in some hell—always escaping disaster by the skin of his teeth and proud of his reputation for swaggering sin.

So proud that he had not been able to resist the temptation to tell her, only an hour before her wedding, that she was his and not his brother Henry's. How he had got into the house, when every servant employed by all the FitzWalden families knew to bar the door to him, she had no idea.

'Poor sickly Henry,' he'd said, his beautiful brown

eyes smiling with malicious glee. 'He wasn't capable any more, but he would never admit it, of course. That would mean facing the fact that you couldn't be his. And haven't you turned out well? The heir to a marquess for a husband. You'll be able to look after your dear father now, won't you, my girl?'

Somehow Cressida had resisted the temptation to scream, or sob, or slap his face. From somewhere had come the self-control to give him an incredulous look, to turn on her heel and go down to the waiting carriage and her brother and keep a calm countenance on the drive to the church.

But her brain had been whirling. Was Charles telling the truth or was this an elaborate and daring attempt at blackmail? And whether it was the truth or not, should she, could she, tell the man she was about to marry?

The answer to that, she realised as the carriage came to a halt at the church, was, no, she could not. If it had been anyone else claiming to be her father, perhaps, but this was the man Lord Easton had clearly forbidden her to have anything to do with.

She was not quite sure why he was so very vehement. He would know Charles's reputation, know that the family had cut him from their lives, so she had not been surprised at the prohibition itself, but it had seemed almost personal in its vehemence.

In the face of that, he would never forgive her for making him the man's son-in-law. Would such a deception be grounds for divorce? Probably.

It had taken her the length of the aisle and then the first blurred minutes of the service for Cressida to make up her mind. No, she could not marry Guy Thurlow and she could tell no one why not.

It only occurred to her, after she had been in hiding with Great-Uncle Rufus in Devon for a month, that not only could she not marry Guy Thurlow, but she could marry no man who might fall victim to Charles's blackmail. And that ruled out anyone of any respectability whatsoever.

She had told Guy just now that she would try to be his friend. The alternatives to that were either to cut him entirely or to move away. And she was not going to do that, not be driven out of her home and away from a community where she was happy, because of what one wicked man had done. The *Dis*honourable Charles FitzWalden had done her enough damage as it was.

Cressida recalled a friend, Arabella Carfax, who had fallen in love with the man who had married her own sister. She had confided in Cressida months after the wedding.

'He never knew how I felt about him, thankfully,' Arabella had told her. 'And they live so close, it has been very hard. But gradually I am learning to think of him as my brother-in-law, as a friend. One day, I suppose, I will forget how I feel about him now.'

If Arabella could do it, then so could she, Cressida told herself. And the cases were different—she was not in love with Guy. The fact that she was feeling so shaken and inclined to tears was because she was still convalescent and was flustered from his lovemaking. That was all.

Guy caught up with Arthur just before his steward turned on to the path that led into the park.

'Get in,' he ordered as he brought his horses to a halt.

'Thank you, but I am enjoying the walk,' Arthur said, with a cheery wave.

'That was not an offer, that was an instruction,' Guy said.

'Oh. Right.' Arthur climbed up, making rather a business of tucking the rolled plans tidily under the seat where Guy had put them before he sat down.

Guy let the reins slacken and the bays started off with more of a jerk than was usual.

'What the devil do you think you are playing at?' he enquired, his voice dangerously calm. 'Think you are Cupid, do you?'

'Er...'

'Miss Williams was not expecting to see me. You lied to me.'

'It was more by omission than an actual untruth,' Arthur protested.

'An officer and a gentleman does not lie,' Guy said, ignoring that. 'My employees do not lie. Not and remain in post, that is.'

'I spoke as your friend,' Arthur said, recovering his nerve and, with it, his dignity. 'But I have offended you and I will resign forthwith.'

'You will do no such thing,' Guy snapped. 'You are a good steward and I see no reason why I should be deprived of your services because you are, on occasion, a damn sentimental fool. I am perfectly capable of flooring you if you offend me, but Miss Williams is a lady and she cannot resort to fisticuffs. You have distressed her.'

'I will apologise to her. Let me down and I will walk back at once,' Arthur said stiffly.

'Not unless you want to experience a left hook here and now. Miss Williams will be best served by you pretending that today nothing happened beyond the examination of those maps. Is that clear? Miss Williams is a friend of mine and that is all. Is *that* clear?'

'As crystal.'

'Excellent. I am aware you meant well which is probably one of the worst things anyone can say about anyone. The matter is now forgotten.'

'I truly did not mean—'

'Arthur—shut up.'

Chapter Eleven

A week later Cressida walked up the hill with Maud to see the maid off on her return to Easton Court. It was the most exercise she had attempted since her near-drowning and she was panting somewhat by the time they reached the market square. She also suspected she was unflatteringly pink in the face.

'I will sit here,' she said, gesturing to the bench in front of Millington's Haberdashery. 'I would like you to take this as a small thank-you for your hard work looking after me. Mrs Grainger chose well.' She pressed a folded banknote into the girl's hand.

Maud beamed and blushed and visibly struggled to compose herself into the image of someone Mrs Grainger would approve of. 'Oh, thank you, Miss Williams. I've always wanted to be a lady's maid, so it was nice to be able to practise. I hope you feel properly well very soon.' She bobbed a curtsy and Cressida watched her make her way across the cobbles towards the track to the Court.

Now what to do? It was pleasant in the sunshine

and this was a perfectly respectable place to sit, so perhaps she would rest here a while longer, then go in and browse through the latest additions to Mr Millington's stock.

Or just stay where she was. Cressida recalled an old man in the village near her childhood home. He was always to be found on the bench by the stocks, his pipe clenched between his teeth, the smoke curling up around his battered billycock hat. One day she asked him what he did there all day to pass the time.

'Ah, missy, that's a question,' he said. 'Sometimes I sits and thinks and sometimes I just sits.'

Just sitting seemed an excellent idea, because thinking was still a painful exercise. At least she now felt more resigned to her unhappiness, although it would be helpful if she could only stop herself drifting off into daydreams where her uncle was not a rakehell, or if he was, he was capable of keeping his secrets to himself. Ignorance really would be bliss.

She was still comfortable on the bench, alone for a moment in between exchanges of greetings and gossip with the matrons of the town who were about their shopping, when a somewhat battered post-chaise clattered across the square and stopped. The postilion touched his whip to his cap and called across, 'Could you point me in the direction of Church Hill, miss?'

Cressida stood up and walked towards him. 'The road right in front of you, slightly to the right,' she had said when the window of the chaise dropped down and Marjorie leaned out.

'Cressida! Jump in, dear.' She beamed as Cressida

settled herself on the seat, squashed somewhat between her cousin, Jane, the maid, and various baskets. Luncheon and sewing, she guessed.

'What a lovely surprise, Marjorie,' Cressida said as they managed awkward cheek-kisses. 'I am so pleased Cousin Harriet is well enough to spare you at last.'

She tried to keep the dry tone out of her voice, but, even so, Marjorie looked a trifle self-conscious.

'It was more nerves than anything, once the danger to little George was past and she'd recovered her own strength somewhat. But with dear Frazer away at sea—and called so suddenly at such a delicate time as well—I felt it wise to remain until I was certain she could cope. I wouldn't have wanted to return again almost as soon as I got there and I knew you were in good hands.'

'I am glad you were not worrying about me. It was such a foolish accident.'

'Oh, no. Mrs Grainger wrote to me almost every day on Lord Easton's orders, so I knew it would be foolish to worry. Such a sensible-sounding woman.'

'She is. Very competent.'

'And how is Lord Easton?'

'Well, as far as I know. I have had no sight of him for a week.'

'No? A week? My goodness.' Marjorie seemed suddenly to recall that Jane was sitting with them. 'He is not much around in the town, then?'

'He and Mr Graham, his agent, are exceedingly busy with work on the estate—' She broke off. 'Here we are, you will be glad to be under your own roof again, I'm sure.'

'I will be glad of my own bed!' Marjorie said robustly as Jane opened the chaise door and jumped down. 'A dreadful old feather thing I found myself in. Now, I must tip the boy—where's my purse, Jane? Oh, here it is. There you are and thank you. Oh, Cook—yes, we are home at last. I hope the kettle is on the hob…'

Marjorie did not stop talking from the moment she crossed the threshold until she and Cressida were seated one each side of the tea tray, with the door closed behind them.

'And how is His Lordship?' Marjorie asked again.

'No doubt as embarrassed as I am by the well-meaning attempts at matchmaking by Mr Graham and yourself,' Cressida said tartly, pouring tea with so much emphasis that it splashed in the saucers.

'I think you would be ideal for each other,' her cousin said defiantly. 'I was sure that it only needed for you to be with him for a time for you to find that your earlier objections to him were less compelling than you first thought.'

The very idea of explaining to Marjorie, let alone Guy, what her objections to marrying him were made Cressida feel nauseous.

'I had managed to almost forget, or, at least put behind me, those objections,' she said now, staring into the depths of her tea as though it might hold some meaning. A tea leaf floated to the surface, that was all. 'Now I find that having to think about them again makes it very much worse, more compelling than ever before.'

'But why, dear?' Marjorie asked. 'Time so often heals wounds, gives us a different perspective.'

'I have no idea,' Cressida said shortly. 'Do try one of these shortbread biscuits—I do believe Cook has perfected that recipe of Mrs Green's.'

In the face of such a comprehensive change of subject Marjorie fell silent.

Cressida bit into the crumbling sweetness of a biscuit which proved hard to swallow. She was not telling Marjorie the truth because she knew very clearly why her secret was assuming such monstrous proportions in her mind.

I am in love with Guy. I really cannot deceive myself any longer. It isn't simply desire or liking. It is love.

She could tell him the truth about herself—her real identity, the revelation of who her father really was—and see him turn away in anger and disgust. Or she could tell him her real name and pretend that her flight was something foolish and, now, unimportant, and pray that Charles FitzWalden would not dare attempt to blackmail her, or extort money from him if Guy was forgiving enough to wed her. If he wanted to.

And then if he does *marry you?* the voice of common sense enquired acidly. *And Charles* does *tell him—then what? Divorce?*

No, nothing that definite. She had been accepted as legitimate by her father. That made her legally, whatever the truth, the person the world thought her to be. There would be no grounds for divorce or annulment, she was almost certain. Which meant that Guy would be tied to a wife who had deceived him, had laid him open to sneers, gossip and scandal. Whatever feeling he had for her now could not possibly survive such a betrayal.

'A penny for them?' Marjorie asked archly, presumably in an attempt to ease the atmosphere.

'Oh, nothing worth as much as that,' Cressida said lightly. 'Let me tell you about the accident and the maps Mr Graham found and the plans Lord Easton is making for the grounds.'

'But what about the house?' Marjorie asked. 'Surely that is a greater priority than the grounds?'

'I imagine that Lord Easton hopes to find his bride during the coming Season,' Cressida said. 'She will surely wish to put her stamp on the house, so it makes sense that what he is doing is simply making the structural repairs—they have begun on the roof already—sorting out the drains and so forth and scouring the house from top to bottom. If it is clean and the existing furniture and paintings arranged with taste, then the new Lady Easton will have a clean slate to make it hers.'

She put down the remains of the biscuit half-eaten. What did Guy want with her, truly? His words during their last conversation had sounded as though he liked and desired her, possibly even enough to marry her, despite what he thought was her modest status in Society. She believed he enjoyed her company, as she did his. He certainly made love to her with care and intent. Such a match was not impossible if she had been the daughter of a gentry household, as Guy believed her to be.

But love? No. Surely, if he loved her, she would sense it and, besides, he would tell her. He would think it would be a powerful persuasion to abandon her reasons for abjuring marriage.

No, he was not in love, but he was 'in liking' and in lust and not at all enthusiastic about undergoing the rigid social round of the Season to find his bride. She would do very well and save him the effort, he was perhaps thinking.

If only he knew…

Guy regarded the silver salver Herring had just presented with resignation. The fact that Arthur, on the other side of the breakfast table, had an even larger pile beside him did not improve his mood.

'Letter from Andrews telling me what a good time he is having at that house party I turned down… An invitation from Lady Landon inviting me to what she calls an intimate, friendly gathering next week—how many daughters has she on her hands? Three or is it four? However many it is, I am not prepared to drive clear across the country to view their charms.' Guy tossed that aside. 'Hoby, the bootmaker, respectfully drawing my attention to their new design of boot for the country gentleman…'

The next was a missive from his father commenting on the last report on the progress to the house and estate. He went on to inform Guy, at length, that he had just acquired a new thoroughbred mare for the stud.

Guy skipped through a page of unwanted facts on horse breeding and turned to the next.

Yr cuz Penelope is causing her parents great anxiety again. It is a consolation to me that I have no daughters to fret me with their foolishness.

What Miss Penelope Thurlow was up to now the Marquess did not divulge, moving on to report, with satisfaction, the arrest of a notorious poaching gang.

Not that Penny's previous escapade had been caused by anything other than her innocence and trusting nature. Together they had combined to make her the prey of a rogue with designs on both her virtue and her dowry. The fact that she had escaped unscathed was largely due to her own innate courage and quick thinking and Guy's presence in Hyde Park at the time.

Her parents—both of them completely failing to understand their daughter, in his opinion—reacted as though she had been wilfully foolish and treated her from then on as though she was apt to elope with some adventurer at any moment. As a result, Penny was still unwed at the age of twenty-two.

Guy was very fond of the chit, as fond as he would have been of a beloved sister, and he worried about her. He was still wondering what he could do to help resolve this latest situation, whatever it was, as he picked up the last letter, addressed in a determined looping black script that looked all too familiar. He broke the seal with a smile.

Dearest Guy—help! it began. Typical Penny, he thought, glancing at the end where it was signed *Your ever loving and desperate Penny.* Now what was she up to?

Five minutes later he looked across at Arthur, who was engrossed in the centre pages of the *Morning Chronicle.*

'We are about to have house guests.'

'We are? Who?'

'My cousin, Miss Penelope Thurlow, her companion, Miss Hobhouse, and their maids. Penny is in disgrace because she wants to marry some man of whom her parents do not approve. They wanted to send her off to a ghastly great-aunt in the depths of Shropshire out of harm's way and she decided she would much rather stay here to, as she puts it, "help me with the house". Her unfortunate parents presumably think she is meekly going off to Great-Aunt Hermione.'

'She is actually on her way, then?' Arthur, his expression faintly alarmed, looked around the breakfast parlour which was serving as a snug bachelor sitting room. Despite Mrs Grainger's best efforts, it was a litter of sporting journals, fishing rods and miscellaneous masculine clutter. 'Will you send her back where she is supposed to be?'

'Certainly not. I wouldn't hand her over even if she had robbed the Tower of London. Her parents are idiots.' Guy flicked the letter with one finger. 'She places every confidence in my ability to assist her in achieving her heart's desire—a gentleman of Kent by the name of Nicholas Foster—and generally, as she puts it, saving her from becoming quite distracted by parental prejudice.'

'Foster of Kent, you say?' Arthur tossed the newspaper aside, got up and, after some rummaging in a stack of books, produced a weighty tome with *The Landed Gentry* in gold on its spine. He dumped it on the table and began to flick through. 'Foster… This could be the man. If it is, he sounds acceptable enough. Owner of Rising Park near Faversham. Father the second son of Lord Travis. What's wrong with that, do you think?'

'He's not an earl. A viscount would do at a pinch and a mere baron would be a last hope. The son of a second son of a baron? No.'

'Miss Thurlow is very eligible?'

'She is perilously close to being on the shelf, is self-willed, too intelligent for her own good—in her mother's opinion—and is taking rather than pretty. Her dowry is exceedingly respectable.' He did not add that it was probably not as much the size of her dowry as the fortunes of her various relatives that must have attracted the man from whose clutches she so narrowly escaped all those years ago.

'But what are we—I mean you—going to do with her here? You have been refusing invitations locally because of the amount of work needing doing which means the house is not suitable for returning hospitality and our neighbours understand that. Surely Miss Thurlow will find this very tedious?'

'Compared with Great-Aunt Hermione and her smelly lapdogs? I very much doubt it. And she knows she will be safe with me. Besides, I am sure Miss Williams would be kind enough to help me look after her.'

It was, Guy realised, perfect. Having Penny around always made him happy, even if she was enough to turn an almost-brother's hair white with worry on occasion, and he was missing Cressida after a week when he had scrupulously avoided any contact beyond a bow as they passed at church on Sunday. Was she missing him as much? He could not tell from her cool smile and slight bow in return. The only thing that had been achieved by the separation was a growing conviction that she would make a perfect wife—but how to achieve that?

He could probably seduce her, he thought, but that was no way for a gentleman to act. He could compromise her, perhaps by seizing her in a passionate embrace where they were almost certain to be surprised by some of the ladies of the town. But that made him just as uneasy. It felt too much like coercion and, much as he wanted her, he wanted her wholehearted consent more.

He could declare undying love, he supposed. That was supposed to be infallible, because apparently no tender-hearted lady could bear to see a man languishing for love of her. But it would be a lie and Cressida would probably detect it. Guy knew himself to be no actor and, besides, he had no idea how a man in love looked or acted. Poetry, mooning about, being distracted and dreaming of the beloved all came into it, if hearsay was to be believed. He certainly dreamt about Cressida and very arousing that was, but he could hardly describe the erotic images as romantic. And he suspected that romance—love—was the only emotion that would be strong enough to overcome Cressida's refusal to contemplate marriage.

None of that could be voiced, of course. What he did say was, 'I'll ride down and see if Miss Williams has any ideas for keeping Penny entertained. And I'll ask Miss Pomfret, too, of course.'

'Of course,' Arthur agreed, his face so straight that Guy suspected he was being teased. 'Miss Pomfret knows all the ladies of the town.'

Chapter Twelve

Cressida was arranging flowers in a vase on the hall table and answered the door herself, a sprig of asparagus fern in one hand.

'Guy! Lord Easton, I mean. What a surprise. I mean, good morning.'

He was dressed for riding and, flustered, she glanced up and down the street as though expecting his bay hack to be tethered to the railings.

'I left my horse at the Raven's Nest rather than risk obstructing your footway,' Guy said, apparently reading her mind, which was disconcerting. She had too many thoughts in her head that she would have died rather than reveal to that clear grey gaze.

'Yes, of course, do forgive me, my mind was all on whether I had cut enough greenery for my arrangement.' Cressida stuffed the fern frond into the vase with more haste than delicacy and found a social smile from somewhere. 'Do come in. Might I offer you coffee? Or tea?'

Or anything else you might want? murmured her body, flooded with disconcertingly wanton sensations.

'Coffee would be very welcome, thank you.' Guy followed her through into the sitting room, leaving the door open wide behind him. Clearly, he had far more willpower than she, or, more likely, he was far less tempted to take advantage of privacy.

Jane brought the coffee pot and cups and Guy made himself comfortable in a deep armchair. 'I have a cousin, Miss Penelope Thurlow, who has just written to say she and her companion intend descending upon me for an unspecified length of time as she is in disgrace with her parents. They do not approve of her choice of husband. I was hoping you might take pity on me and help me entertain her from time to time. I think you would find her good company.'

'Yes, of course,' Cressida said, without having to consider it. 'Poor girl. She is not of age, I assume.'

'No, she is twenty-two or three, I believe.'

'Then why does she not marry the man regardless? Or is he so very unsuitable that one ought not to be encouraging her?'

'I assume she is hoping to persuade her parents, rather than defy them, in order to prevent a rift. She is high-spirited and intelligent, but it would distress her to cut herself off from them. The man himself sounds perfectly respectable, but Penny found herself embroiled with a rake a few years ago and her parents cannot be brought to believe this does not show some fatal weakness in her character. Combine that with their serious ambitions to marry her well and the result is she finds herself almost on the shelf.'

'If he is a decent man and they love each other, then she should marry him regardless,' Cressida said firmly.

'You believe that love is the most important consideration in marriage, then?' Guy asked, his tone almost challenging.

'I think it the most desirable,' Cressida retorted. 'Of course, matches with mutual liking and respect can be very happy, but love, surely, is the ideal—that depth of desire and affection, that closeness...' She let her voice trail away, afraid her own longings were all too apparent.

But Guy was frowning into the depths of his coffee cup. 'How the devil is one supposed to know what love is?' he asked. 'Easy enough to tell whether one likes a person or not, whether one trusts them, whether one desires them. But love?' He shrugged, the picture of the male confronted with difficult emotions. 'It seems a hostage to fortune. A huge risk of hurt and betrayal and disappointment.' He put down his cup and saucer, the fine china hitting the polished mahogany just a little too hard.

'Loving someone is overwhelming,' Cressida said, watching his hands, the long, sensitive fingers interlinked, the tendons stark under the lightly tanned skin. Those fingers had held her, caressed her, saved her from drowning. 'I can only imagine what it must be like if that love is returned. How powerful that would be.'

'Is that what happened?' Guy asked, looking up, catching her gaze. 'You lost someone you had that shared love with? Or you loved and it was not returned? Is that why you will not contemplate marriage?'

'No,' Cressida answered abruptly. 'No, love had absolutely nothing to do with it. Nothing. Anything but love.'

'I apologise, I should not have mentioned the matter.' He straightened in the chair as if to emphasise a change of subject. 'I trust your judgement over Penny's feelings for her young man. If you think it right to encourage the match, I will see what influence I can bring to bear.'

'You can persuade her parents?'

'I can persuade my father and what the Marquess of Thurlow wants tends to be law in the extended family,' Guy said wryly.

'One day you will wield that power yourself,' Cressida said. 'A huge responsibility. Will you take your seat in the House of Lords?'

'I suppose that, too, would be my duty. Fortunately, the day when a coronet complete with its four strawberry leaves lands on my head is far distant. My father is hale, hearty, not yet sixty and looks fit for thirty more years at least, provided a fit of temper does not carry him off first.'

'That is good to hear. More coffee?' Cressida asked. Guy picked up his cup and saucer and held it out, their fingertips brushing as she took it from him. His skin was warm, slightly roughened—and gone in an instant. She took care to pour without a tremor and passed the cup back, keeping her fingers well clear of his this time.

'When does Miss Thurlow arrive?'

'Goodness knows. I have a sinking feeling it might be at any moment. Her parents believe her to be going to her great-aunt in Shropshire. I am certain Penny will give the postilions my direction at the very first change of horses.'

'Her companion will not try to prevent her?'

'I doubt the Household Cavalry could control Penny when she has made up her mind to something.' Guy drank his coffee in one gulp, put down his cup and stood, all in one continuous motion, as though he could no longer bear to linger. 'I should not keep you and I must go and see that Mrs Grainger has all she needs to create two suitable guest chambers. My regards to Miss Pomfret. I will invite you both to tea as soon as Penny is settled. Good day, Miss Williams.' Guy stopped halfway to the door, turned and sent her a smile of surprising sweetness. 'Cressida.'

Quite how she got there she could not afterwards recall, but Cressida found herself standing in front of him, one hand lifted to just touch his cheek. Why were her fingertips so sensitive to the slightest touch of his skin? First his hand, now the faint prickle of stubble from his shaven chin, the tension in the muscle.

'Don't worry about your cousin. I will do all I can to help her, or at least, to take her mind from her troubles.'

If that is ever possible...

'I know you will.' Guy turned his head as he spoke, his lips touching her hand with the most fleeting of pressure. Then he stepped back, leaving her breathless, as though he had kissed her full on the mouth.

She was still standing where he left her when Marjorie came in through the front door. 'I met Lord Easton just now, striding up the hill and whistling! Positively whistling, like some errand boy.'

'Relief, I expect. He has a cousin coming to stay with him, Miss Penelope Thurlow. She is in disgrace at home over some love affair and I have promised we will help entertain her.'

'That's nice, dear,' Marjorie said vaguely, but Cressida noticed the look she gave her was sharply assessing.

'So, has Guy asked you to find out everything about Nicholas?'

Miss Thurlow perched on the edge of the balustrade overlooking what, with more attention, would one day be the front lawn sweeping down to the ha-ha. The summer evening light that lingered was still golden, although the heat was beginning to fade.

Guy, the Vicar and Arthur were discussing whatever men talked about over their port; Marjorie, Miss Thurlow's companion and Mrs Truscott had gone in search of Mrs Grainger to see if she could be persuaded to part with her recipe for lemon and beeswax polish and Penelope and Cressida had wandered out on to the terrace.

Cressida had not expected such a direct attack. This small dinner party was the first time she and Guy's cousin had met since Miss Thurlow had arrived, the day after her letter to Guy. He had wasted no time in introducing her, arranging this gathering for the very next evening.

At first his problematic cousin had appeared to be a quiet, rather mousy young lady, not given to anything but polite small talk. Now there was some colour in her cheeks and her eyes sparkled with what might be indignation.

'Lord Easton asked me to help him entertain you,' Cressida said. 'And he told me a little about the reason you have left home. So I did not say anything tactless, I assume.'

'Hmm.' Penelope wriggled more comfortably on to the warm stone ledge and slanted Cressida an assessing look. 'He is carefully not saying anything to me about it. It is like having a large carthorse in the drawing room and everyone pretending it doesn't exist.'

'Do you want to talk about it? About your Nicholas?'

'Then you can tell Guy?'

'Not unless you want me to. Or you could tell him yourself. If he is offering you sanctuary, I would have thought you could trust him, Miss Thurlow.'

'Of course I can trust him,' the other woman said indignantly. 'Call me Penny, all my friends do,' she added. This time the slanting glance was warm. 'We are going to be friends, aren't we?'

'I hope so. Tell me then.'

'We met at a mutual friend's house in London. He has a small estate in Kent—essentially, Nicholas is a gentleman farmer. He is kind and funny and strong and he makes my toes curl.'

'He sounds wonderful. So, what is wrong with him?'

'He is not the Earl of Whittleford, who is dull and snappish and has no chin. And he isn't the Earl of Easton, either.' There was that look again.

'Your parents want you to marry Guy?'

'Any earl would be excellent, but one who is heir to a marquess is better. Not that I have any desire to marry my cousin, you will be glad to hear.'

'Will I?' Cressida said faintly.

'He's in love with you and you're in love with him, aren't you?'

'Whatever— Of course he is not in love with me.'

'He looks at you when you aren't looking at him. And then you do the same to him. I catch Nicholas doing it to me.'

'Lord Easton is an attractive man,' Cressida managed to say. 'Naturally he tends to, er, draw the eye. But this is not about me, or your cousin. You are of age—why do you not marry your gentleman farmer regardless of what your parents say?'

'Nicholas has scruples,' Penny said, as though the man had a nasty skin disease. 'I would marry him tomorrow, but he wants Papa's blessing.'

'Difficult. Perhaps Guy—Lord Easton, I mean, will find a solution.'

'I am placing my faith in him. He has always looked after me and he rescued me before.'

'He did?'

'Oh, yes, I was in such a pickle and although I was screaming my head off, I didn't think anyone would come— Oh, here is Amanda.'

Miss Hobhouse, Penny's companion, stepped out on to the terrace. 'May I join you? I confess to having little interest in furniture polish and even less in recipes for pickles, which is what the ladies are discussing now.'

She was a composed young woman, a clergyman's daughter fallen on hard times with the death of her par-

ents, Guy had told Cressida, who liked her on sight.
And so, she suspected, had Mr Graham who had part-
nered her at dinner.

'The gentlemen are coming out now, I think,' Miss
Hobhouse added as masculine voices filled the drawing room behind her.

No sooner had they appeared than Mrs Truscott
and Marjorie joined them, sweeping Penny off to one
side to interrogate her on what amusements she might
enjoy. Picnics? Sewing parties? The ladies' reading
group?

The Vicar excused himself, murmuring something
about a book in the library that Lord Easton had said he
might borrow and Arthur Graham, a trifle pink about
the ears, asked Miss Hobhouse if she would like to see
the view of the lake from the other end of the terrace.

'We have been abandoned,' Guy said, lounging
against the balustrade at Cressida's side. 'Has Penny
poured out her heart to you?'

'She spoke affectionately and sensibly about her
Nicholas, a gentleman farmer it seems. He sounds perfectly acceptable to me—his very reluctance to simply marry her out of hand must show his intentions
are honourable.'

'So, he is being the perfect gentleman and she is
despairing of him?'

'Miss Thurlow has every confidence in your ability
to rescue her, she tells me.' The setting sun was in her
eyes and Cressida shifted position a little. It brought
her very close to Guy. 'The sun was in my eyes,' she
explained, self-conscious. 'I was dazzled.'

'And I thought I was,' he murmured, which was

strange, given that his back was to the light. Surely Miss Thurlow had not been correct? Did he look at her? No, surely he was merely flirting.

She made herself concentrate as, with a glance along the terrace to where everyone else was out of earshot, Guy added, 'I need to be certain of the man—I couldn't forgive myself if he turns out to be less than she thinks him.'

'Surely your man of law has access to confidential enquiry agents?' Cressida asked. 'Papa—I mean, a friend of my father's was always using one to check on senior servants before employing them, or to ensure that businesses he might invest in were as sound as they appeared.'

For some reason Guy was looking uncomfortable. He shifted his gaze away from her and straightened up. 'Yes, I suppose that would be prudent. I… It did not occur to me to use such services in this case. We should go inside now. The insects are beginning to swarm.'

There was hardly a midge in sight, but Cressida did not demur. It would be far more comfortable to have other people around them. Or perhaps *safer* was the word she was looking for. The temptation to lean a little closer, to allow her hand to brush against his sleeve, to close her eyes and inhale the faint but heady mixture of citrus and linen and man—that was kept firmly under control by the sharp eyes of Mrs Truscott, the benevolent smile of the Vicar and Marjorie's affectionate curiosity.

His father, the Marquess, employed many men of law and for this, a far less sensitive matter, Guy wrote

to the most conservative, most cautious and traditional.
If Mr Augustus Weston passed Penny's Nicholas as an
honest, respectable gentleman, then his word would be
sufficient to sway the Marquess in her favour.

He told her what he had done late the next morning
when he encountered her in the market square. He had
made a detour from riding right around the bounds of
the estate in order to drop the letter at the receiving
office to catch the next Mail to London. Penny, driven
down earlier in the gig with Miss Hobhouse by one of
the grooms, was in company with Miss Pomfret and
Cressida on their way to a meeting of the Stowe Easton
ladies' reading circle.

Guy swung down from the saddle and looped the
reins over his arm before raising his hat to the ladies.
'Good day, Miss Pomfret, Miss Williams. Might I have
a word, Penny?'

He took her to one side to tell her discreetly what he
had done, but that was a wasted delicacy. She gave a
squeal of delight and threw her arms around his neck
to give him a resounding kiss on his cheek. To keep
their balance on the sloping cobbles he put his arms
around her in a tight hug.

'Darling man! That is just the thing to convince
dearest Uncle. Mr Weston is the stuffiest thing in cre-
ation, but he is a fair beast and Nicholas has nothing
to hide.'

Over Penny's shoulder Guy saw Miss Pomfret's
raised eyebrows at the embrace and the complete absence of emotion on Cressida's normally expressive
face. Was she, could she be, *jealous*?

Despite his aunt and uncle's ambitions and the fact that he was very fond of Penny, Guy would no more consider marrying her than he would his own sister, if he had one, but Cressida would not be certain of that—cousin marriages were a common enough strategy for keeping wealth and land within the family circle.

It was probably reprehensible to feel something like smugness at the thought Cressida was jealous. But perhaps it was not smugness, he thought as he set Penny back on her feet and told her, with mock severity, to behave herself in public. Perhaps it was hope. And that was a disconcerting idea for a man who was beginning to feel a very unfamiliar uncertainty.

Riding away from the square and down the hill past Cressida's home, Guy struggled to analyse his feelings. What the devil was the reason for the small, cold lump that appeared to have taken up residence in his stomach recently?

Study of the estate maps had shown him the location of a lane that gave access to the park and as he found it he realised what that unpleasant sensation was: fear. Not the thrill of the nerves, the chill in the blood that he was familiar with from the battlefield, or the sensations that had flooded through him at the first sight of the enemy. No man, if he was honest, denied feeling fear then—you were foolishly reckless, or had completely underestimated the situation if you did not. Duty, experience, training carried you through until the moment when the heat of battle was on you and there was no time, no room, for fear.

No, this was the nasty, cold sensation that came in the night before the battle, the terror that each man wrestled with in silence and alone while his imagination ran riot. Guy knew he was afraid now—afraid of losing Cressida. Was this love, then? If it was, it was thoroughly unpleasant.

Guy swore at his mount as the big black gelding fidgeted and sidled, unaccountably unwilling to back up and let him open the gate as it had been trained to do. Then he realised his hand was tight on the reins, its signals at odds with what the shift of his weight was telling the animal. He relaxed his grip, gave Blackjack an apologetic pat on the neck and opened the gate.

He would control this fear as he had dealt with those night-time ghouls: with sheer willpower. He would wait until he had Brent's report, then he would know what he was dealing with. One stubborn young woman with blue eyes he could drown in and a mouth that made him lose all grip on reality was not going to succeed where Napoleon's forces had failed.

The scar on his left wrist chose that moment to give one of its periodic twinges, reminding Guy that Napoleon had succeeded in wounding him, leaving a mark that would never heal, severing part of him for ever.

In the breast of his coat was the letter he had picked up that morning from the receiving office and had put off opening because he recognised Brent's handwriting.

Now, with Blackjack walking sedately along the margins of a field, Guy let the reins drop, took it out and opened it.

I beg to report that, having returned from North Britain, I have begun my enquiries with the

*whereabouts of the Hon Miss V. F. These ne-
cessitate my travelling into the West Country, a
journey I am about to embark upon.*

*I trust that this will yield useful intelligence.
As for the matter of Miss W., there are curious
circumstances which may be coincidental. I trust
that I will be better placed to inform Your Lordship on the matter shortly.*

In my respectful duty,
Wm Brent

No news, then, just mysterious hints and the agent
off on yet another lengthy journey. Guy forced his
mind away from thoughts of women, past and present, focused on the state of the boundary wall and did
his best to bury aching uncertainty under a severely
practical assessment of crumbling mortar and missing bricks.

Chapter Thirteen

'Arthur... I mean, Mr Graham asked me to give you a message, Miss Williams,' Miss Hobhouse said as they sat down to luncheon at Mrs Whitlow's loaded dining table. The ladies of the reading circle took it in turns to host the gatherings and served what was supposed to be a light luncheon, but which had become an exercise in competitive catering with each vying to produce the most exquisite repast.

'Oh?' Cressida made a business of shaking out her napkin to hide her smile at the revealing use of Mr Graham's name.

'He wondered if you had had the opportunity to think about the second temple, the one on the rise opposite the Temple of the Winds. Should he have a carriage drive cut through to it, or would a winding path be more suitable? He is not certain which would make a better picnic spot.'

'I see no reason why they cannot both be used for that, but I see what he means about paths and rides.

One would not want to spoil the woodland by cutting too many wide drives through it.'

The luncheon table chit-chat was no help in thinking through the problem and Cressida could not envisage how steep the slopes were or how heavy the woodland.

'I will come back with you in the gig as far as the main drive,' she said finally as they did their best to make admiring remarks about dessert, an over-elaborate confection of cream, dried fruit and pastry. 'I can walk up and see for myself. Perhaps you could tell Mr Graham that I will send him a note with my thoughts, although, of course, Lord Easton must be the final judge.'

The distant chimes from the church belfry striking two o'clock reached Cressida as she made her way up the winding, overgrown path leading to the second little temple. She was regretting Mrs Whitlow's *crème delice des fruits Parisienne* as she climbed, but at least the exercise should help digestion, she told herself, dealing with yet another bramble determined to trip her up.

When she finally reached the summit of the hill and walked around the temple, she saw her heated struggles had been quite unnecessary. 'Oh, rats,' she muttered. On one flank of the hill leading down to the parkland there was open ground, with rabbit-cropped grass and only scattered bushes and small trees. The underlying rock must be different, or perhaps some long-ago fire had so damaged the woodland here that it was only just recovering.

'That answers the question about a route for carriages, at least,' she informed the ivy-clad goddess who was peering coyly out at the world by the steps up to the temple platform. 'It can wind down to the park and then curve around the foot of the hill to join the main drive.'

The goddess had nothing to say to that, nor did the wicked-looking faun who was leering at her. Cressida found several more statues, some toppled, others entangled in the undergrowth. To her untutored eye they looked of good quality, although whether they were genuine antiquities brought back by some Thurlow ancestor from his Grand Tour, or more modern reproductions, she did not know.

This temple was square with a row of columns at the front, with behind them a porch and stone benches. Double doors, massive and studded with bronze nails, stood firmly closed. She had intended walking back down the hill and returning home—now the very strength of the barrier roused a stubborn determination to get inside.

There did not appear to be a keyhole, only handles formed of giant rings. Cressida turned and twisted them to no avail, then simply put her shoulder to the join and pushed. The doors creaked open, with a sound that would have chilled the marrow of any reader of Gothic tales, to reveal not some haunted tomb or ancient crone, but a charming room. It was set out with stone seats, a table with benches running along the walls and, in a central alcove flanked by doors, a wide platform.

There were cobwebs, but very little dust and she realised as she explored that the heavy doors had kept out damp as well as vermin, because the seats and benches still had cushions of faded red velvet. The dais in the alcove was scattered with more cushions, conjuring up images of picnickers, replete with chicken and wine, taking refuge there from the summer sun like so many sultans in an eastern palace.

Cressida explored the tiny rooms on either side. One held a dank privy, and a good many spiders, the other a tiny pantry where, presumably, the servants prepared the feast. It could be a magical place, even in winter, because there was a fireplace.

When she pummelled several of the cushions into a comfortable perch on the edge of the dais they gave off puffs of dust, but no leaks of feathers, so she sat down and looked out of the open doors. Only the sky was visible from this far back in the temple. It was the intense cloudless blue of a hot August afternoon, but a faint breeze crept in, bringing with it the scent of green growing things, the sound of birdsong.

The enchantment she had felt for this park ever since she had first ventured to trespass into it swept over her: peace, the sensation of time standing still, of detachment from all the troubles of the world.

Fortunate Guy, she thought, watching a kestrel through eyes half closed against the light. And with that crept in another thought, far less generous. Lucky Lady Easton, whoever she would be, sharing this place with him. She should be glad for that unknown woman, hopeful that Guy would find someone who would cherish his home as much as she cherished him, but it was very hard to find any emotion except resentment.

It made her even sadder to discover she could feel

like that. Cressida brushed away the moisture on her cheeks. She should stop staring out at that brilliant sky—it was making her eyes water. But it wasn't the sky that was at fault, she knew that. She was weeping for what she could not have, for the man she now knew she loved.

When she curled up into a miserable ball the cushions gave off a musty smell, but that somehow felt only proper and fitting for her unhappiness.

When was the last time she had wept? She couldn't remember. Not since she had found her new life with Marjorie and perhaps not even before then. The blow of discovering who she was—and who she was not—had been numbing, an ache of misery and confusion, but it had never occurred to her to cry then.

Best to get this over with, she thought grimly, racked with sobs. Then she would walk back past the stream, wash her face and, perhaps by the time she was home again, the state of her could be explained by a long, hot, difficult walk.

The storm passed as quickly as it had come, leaving her with an aching chest, a sodden handkerchief and bleary eyes. Exhausted.

I am too tired to walk home yet, she thought miserably.

She would rest here, perhaps sleep, then she would surely feel better.

The grit of pebbles against stone had her blinking awake, twisting around so that when the tall figure stood in the doorway, a black silhouette against the blue of the sky, she was still huddled on her makeshift bed, the light unmercifully on her face.

'Cressida?' It was Guy—of course it was. It couldn't be some passing shepherd who would shrug at the odd ways of the gentry and be on his way, or Mr Graham, kind and rather shy around women. No, it had to be the man she had just wept her heart out over and she must look a complete, pathetic mess.

'Cressida,' he said again, crossing the space between them in six long strides. 'What is wrong? Who has hurt you?'

'Nobody,' she muttered as Guy knelt beside her. 'Nothing. It isn't important.'

'Cressida,' he said again and something in the way he said it, the tenderness, the concern, broke through the barriers.

'Oh, Guy.' She swayed towards him and he gathered her close, murmuring something soothing. But she did not want soothing, she wanted him, to lose herself in him, to show him, without the words she could not utter, how much she wanted him. Loved him.

The flood of tears had scoured her empty of inhibition, doubts, caution. This place, lost in time for so many years, was not real and nothing mattered in here but the two of them.

'Kiss me.'

The pressure of Guy's lips, the way he held her, was gentle. He thought she needed comfort, although she could feel the tension thrumming through his muscles, the effort it was taking to hold back.

'No.' Cressida pulled back until she could look into his eyes. 'Kiss me. I need you to kiss me.'

I need you to love me, make me yours, just for this moment.

She ran her fingers into his hair, pulled him down, arched her body into his, as explicit in her desire as instinct could make her. For a moment she thought he would resist her, then they were sprawled together on the old cushions, his mouth hungry on hers, his hands moulding her body to his.

As much as a respectable young lady could, Cressida knew what happened between a man and a woman in bed. And no woman, however modestly brought up, could avoid knowing just how different male anatomy was—not with the vogue for Classical statues and the tightness of fashionable breeches.

But this... This was not a question of body parts and biology. This was a maelstrom of feeling, sensation that had nothing to do with rational thought at all.

Somehow Guy's coat had gone, and his waistcoat. He ripped off his neckcloth one-handed, the other hand moving over the bodice of her light summer dress. It was held in place by a few ribbons and a hidden button which surrendered without a struggle to fingers that knew precisely what they were doing.

Then his hand stilled on her breast as he rose up over her. His kiss became slower, deeper, as though he had all the time in the world to explore her, taste her. And she could taste him, familiar and yet now with a sharper edge that must be her passion meeting his. Their bodies were speaking without words.

The scent of his skin was familiar, too, but muskier now—male and dangerous. Thrilling. Cressida followed his lead, let her tongue tangle with his, pulled back to nip at his lower lip, making him growl.

The hand on her breast was no longer still, the fingers exploring under the lace of her camisole, down to the edge of her light corset where it cupped her breasts. His thumb slid beneath the firm linen, found the nipple, fretted it.

Sensation lanced like hot wires from the pad of his thumb to the aching place between her thighs making her moan against his lips. She wanted more, wanted something... She pressed her legs together tightly, trying to control the sensation, only to make it worse—better—she could no longer tell the difference.

'Shh,' Guy murmured as he shifted position, his body almost over hers, his free hand sliding down her body, over the swell of her belly, down to the intimate triangle. He paused for a second, just pressing lightly until she arched against his hand, then the strong horseman's fingers slid down, caught at her skirts, dragged them back up, baring the skin above her garters until his fingertips brushed against the nest of curls that were all the protection between the aching need of her and his exploration. 'Ah, Cressida, there you are.'

And then he laid his hand over her there, cupping the mound, gently pressing, and went back to kissing her.

It was intolerable. Torture. She wanted... She wanted *something*, something she had no words for. She needed to touch him, to torment him as much as he was tormenting her. Her fingers dug into the waistband of his breeches, fastened on his shirt, pulled and tugged until it came free and she could put her hands on the bare skin beneath. Heated, muscled, smooth, then, as her hands moved up, rough with hair. She scratched lightly and was rewarded with his gasp, followed the trail of hair downwards, back to his breeches. Why was the rasp of hair under her palms so exciting? What would happen if she was bolder still?

It was hard to concentrate now because the hand that had been so torturously still was moving at last, one long finger pressing through the curls into secret folds, hot, damp folds that felt swollen and aching, yearning.

Her own fingers found the fastenings of the fall of Guy's breeches, tight against the flat muscles of his stomach. Cressida struggled with them, freed them and pushed them aside, curling her fingers around him just as he found a place that had her arching up against him, crushing their hands together.

'*Oh!*' she gasped, falling back, her hand sliding on the rigid length.

'Yes,' Guy said as though the word was wrenched from him. '*Yes.*'

She did not understand him, but her body did, her hand knew what to do, although she thought hazily that she must be clumsy, must be hurting him, because his breath was ragged now.

But it was too late to stop, to ask, because that exquisite spot he had found so unerringly had become the centre of her being, a tormenting pleasure tightening to the point of torture. That, and the silken slide of flesh against her fingers, was all she was aware of.

'Now,' Guy gasped against her breast. 'Come for me, Cressida. Now—'

Her fingers tightened on him as the pleasure exploded. She was conscious of Guy thrusting into her grasp, of wet heat, of her own body pressed against his, of sensation flooding through her and his cry mingling with hers.

'Yes.'

Cressida drifted back into consciousness, opened her eyes and stared up to a stone ceiling through dust motes dancing in shafts of sunlight. There was a heavy weight on her bare shoulder, a tickle of hair against her cheek, another weight slung across her waist, the sound of breathing, deep and regular.

Her body felt heavy, boneless. Tiny, disturbing flickers of sensation ran through her limbs, ghosts of the wave of pleasure that had swept her away.

Swept her away in Guy's arms, she thought as she came fully to herself. And Guy was here, his head pillowed on her breast, the prickle of stubble against the sensitive skin a delicious almost-pain. His arm lay across her waist, protective, possessive.

The temptation to touch his hair was too strong, but even a feather-light stroke roused him. Cressida felt the brush of his eyelashes, a tickle as light as butterfly feet, then he raised his head, shifted his weight and sat up.

'Are you well?' he asked.

'I have no idea,' she confessed, managing somehow to meet his gaze. 'Am I supposed to feel like this?'

'Bemused, somewhat befuddled and relaxed in every limb?' His smile was amused, but sympathetic.

'Precisely. I suppose,' Cressida ventured, despite

her blushes, 'that is the consequence of losing my virginity.'

'But you haven't.' Guy sat right up, slid off the dais and began to put his clothes in order, tactfully half turned from her.

'But we…but you… And then I…'

'We made love, pleasured each other—something it is perfectly possible to do without any risk to your maidenhead, Cressida. And with no risk of anything else either,' he added drily.

It took her a moment to realise what he was talking about. There was no risk that she might be with child.

I never even thought about that, Cressida realised with a wave of shame. *And I should have done. I did not consider my own virtue either and Guy took responsibility for both those things.*

'I am ashamed of myself,' she said out loud.

'No.' He turned towards her, his face intent, serious. 'You have nothing to be ashamed of.'

'I mean, I should have thought about the risk of a child. I should not have left it to you to think of these things. And I cannot plead ignorance,' she added, determined to accept all the blame that was due her. 'I know perfectly well what causes pregnancy.'

'Knowing the theory is not the same as understanding the practice,' Guy said, the quiver of amusement back in his voice as he turned away again to allow her to wriggle off the dais and restore order to her rumpled gown. 'I have found that applies to a great many things in life, from lovemaking to military tactics.'

He, no doubt, had a great deal of practice at both, Cressida thought with a sudden stab of unhappiness.

The mists of physical pleasure, of dizzy happiness, were fading fast now, leaving her all too well aware that she had flung herself into this man's arms, more or less begging him to make love to her.

Guy must assume she wanted to be his mistress, or that she was simply a wanton. He must have taken pity on her, she thought, lashing herself with the shame and misery now. He cannot have desired her, not looking like a badly wrung-out dishcloth. It had been pity, that was what it had been.

'I must go now,' Cressida said as she found her slippers kicked halfway across the marble floor. 'I expect by the time I have washed my face in the lake and walked home I will look merely windblown and overheated and not... Not such a complete wreck.'

'Have you no idea how you do look?' Guy asked. 'Your cheeks are flushed, your eyes bright, your mouth deliciously swollen with kisses. You look like a lovely woman who has been well loved.'

When Cressida made an abrupt gesture with one hand he added gently, 'What was wrong? Why had you been weeping?'

'For what I cannot have,' she said, shaken into honesty by the look in his eyes. 'I sat there and looked out at the sky and listened to the birds, sensed the perfect peace of this place and felt desolate. I never cry,' she added, defensive now when Guy did not reply. 'I don't know why I did now.'

'Tell me, Cressida. Tell me the secret you are keeping that weighs so heavily on you. I will not betray your confidence, I swear.'

It was suddenly too hard to fight, to keep it all a secret any longer. If she told him part of the truth, then, surely, he would turn away from her for ever. It would break her heart, but at least this would be ended, she could stop pointlessly dreaming, hoping.

'My father is not the man to whom my mother was married.'

Chapter Fourteen

'**O**h, hell.' Guy dropped on to the nearest stone bench. 'That is…'

'A problematic circumstance, I am sure you would agree,' Cressida said. She sat down on the edge of the dais and appeared to be doing something about her tangled hair. Anything rather than look at him, he supposed.

'She did not marry twice, I presume?' he suggested hopefully.

'No.'

'But your… The man to whom she was married accepted you as his child? A child born in wedlock is assumed to be legitimate unless the father repudiates it.'

'I do not believe he knew,' Cressida said. She gave up on her hair, absently tucking a straggling lock behind her ear. 'But I do, you see.'

And, of course, her conscience would make that a burden and a secret she had to keep. No wonder she had resolved never to marry and face the dilemma of whether or not to tell her suitor. Most men of her class would baulk at a bride of irregular parentage.

'Your mother told you? It was a deathbed confession?' Of all the selfish things to do, he thought savagely. What possible good could that do? And the harm to her daughter by that knowledge was devastating. 'She might have been rambling, delirious.'

'He told me himself,' Cressida said tightly. 'He was quite sober at the time, I think, and in good health.'

'And he is still alive?' Hopefully the man was dead and the secret belonged only to Cressida.

And now to me.

'He is. So you see? It is an impossible situation.'

'Difficult, certainly.' Impossible, in fact, unless she married a man to whom irregular birth was no concern and who was strong enough to protect Cressida from attempts to blackmail her, which must be a constant danger. It went without saying that her father was a man of no principles at all, otherwise he would never have told her who he was.

'Impossible,' she repeated.

Guy felt a strong desire to smash something, preferably the face of the man who had fathered Cressida, but the nearest breakable item would do. Unfortunately, the solid marble interior held nothing he could demolish. Instead, he took a hold on his temper.

'This is why you feel you can never marry,' he stated.

Cressida nodded. Despite the tear stains on her cheeks, the crumpled gown, the tangled hair, she had dignity now. Dignity and pride and strong scruples. 'Why I should not even be your...friend. Most people would say I should not be associating with your cousin.'

'To hell with that! How can you be blamed for your parents' failings, your father's lack of character? We are friends, Cressida. Just now we were rather more than that. We can still be friends. I would be reluctant to let you go, my dear.'

'Thank you for not pointing out that under the circumstances I should be grateful for the offer of a carte blanche.'

That almost cracked his fragile hold on violence. Guy slammed his clenched fist down on the bench beside him. It hurt, but not as much as the pain inside him now. 'I want to help you, not ruin you, Cressida. Who is he?'

She shook her head at that. 'I am never going to tell. And you cannot help me, except by keeping my secret. It would cause a stir in the town if it was known and Marjorie would be shamed—she does not know, you see. And once they know in Stowe Easton, gossip would spread, would reach London.

'My mother's name would be blackened, and I have no idea whether she was un—unwilling and forced or his willing lover. My young relatives who are to make their come-outs next Season would be tarred by association.'

Interesting, Guy thought, fleetingly distracted. *She has London relatives wealthy enough to launch more than one daughter on to the Marriage Mart with all its expenses.*

'Upon my honour your secret is safe with me,' he said and was warmed by the immediate belief he saw on Cressida's face. She did not doubt him, she trusted him with her honour, just as she had trusted him with her virtue. If only Brent would finish his investigation and write, then he might be in a position to discover who this cur was who not only planted his child on another man's wife, but was so lacking in care for that child that he tormented her with the truth about his identity.

'Did he try to blackmail you?' he asked. 'Is that why you have come to live with Miss Pomfret?'

Cressida Williams was, in all likelihood, not her real name, he realised. That was not going to help Will Brent's investigations. He needed to discover who Cressida's real father was and then deal with him, shut the man's mouth. Quite how that was to be achieved, Guy was not certain. A duel, of course, if the swine had pretensions to be a gentleman, although that would not be certain to silence him unless Guy killed him. It was a solution, but having to leave the country while his father dealt with the consequences did not appeal at all.

Visions of a convict ship bound for Australia flitted through his mind. Or the many dangers involved in the East Indies, life before the mast in the Royal Navy...

Guy gave himself a mental shake. Time to work out how to deal with the man once he knew who he was. In the meantime, he had a distressed young woman on his hands and he was not going to try to bully the name out of her.

What had she thrown at him just now? *'Under the circumstances I should be grateful for the offer of a carte blanche.'*

He wanted to make love with Cressida again and he

wanted more, to make her his. Many people would say that it would be perfectly reasonable for him to make her his mistress under these circumstances.

But this was Cressida and he would not do that to her, not add to her shame and her sense of guilt. One man had effectively ruined her life, this one was not going to make it worse.

I shall marry her.

The clarity of the thought startled him so much that he sat staring at her while the thoughts jostled and tumbled through his brain.

I can deal with any blackmailer, even if rumours escaped: it is logical that some criminal would try to extort money from the heir to a marquess, so people would believe me when I said it was an opportunist act. I like her, desire her—even more now—and she has intelligence, courage, presence. And I would not have to waste my time in the overheated reception rooms of the London ton *seeking a bride I can tolerate among the unformed green girls assembled to compete for the largest fortune, the most prestigious title.*

And she seemed to like him. She certainly returned his desire. And Cressida loved this place, the house and estate he was shaping to be his home. She would make a fine chatelaine for Easton Court.

'Why are you looking at me like that?' Cressida's question cut across his thoughts.

'Like what?' Guy demanded.

'As though you were plotting something,' she said. 'Please do not. You cannot help, I do not want you to help. There is nothing you can do, unless you can travel back in time and stop him.'

'And then you would not have been born, or, if you had, it would not have been you,' he pointed out.

'That is too complicated to think about,' Cressida said with a smile and he saw, with relief, that she was regaining her composure. Her spine was straight, her chin raised, her gaze steady, despite her puffy eyes. Yes, she had the poise, the determination, the sheer style, to make a marchioness. But he could not ask her now, not while she would think it simply a proposal forced by honour because he thought that he had ruined her.

'Let me drive you back to the Court,' he said, instead of the words that were on the tip of his tongue. 'You can wash your face, comb your hair and take a cool drink. Then I can return you home feeling rather less tumbled.'

'Yes,' Cressida said, with a twinkle in her eyes that made his heart catch. 'I do feel very thoroughly tumbled at present.'

'Come then.' He held out his hand and felt ridiculously happy when she put hers into it without hesitation. 'Will you ride back behind me?'

'On that great creature?' Cressida stood regarding Blackjack with doubt written all over her face. 'How do I get up on such a monster, pray?'

'I mount, ride alongside the steps, then take your hands and pull you up behind me.' He saw her bite her lip and added, 'And if you ask me if my back will stand it, as you have twice before, then I will simply throw you over my saddlebow and ride off with you.'

'Like Young Lochinvar?' Cressida enquired as Guy

mounted, taking what he knew was quite exaggerated efforts to do so as athletically as possible.

'Exactly like Lochinvar,' he said, edging the big horse against the steps. 'And don't you dare laugh at me, you minx.'

She reached up her hands from her position on the top step, trusted him to swing her safely up behind him on to Blackjack's broad rump and then wrapped her arms around his waist.

Why that trust affected him so, why the feel of her body pressed against his made him feel so ridiculously happy, he could not fathom until he was halfway down the hill.

I have fallen in love with her, he realised. *I love Cressida and that is why I want to marry her. Not for convenience, not because she would be acceptable or because it would help her. I love her.*

It was a shock and it silenced him. Guy rode on, keeping his horse to a steady walk, conscious only of the ripple of sensual satisfaction that was the afterglow of lovemaking, of the warmth of Cressida's body, of the faint, tantalising thread of her scent that the heat of their loving had stirred into life.

'I'm going to fall asleep in a moment,' Cressida murmured against his back.

Guy laid one hand over hers where they were clasped in front of him. 'Sleep then. I've got you.'

I've got you.

He closed his eyes and let Blackjack plod on through the heat of the late afternoon, apparently now as sleepy as his riders. Were there any more satisfactory words in the English language? *I love you, too,* perhaps. Yes, those would be wonderful to hear.

When should he tell Cressida how he felt? When should he ask her to marry him? Instinct told him to wait a few days, to make it quite clear this was not an offer he felt honour-bound to make. A picnic luncheon, just the two of them, at the temple. Light, delicious food, fine wine. Flowers. *New cushions.* Guy made a mental note.

His mother's diamond and ruby ring—a proper proposal, romantic, yet formal.

With his plan fully formed, Guy woke from the light doze he had fallen into, just as Blackjack came to a placid halt before the sweep of steps to the Court's front doors.

'We are home.' He squeezed the hands lying under his and felt Cressida stir into wakefulness behind him.

'Oh. So we are.' There was a tiny pause. 'Your home.'

It was the first time he had thought of Easton Court as 'home', Guy realised. Why was that? Because he had become used to the place—or because where he and Cressida were would be *home*?

He kicked his feet free of the stirrups, threw his right leg over Blackjack's neck and slid to the ground.

'Slide down to me,' he said, holding up his hands to Cressida.

She jumped rather than slid, launching herself as though she had every confidence that Guy would catch her.

To tease, to prolong the pleasure of having her slim waist between his hands, he held her in mid-air so she had to put her hands on his shoulders to steady herself as she laughed down at him.

'Beast! Put me down this instant.'

No one ordered earls about, except their parents, and it was a perverse pleasure to have this laughing woman tell him what to do.

'Very well,' Guy said meekly, then lowered her, inch by inch, so she slid down against his body, torturing both of them.

'Guy,' she whispered as her feet touched the ground and her hands left his shoulders to curl around his neck.

Does she know how erotic that innocent demand is? he wondered, as he bent his head to kiss her.

She kissed him back without hesitation, although when he shifted his stance to take her more securely in his arms, deepen the kiss, she wriggled free.

'Guy, we are right in front of the house—anyone might see us.'

'Why do you think I ride such a large horse?' he asked. 'He provides a perfect screen for kissing country maidens behind.'

Cressida fetched him a buffet on the shoulder. 'I do not believe that for an instant, My Lord.' With exaggerated dignity she lifted her crumpled skirts and walked towards the house.

The doors swung open as she approached, which meant, Guy thought ruefully, that at least one footman had, indeed, viewed his master making an exhibition of himself in public. He was not shy about such matters, but it did concern him that Cressida's good name might suffer from that kiss.

It was a relief to see Herring's impassive countenance, and not a footman, as they came in through the double doors.

'My Lord. Good afternoon, Miss Williams.'

'Could you ring for Mrs Grainger, Herring? Miss Williams has been visiting one of the temples and has found it a wilder and rougher climb than she imagined.'

The butler met his gaze, his own expression holding something very much like reassurance. 'It is indeed very hot today, My Lord. I have the staff working on the cooler north side of the house,' he added. 'It is fortunate that I happened to hear your horse or there might have been a delay before the door was opened.'

In other words, Guy thought, giving Herring a nod that implied appreciation for tact, *no one saw you kissing Miss Williams*. What good butlers saw did not count.

Mrs Grainger came down to find Guy standing with one foot on the drawing room fender and Cressida sitting on the window seat, the pair of them making polite conversation about the latest Court news.

'The Regent's presence in Brighton makes an otherwise very pleasant resort positively uninhabitable to anyone of any taste,' Guy remarked loftily. 'His hangers-on are intolerable tuft-hunters... Ah, Mrs Grainger. Miss Williams unwisely undertook to explore the more distant temple and a combination of the heat, the steepness and the overgrown shrubbery has been unfortunate.'

The housekeeper made a tutting sound. 'Dear me. We will draw a cool bath for you, Miss Williams, and the girls can restore that gown to order while you rest.

If you would care to come up to the bedchamber you occupied before?'

They left Guy alone in the drawing room where he indulged in a pleasant hour planning the renovation of bedchambers. At present he and Arthur had taken a small chamber each on the grounds that the larger rooms, let alone the master suite, would take the staff days to make habitable.

Now he sank down on one of the sofas, put his booted feet on the nearest occasional table and closed his eyes, the better to think. The master suite—bedchamber, dressing room, study and sitting room—had next to it the suite of the last Marchioness to occupy the house. Guy had not done more than open doors, grimace at tattered silks and stained wallpapers. Now he wondered whether Cressida would prefer to plan every detail of her own suite or would enjoy being surprised by whatever he could dream up.

He could hardly ask her, not yet. Perhaps Penny would advise him on how a woman would regard that problem but, whatever the answer was, one thing was definite—the bed was going to be new. And large. The bed in the master suite was vast, probably dated from the seventeenth century and must have involved the felling of a small copse of oaks to build it.

It cried out for rich, dark draperies, whereas the other bed must be light, romantic, charmingly feminine. Then they would have a bed to make love in for whichever mood took them...

Cressida tried to suppress her laughter, but it escaped as a giggle.

That was enough to waken Guy, sprawled on the

sofa. He opened one eye, then got to his feet, sending the little table he had been using as a footstool rocking.

'I was just resting my eyes,' he said. 'The better to admire you.'

She was certainly feeling more worthy of admiration now that she was cool, bathed, brushed and wearing a gown that no longer belonged in the rag bag. 'Resting your eyes for over an hour?'

'I was thinking about interior decoration,' he said with dignity. 'Are you well?'

Those had been his first words when they had come to themselves after making love and they made her blush all over again.

And all over, Cressida thought. She wanted to walk into his arms, but now Guy was showing the discretion he had forgotten outside and, although the expression in his eyes as he looked at her was warm, he made no move to come closer.

'Have you been offered refreshments?'

'I have been treated to tea and the most delicious cakes, thank you.' Cressida felt awkward now. Should she sit and make polite conversation? Should she ask to be driven home at once? What was the etiquette when taking leave of your...lover? Was a man one's lover if it had happened only once?

Guy answered at least one of her worries by tugging the bell pull. 'I'll have the gig brought around. Bates can drive you back—I think that might be the most discreet thing.'

'Yes, of course. Thank you.' Already what was between them had become something that must be hidden, something that would ruin her if it was known, something that Guy must be regretting.

And of course, that was perfectly right and proper. There was no future for them, after all.

Guy escorted her to the door, down the steps, handed her up into the gig where Bates, cheerful and solid, held the reins of a smart bay cob.

'Thank you, Miss Williams, for your advice on how I can use that second temple. Most valuable.'

Cressida smiled and bowed and tried not to blush yet again at his words. But, as the gig bowled along towards the road, she felt a flash of annoyance. She had shown him how he could use the little temple for dalliance, had she? With this yet-to-be-decided wife or a mistress or two?

No, it was not annoyance. It was, quite simply, jealousy.

Chapter Fifteen

The letter from William Brent that arrived with the afternoon post on Friday was disappointing. Guy flicked its edge irritably with his thumbnail as he read it for the second time.

Yes, the agent had arrived in Devon and had located the estate of Viola FitzWalden's great-uncle. So far, so good, but then he had run up against a wall of silence. The old man was definitely dead—being of a suspicious disposition Brent had been to inspect his gravestone in the churchyard. Yes, a young lady, his great-niece, had lived with him for several years until his death. A very pleasant lady, but quiet, kept herself to herself. The two did not socialise much, but then, the estate was miles from the nearest neighbours of any social standing and the old man was frail.

Brent had tried gossip, but could find not a single person who would as much as speculate on where Miss Viola had gone after the funeral. He reported, barely hiding the frustration, that the local people would not even describe her to him. The old man's housekeeper had shut the door of her cottage in his face and, when he had offered money, she had produced a shotgun.

In old age Mr Rufus FitzWalden had reduced his stables to a gig, a pony to go between the shafts and a riding horse for Miss Viola. Therefore, Brent deduced, when she had left it must have been by hired vehicle, unless someone had collected her. His next move would be to interrogate all sources of hired vehicles for ten miles around.

If Your Lordship has any further information regarding the other young lady in question, then I would be most interested to receive it, as that part of the investigation is proving—

Guy squinted again at the heavily crossed-out words. Damnably confusing.

—elusive, with a number of confusing coincidences.
I remain Your Lordship's obedient servant,
Wm Brent

Guy folded the sheets together and tossed them on his desk. He wished now he had told the agent to make Cressida his priority, but the man was in Devon now and it would be ridiculous to call him off that chase before he had exhausted all the lines of enquiry.

But then, when he had proposed to Cressida, told her he loved her and promised to deal with the man who had fathered her, she would feel free to explain everything, would feel safe in confiding her whole story to him, including the man's identity.

Then it would be straightforward, Guy thought, getting up and beginning to pace up and down the gloomy study considering possibilities. Either her real father had never intended extortion, or had thought better of it since and merely needed warning of the consequences of indiscretion, or he was an out-and-out rogue and threats would be necessary.

Guy's instinct was to kill anyone who threatened Cressida, but that was not the answer if the threat came from her own father. He could hardly challenge the man to a duel, he realised now he could consider it more calmly.

Probably a moralist would say that bribing the nearest press gang to seize him, or having him knocked on the head and transported to some distant and disease-ridden part of the world, was equally unacceptable behaviour. How distressed would Cressida be to know her own father had been summarily disposed of?

She had no reason to like the man, let alone love him, but he was her own blood, after all. There might come a time when she regretted what had been done, even blamed herself and that might happen when she had her own children, realised that her own father had been given no chance of redemption, of knowing them.

Negotiation, then. Guy heaved up the long window that opened on to the rear terrace and ducked out into the sunshine, then carried on pacing. He would make it clear that anything approaching extortion, gossip or embarrassing behaviour would have dire consequences. But if the man was prepared to make his peace with Cressida, show that he could be trusted, then a place might be found for him as some distant relative, or old acquaintance.

It went against the grain to be conciliatory towards someone who had so hurt the woman he loved, but if that was what she wanted, then that was what he would do. One step out of line, however…

There was a tap on the study door and he looked through the window as Arthur and Mrs Grainger came in.

'I have sent workmen up to the Temple of the Moon to scrub it inside and out and a man to sort out the privy and clean the rainwater tank,' Arthur reported.

'And I have had the cushions brought down here to act as patterns for new ones,' the housekeeper added. 'I thought a good sturdy cotton would be most suitable, with oilskin on the underside so they can be taken outside and used on the grass. Two of the girls are working on them now, so they should be completed by Monday.'

'Monday? I had said the day after tomorrow.'

'Which is Sunday, My Lord. That must have slipped your mind.'

Damn. Presumably a man may not take his love off into the country on a picnic on a Sunday, seduce her on a Sunday, propose on a Sunday.

'The workmen should have finished by then also,' Arthur said. 'A graded carriage route will take longer, of course, but I have sent groundsmen to make a passable way for a pony cart.'

They stood there side by side, regarding him with near-identical expressions which clearly said they were itching to know why he wanted that temple put in order so urgently, but were, of course, far too polite to ask.

Guy had absolutely no intention of telling them. Instead he thanked them and added, 'I would be obliged if you would send Griggs to me.'

Guy would trust his old batman, now valet, with anything. He had certainly trusted him with his life before now. The man was stubborn, argumentative and appallingly frank in voicing his opinions, but he was rock-solid honest and as tight-lipped as an oyster about Guy's business.

He came out on to the terrace, and, as always, Guy was surprised to see him in a valet's discreet black clothing, not in his scarlet coat.

'I want you to go to Thornborough Chase and take one gem from the safe in my suite.'

'I brought all your valuables with us, My Lord. All your stickpins and fobs and seals and chains. The rings, too. Even the stuff you never wear.'

'This is from the box of ladies' jewellery in the bottom of the safe. My mother's gems. There is a green leather ring case with a diamond and ruby ring. I'll give you a sketch of it. That's all I want. If you could avoid informing anyone of your purpose, I would be obliged.'

'Aye, My Lord.' Grigg's undistinguished face was expressionless. 'Don't want that lot prying into our business.'

'That includes the Marquess, Griggs.'

The man just nodded, but now there was knowing amusement in the brown eyes.

'Leave now, take a good horse and change whenever

you need to. I want that ring here by noon on Monday without fail.'

Griggs sketched a salute. 'Yes, Colonel, sir.' He turned to leave and added, just audibly, 'Will look right pretty on the lady, that will.' He cleared his throat. 'The gossip in the town is that pretty new doctor is making up to the Vicar's eldest daughter.' He was gone before Guy could damn him for his impudence, protest that he never thought about the confounded doctor. Which was true. Cressida would never kiss him as she did if she had desires for another man.

Was it possible to keep anything secret from one's valet? Guy wondered. He suspected not. The valet, or his military equivalent, the batman, saw his master at his most vulnerable, glimpsed his moments of weakness, had to endure his bad moods or enjoy the reflection of his happiness.

Some men, Guy knew, confided in their valets, used them as a sounding board, treated them as extensions of themselves with no independent life, without considering the risk they took in sharing that information or the burden they placed on their servants to remain discreet.

Guy had never let slip military secrets to Griggs because it was his duty to guard them close. But the man was intelligent, experienced and more than capable of putting two and two together and coming up with exactly four. Guy never had to spell out whether he was going on patrol, into battle or spending a day in camp: the correct gear was always ready. Apparently, Griggs was making deductions with equal accuracy now.

The problem was, Guy could never recall feeling

quite this degree of gut-wrenching anxiety about the outcome of a battle before. And this was going to be a battle, one fought against Cressida's scruples and anxieties. If he knew whether she loved him or not, then he would have some tactical advantage, but he wasn't even certain about that.

Did a principled, gently bred virgin allow a man to make love to her, as Cressida had done, unless she loved him? Guy had never made love to a virgin, had never attempted to seduce one. His mistresses had always been ladies of experience who knew exactly what they were doing, what, and who, they wanted and on what terms.

What if he was reading too much into Cressida's responses? What if this first experience of lovemaking had overwhelmed her and she had been swept along by it, far beyond limits she would normally set? What if it was sensuality, not love, that had brought her into his arms, put that soft light in her eyes? What if it was need, not trust, that he sensed?

And I am doing just what I used to tell inexperienced young officers not to do. I am allowing my imagination to run riot, I am forming opinions or creating doubts on no evidence whatsoever.

Guy gave himself a brisk shake. He was going to avoid Cressida until the day after tomorrow when he had set his scene. He would take her to the temple that he would have made as comfortable, as romantic and as private as he could and he would propose to her. He would tell her he loved her, ask her if she felt anything for him.

If she did—and he did not believe she would lie

to him, not without him being able to detect it—but refused him, then he would set about convincing her.

But if she did not love him, had lain with him only because their mutual passion had swept her away, then what did he do? Could he, in all conscience, try to persuade her into marriage? He probably could do it. Point out that by allowing him to make love to her she was, effectively, ruined. Tell her that his honour demanded that he wed her. Dangle the lures of title and wealth in front of her—and the promise of removing the spectre of her real father from her life or of drawing the poison from his fangs.

Yes, he could do it, Guy thought. But he knew, deep down, that he could not bring himself to do so. It would be like trapping a linnet in a cage and expecting it to sing and be happy.

For some reason he thought of Viola FitzWalden. Men—her brother, his father, he himself—had captured her and tried to put her in that cage. Had anyone asked her, really asked her, what she wanted and then listened to her answer?

But Viola had broken out of the net, had flown free and found sanctuary with her great-uncle. The fact that a seventeen-year-old girl had chosen a life of social isolation with an old man in the middle of some blasted heath rather than marry him should have told him something, Guy thought grimly.

If Cressida could not find it in her to love him, then he had lost her.

There was no sign of Guy on Friday, no word either. Saturday also passed without Cressida seeing him.

The emotions she felt ran from disappointment, to irritation to unhappiness and then, by tea time on Saturday, back to something very like anger.

They had made love. He had been tender and caring. She had thought him on the verge of a declaration of…of something.

If that declaration was one of love, of marriage, then what could she say except, *I love you, but actually I am Viola FitzWalden, the woman who jilted you and, by the way, what I told you about my father is perfectly true.*

That would be the end of everything because, sheltered from London society as she was, even she could imagine the scandal that would provoke. The Earl of Easton marrying the woman who had left him so humiliatingly on the altar steps all those years ago?

What if Guy offered her a carte blanche after all? Perhaps the reason for his silence was that he was thinking it through, deciding how to frame an offer she would accept.

Would I?

Two days ago, Cressida would have slapped the face of any man who made such a proposal. Now, with the memory of Guy's caresses, of the look in his eyes, of the feeling of lying in his arms, Cressida was not so certain any longer.

She would have to leave everything behind her, probably change her name again. Leave Marjorie, leave Stowe Easton, cut herself off from her brother and the rest of her family. Guy would set her up in some little villa just outside London—Highgate, perhaps, or Chelsea. Her life would revolve around him and he would spare her what time he thought fit.

He would be married, of course, but the image of his future wife was vague, unreal, not a real woman she would be hurting. It would be adultery, a sin. Probably she should no longer go to church.

All that sacrificed for love.

And when he no longer wants me?

Guy was not a man to cast a mistress off and leave her destitute, Cressida was certain of that. There would be a pension for life, no doubt. She could move away, find a new home in some little market town far from anyone she knew. Make a new life without Guy, without children, without family.

By Sunday Cressida was feeling so low that she had to pretend to Marjorie that she thought she had a head cold developing to account for her heavy eyes, her listlessness and lack of appetite.

'Should you go to morning service, dear?' Marjorie peered at her closely as they stood in the hall pulling on their gloves before setting out for church. 'Wouldn't it be better to stay at home and rest in bed? You could read from the Prayer Book, find a sermon to study. This might be a recurrence of whatever you caught when you fell in the lake.'

'No, I just have what Papa used to call Black Dog. I am gloomy and all I need is fresh air and a walk and I will be much better.' Cressida found her prayer book on the hall table and opened the front door. 'Look, the sun is shining.'

Some quiet contemplation in church might help her

find the balance to make the right decision, if she was faced with one. Or the resolution to live a full life if she could not experience it with Guy, as she was very much afraid must be the case.

For the first time she let herself feel hate for Charles FitzWalden. Then, as they climbed the long slope towards the church, another possibility for Guy's absence struck her. What if he now despised her, thought her wanton, as unprincipled as the man who had fathered her? Men were prone to such double standards, she knew that. For a man to take lovers only proved his virility, for a woman to be caught kissing another man was to condemn her as lost to all decency, ruined for marriage.

That was the only explanation for two days' silence.

I hate all men, Cressida thought bitterly as they walked into the churchyard. *I shall remain a spinster and revel in my independence from the entire sex.*

Guy and his party from the Court entered the church just after Cressida and Marjorie. She had warning as they came down the aisle because the verger hurried before them to open the door of the pew.

Cressida kept her gaze fixed on her prayer book, but out of the corner of her eye she saw Miss Thurlow on Guy's arm, followed by Miss Hobhouse supported by Mr Graham. An involuntary glance upwards showed her how carefully he handed Penny's companion into the pew, the look on his face as he followed her.

Lucky Miss Hobhouse. A man who was clearly falling deeply in love with her and no apparent reason why they should not marry and be happy together.

Hate, anger and now envy. Cressida told herself that

these feelings only did her harm, that she must culti-
vate resignation and a generous spirit. Just at that moment it felt very hard to do, even in church.

When she and Marjorie came out of the porch the
Vicar was there as usual to shake hands. Marjorie
paused to ask him a question about some matter of parish business, so Cressida walked out into the sunlight
and stood fiddling with the tricky catch on her parasol.

'Miss Williams.'

Guy spoke so close behind her that she jumped,
dropped the parasol, then found herself without a word
to say.

'Allow me.' He stooped and picked up the parasol,
shook off the strands of dry grass clinging to it and
handed it to her. 'I am sorry I startled you.'

'I…I was not expecting you to speak to me.' It came
out stiffly, but at least she managed not to demand why
he had made love to her, then ignored her for two days.

But however carefully she had spoken, she saw the
realisation dawn that he had hurt her and felt an overwhelming sense of relief. It had not been deliberate or,
rather, it had not been intended to cut her off, to signal
to her that Lord Easton no longer had any time for the
wanton Miss Williams.

And, being Guy, he went directly to the point. 'You
thought I was ignoring you. I am sorry, that was not
my intention. I thought perhaps you needed a little
time to reflect on what has passed between us before
we talked again.' There was the barest hesitation on
talked, but she felt the colour come up on her cheeks.
He wanted her again.

And I want him.

And standing on the very threshold of the church was not the place for respectable maiden ladies to be thinking carnal thoughts about any man, let alone earls who were entirely out of their reach.

'I hoped you would join me for a picnic at the Temple of the Moon tomorrow.' Guy stood there, hat in hand, and Cressida found she could not read his thoughts, or his intentions, at all. Was this an invitation to an *al fresco* meal or to lovemaking? Or was it a private meeting where he could explain to her what an awful mistake it all was and how it was best if they never saw each other again?

That *would* be the best thing, Cressida thought bleakly. She could stop hoping, stop dreaming, stop this endless mental twisting and turning to find a way to escape from the fact that she was the woman who had jilted him.

'Cressida?'

'Oh! I'm sorry. Yes, that would be delightful, thank you.'

'I will call for you at eleven,' Guy said. He put his tall hat back on his head, smiled and strode off down the path to where the rest of his party were waiting at the lychgate.

He looked so sure, so strong, so perfect, she thought, watching the broad shoulders vanish from sight. And tomorrow she must put a stop to this, whatever it was. End it definitely, cleanly. Then learn to live with the consequences.

Chapter Sixteen

The sun was shining again on Monday morning. Cressida, who had risen at dawn to water all the pots and urns in the garden, wondered if it would ever rain again. She washed the earth from her hands and set the watering can back beside the water butt, now almost empty, and watched Percy, belly flat on the grass, stalk across the lawn towards a small flock of sparrows.

'They can see you perfectly well,' she told him. 'A fat white blob oozing along.'

The only answer was an irritated twitch of his tail-tip. Cressida walked to the back door, the sparrows flew up into the rose bushes and Percy sat down and began to wash himself as though that had been his intention the entire time.

She had spent what remained of Sunday deep in thought, striving for some balance, some peace. Now, after a night where, strangely, she had slept soundly, she thought she had found resignation, at least.

For years she had known she was not going to marry and that the reasons for that were fixed, unchangeable. These weeks of knowing Guy again, of falling in love with him, were like a dream where the impossible becomes possible. Now she had woken up and nothing had changed: those reasons were what they had always been. Nor would she become Guy's mistress. She owed too much to her family, to her own future, to consider it.

Waking to that conclusion brought calm along with the sadness. How long that would last, how long it would take her to recover from Guy Thurlow, she had no idea. Perhaps she never would.

Guy drew the gig to a halt outside the little house on Church Hill, wishing he could have brought the curricle, a vehicle with far more dash—but one more than likely to overturn on the rough climb up to the temple. A suitor who had any hopes of success did not jeopardise them by overturning the lady in a nasty carriage accident just before proposing.

He had come prepared with a tethering weight to secure his horse while he went in, but Cressida had been waiting for him and the front door opened almost as soon as he reined in. He had been smiling to himself at a ludicrous mental picture of a dishevelled gentleman emerging from the wreckage of an overturned carriage and proposing to his lady love, her bonnet over one eye as she struggled out of the hedge. But the laughter died as he looked at her to be replaced by a still, very serious certainty.

She was not a great beauty, he knew that. But he did not want beautiful, he wanted Cressida, her lovely face full of intelligence, her graceful figure, her expressive eyes, her… All of her.

'You look delightful,' he said as he wound the reins around his whip and jumped down to hand her into the gig. 'The image of a summer's day.'

She did not turn the compliment with a false modest smile, a murmur of, 'Oh, this old thing', as young ladies were trained to do. Instead, she smiled, a little serious, and said, 'Thank you. I confess I spent some thought and effort on this gown and bonnet, although I fear that the copies of the *Lady's Monthly Museum* from which I drew my inspiration are at least three years out of fashion.'

'Loveliness is always in the mode,' Guy said, turning the gig to send it back up the hill.

He received no response and sent her a rapid sideways glance. Her profile was unreadable, but, it seemed, Cressida was not in the mood for flirtation and had probably not realised that his words had been far more serious than that. Was she as nervous as he was beginning to be himself? Had she guessed his intent, or did she think he was taking her on a picnic with the intention of making love to her again, perhaps going much further this time?

'The view from the Temple of the Moon is very good,' Cressida remarked after perhaps a minute. 'It gives a bird's eye view of a section of the park one cannot otherwise see very well. You can decide whether or not you want to add some new plantations.'

Plantations were the last thing in Guy's mind. As far as he was concerned, just at that moment, Cressida could tell him to add a pagoda, a herd of reindeer or a maze, provided he did not have to take his concentration away from making his declaration.

He had to divert some of it to getting the gig safely up the hill, but the horse was sensible and steady and they lurched upwards without mishap. Then the temple came in sight.

'Guy, it is clean! Oh, look how white it is. And the grass in front has been cut. The doors are open.'

She jumped down as he came to a halt and ran up the steps, stopped on the threshold. 'This is clean, too. And there are new cushions and the table is laid. But there has only been two days and Sunday since we were here. How have you worked a miracle?'

'Not I. Wait a moment while I unhitch the horse and tether him in the shade with some water,' he called, but she had already vanished inside.

When he joined her Cressida was exclaiming over the cool little pantry at the back with its shining marble slabs holding platters of food under muslin cloths. 'Perfect.'

'See the other room,' he suggested and she went to open the door with some caution on what had been the spider-infested privy. It was still a privy, but spotless under a fresh coat of whitewash. Bunches of lavender and fragrant herbs were hung about the walls, a shelf bore a basin and ewer with a mirror above, and what had been a rough wooden hole in a plank was now a discreetly lidded slab of polished mahogany.

'My goodness, there are houses less well equipped than this.'

'You like it? It is all down to Mrs Grainger and Arthur and their people.' Guy took her hand and led her back into the main room. She curled her fingers into his for a moment, then abruptly let go and retreated around the table. He felt the return of the reserve he had sensed on the drive.

'I think it is beautiful. Absolutely perfect.' Cressida sat down on one of the new cushions, her flower-sprigged skirts spreading like a meadow over the blue fabric. But she had chosen to sit on a bench, not on the dais where they had made love, he noticed. 'You are going to be able to enjoy this for years. I am certain it will become a favourite place.'

'It already is.' Guy had meant to say nothing until after they had eaten; now he found himself moving restless around the space, more unsure than he had ever been in his life of what he should say, how he should say it. What he should do.

Is this what love does to you?

'I see my family here,' he said abruptly. 'Children playing on that grassy slope when it has become a soft greensward, my wife sitting in the shade of that sweet chestnut tree watching them. When I stand here,' he said, his gaze fixed on the horizon, because he did not dare look at her, 'I see the future and I hope.'

Cressida was so silent so long that Guy was forced to turn. She was pale and her lips were tight, but when she caught his eye she said, 'Then you must find a bride who loves the country and who will love this place.'

Oh, hell. What have I said? She thinks I mean—

'I thought I had,' Guy said.

It did not flatter her, but seeing Cressida's jaw drop, seeing her trying to believe what her ears were hearing, warmed his heart. She closed her mouth with a snap, regained her poise, a little, but she understood his meaning.

'You will have to be…to be clearer,' she said, her gaze wide on his face. 'I cannot cope with riddles.'

'I love you.' He had never said it to any woman before, had never wanted to say it. He had expected it to be difficult, embarrassing to say in broad daylight, but it was easy. 'I love you and I want to marry you.'

Of all the things Guy expected—tears, joy, kisses, confusion—he had not expected Cressida to jump to her feet sending the cushion spinning to the floor, rejection in every line of her body.

'No. *No.* How could you be so cruel? You know I cannot. Why did you have to tell me you loved me? Why?'

Guy moved towards her, then stopped when she fended him off with raised hands.

'I told you because it is the truth and I want to marry you and I did not think you would consider it unless I loved you. So I had to tell you,' he added, confused that somehow she was not reacting as he had hoped.

'But I cannot marry you, you know that.' She sat down again without noticing it was on to cold, hard marble.

'I can deal with the man who fathered you. I can buy him off—once only. If that does not work, then I will deal with him some other way. If any word leaks out, then both my father and I will be talking loudly about how this criminal was attempting extortion—there is only danger if it seems we have something to hide. The Marquess, my esteemed Papa, is known to be utterly intolerant. He would never accept you if that accusation was the truth.'

'But it is,' she protested.

'I will tell him it is not and he will believe me because he thinks I am as high a stickler as he is.'

'You would lie to your father?'

'For you I would lie to the Archbishop of Canterbury.'

When Cressida only looked at him as though he was talking Russian he walked across, ignored her abrupt gesture of rejection and sat next to her.

'But why do you want to marry me?' she asked.

'Because I love you. And I think we would suit very well and because, when I stand there—' he jabbed a finger towards the doorway '—it is you I see sitting in the shade of that tree and it is children with your eyes I see playing on the grass.'

Cressida gave a little gulp as she buried her face in her hands.

Guy put his arms around her, pulled her close so her forehead rested against his shoulder. 'My love, must you fight me?'

She nodded, painfully, against his collarbone.

'Couldn't you love me?' Words he had thought his pride would never let him say, words that came easily now, desperately.

Cressida reared back against his embracing arm, her face pink and creased from the lapels of his coat. 'Of course I could. I do. I love you so much it hurts. Why did you make me love you, you wretched man?'

'You love me? But that is wonderful. A miracle.' All dignity, all prepared speeches abandoned him. Guy found himself on his knees in front of her, her hands in his. 'Cressida, my darling.'

'I cannot marry you,' she said again, but he saw the hope in her eyes, the way her lower lip trembled, just a little, felt her fingers tighten on his.

'Yes, you can. And you will,' and then she was in his arms again and her lips were on his and her heart pounded against his chest.

Guy stood with her in his arms and carried her to the dais where they had made love before and sat her down on the edge, on the plump, clean, soft cushions where he had every intention of making her entirely his, now and for always.

'This bonnet, however enchanting, has to go.' He tossed it aside and began to unbutton the short spencer she wore over the bodice of her gown. 'And this. And this.' Cressida watched him, silent, as he took off his coat, his neckcloth, sat to pull off his boots, tugged his shirt loose then pulled it over his head.

'What are you doing?' she managed to ask.

'Undressing us. Then I am going to make love to you, completely, and then we will eat our food and drink some wine and make plans for a wedding.' He cocked an eyebrow at her. 'Unless you object.'

'There is something I must tell you,' Cressida said. Terror, joy and something almost of resignation were flowing through her veins, fighting against the sensual pull that the touch of his hands, the sight of his naked torso evoked.

'You do not love me?' She shook her head. 'You

do not want to marry me.' Another shake. 'You are already married?'

'No. Certainly not.'

Guy gestured towards the piled cushions. 'You want to wait until after we are wed.' He sat back on his heels, his hand stilled on the waistband of his breeches. 'Of course. Forgive me.'

'No, not that,' she said, suddenly very sure about it. Perhaps some miracle would happen and they could marry, but if not, she wanted this, wanted the knowledge of all that Guy was.

'But?' he said.

'I have a secret that you must know before you marry me. It may change your mind about me. It probably will.'

She should tell Guy now, tell him that she was Viola FitzWalden and that she had been deceiving him from the moment they met. But then, if that changed everything, killed his feelings for her, then she would never know what it was like to be loved by him. No. She must not keep secrets from him. Cressida took a deep breath and summoned the courage to do the right thing and reveal her identity. 'Guy, I am—'

'Tell me later,' Guy said. 'Do not spoil this moment with tales of dark family secrets or pitiful dowries or whatever the problem is. Let me love you.'

And he touched her and kissed her, and they fell back on to the cushions and every scrap of willpower deserted her.

Her pretty gown seemed to melt away under Guy's hands and she only realised her stays had gone because, when she sighed with pleasure, she felt utterly free.

He knows what he is doing, she thought, her emotions a mix of amusement and jealousy for his past lovers, and then she was beyond rational thought as those knowing fingers caressed and teased and tormented.

The sensation of skin against skin from breast to legs had her eyes blinking open to discover they were both naked, right in the midst of the dais cushions now. Her body felt so sensitive that the merest touch of his hands had her aching, writhing, trying to get closer even though Guy had not touched her yet where she needed him the most. He was even avoiding her breasts, she realised in a rare moment of clarity.

I am too passive, she thought. *Too ignorant*, her weaker self thought. But she pushed against the shyness, the lack of confidence and the drugging caresses, and touched Guy's chest, pressing against the coarse chest hair. He seemed to like it, so, courage rising, she slid her hand over so his nipple was beneath her palm. It hardened, instantly. She touched the other with the same result, then scratched with her nails, very lightly, provoking a growl as his hands stilled on her body.

Fascinated, she followed the trail of hair down to his navel and he lay still, letting her explore. She did not dare look up into his face, or down at what she was doing, but the nerves twitching beneath her fingertips told their own story and the tension in the hard muscles betrayed the effort it was taking for him to control himself.

What possessed her to bend her head, touch her tongue tip into his navel she had no idea, but the purring growl became a gasp and he moved, twisting over her, his weight pinning her into the soft down beneath them as his mouth took hers again and his fingers, at last, found the wet, desperate heat between her thighs.

Before, he had taken her up into a spiral of pleasure until she lost herself; now the teasing fingers left that perfect spot alone and probed, stroked, slid within her while she gasped and struggled against him, the hard heat of his arousal pressed against her thigh.

Cressida clung to his shoulders, tried to ride the storm until one stroke of his thumb sent her tumbling over again. But this time, through the swirling fog of pleasure, she felt Guy's weight come over her, his legs nudge hers apart and then, with relentless care, he was inside her.

It was tight, it hurt, she came out of the clouds with a gasp of protest and those long fingers pressed between them, stroked and cajoled as Guy moved within her and suddenly it was all right…more than all right. It was almost perfect. If she could only find just the right rhythm, join him in that pounding, swooping dance for two.

She lifted her hips, caught the timing, wrapped her legs around the slim hips and rode the storm of pleasure, eyes wide open, her gaze locked with his as he stared into her soul.

'Now, Cressida.' It was wrung out of him as his eyes closed. 'Let go, come for me.'

She did not understand the words, but her body seemed to. The impossible tension peaked, snapped, the world went black and stars exploded against her eyelids. As she fell she felt him withdraw from her, heard his shout, felt the wet heat on her belly, then there was nothing.

Chapter Seventeen

Cressida woke to the sensation of cool breezes on her bare skin and of something heavier, slightly rough, caressing down over the curve of her hip, around to drift across her stomach.

She opened her eyes slowly to find Guy lying on his side next to her, propped up on one elbow, and he was letting the other hand drift over her body. The expression on his face was tender, possessive and, she realised, verging on smug.

Yes, he is very definitely a man, she thought, amused by both the smugness and the possessiveness.

After all, she felt very smug herself, from her earlobes to her toe-tips and everywhere in between.

'Are you well?' he asked as he had before and she nodded.

'Very well.' Now she came to think of it she was rather sore, somewhat sticky and the braid from one of the cushions was digging into her shoulder blade, but none of that mattered. Guy loved her and he had shown how very much he did.

In the back of her mind there was a small black cloud, slowly growing, but she pushed it away, conjuring up a wind to disperse it like smoke.

Not now. Tell him later. Much later.

Guy had stopped caressing her flank and had begun to remove what pins remained in her hair, running his fingers through it, fanning it out over the cushions.

'Lovely. So lovely.'

She had never thought it very special, but it was deep brown, with conker-russet highlights where it had caught the sun when she'd been gardening without a hat. And it waved and it was long and Guy appeared to find it satisfactory.

'One day we will make love with you on top—yes, it can be done, don't look at me like that—and your hair will fall down like a waterfall of silk all around us.'

Guy abandoned her hair, apparently satisfied with the effect he had achieved, and leant over to study her face, trailing one finger up her nose, which made her laugh, running the pad of his thumb around the arch of her eye sockets, ruffling her eyebrows.

'What is it?' she asked, instinctively putting up a finger to smooth them back into their disciplined curves.

His hand had stilled and he was looking down at her, a slight frown between his own brows. 'I do not know.' He sat up abruptly. 'Just some ghost of a memory, something from long ago, I think. I have no idea what.'

With a shake of his head as though to shed the impression he slid from the dais and walked across the circular space to stand in the doorway.

It was as though a Grecian statue had come to life, naked, but with warm flesh instead of cold marble. Cressida pushed up to sit so she could admire him better. The long horseman's legs, the tight buttocks, the triangle from broad shoulders to narrow hips, the dip of his spine between hard muscles.

Then he moved out on to the platform. 'Guy. You have no clothes on!'

'Neither have you,' he pointed out, turning so she, blushing, found herself staring at the even more impressive front view.

Hiding behind a cushion was tempting but undignified, and, now she was an experienced woman of the world, she should not be shy in front of her lover.

Rather unsteady, Cressida stood up and then almost sat down again when she saw the expression on Guy's face. If she'd had any doubts that the man loved her they would have vanished in that moment as he looked at her naked body with a tenderness, a longing that took her breath.

'You are so beautiful,' he said simply.

'I—' The denial was automatic.

'Oh, there are women who would be accounted far more beautiful than you,' Guy said, matter-of-factly. 'Your chin is perhaps a little too decided for fashion, your nose just a little too long and you have allowed your skin to be touched by the sun. You should wear your sun bonnet when you are working in the garden the fussy matrons would say.

'But everything balances, everything makes up... you. I could look into your eyes all day, all night, because I can read your thoughts there. I could watch you move, so graceful, whether you are behaving like a lady in town or scrambling like a hoyden over rough grass and through undergrowth. I could lie with you and delight in how exquisite you are in the throes of passion.'

He moved a little closer, studying her with the intensity of a scholar deciphering a difficult text. 'Whatever you do has such honesty about it. That is what I fell in love with first, I think. You are clear and open and always yourself, not what convention demands. Not the shrinking little spinster, but not the brash, defiant rebel either. You stood up to me about the park and its beauties and what it needed with simple courage and purpose when I must have been intimidating and dismissive. I trust you to be yourself with me, always.'

Cressida ran to him then, forgetting to be shy, forgetting everything except the love she felt for him, from him, and Guy held her close, his lips in her hair, the pair of them bathed in the sunlight striking through the pillars.

After a while he said, 'There is a pail of water standing in full sun to take the chill off it. I will carry it through so you can wash. There are robes on that chair, so there is no need to dress yet.'

Half an hour later, when both of them were clean and dressed in the splendour of the silk robes that made them, Guy said, look like characters from a sultan's court, they took food outside and ate it sitting on rugs and heaped pillows under the shade of the sweet chestnut tree.

They spoke little and then of matters that were

not personal. It seemed that there was no need for love words while Guy's fingers played with the loose strands of Cressida's hair, or while she pulled fat white grapes from their stalks, shook the cooling water from them and fed them to him, one by one.

'Do you think that Mr Graham is falling in love with Miss Hobhouse?' Cressida asked while they were slowly packing away the empty plates and platters, the wine glasses, into the baskets they had been carried in.

'I suspect he may be,' Guy said. He held up a wine bottle to the light, then shook the dregs on to the grass. 'But would a woman be attracted to a man with one arm missing and no home of his own?'

'I do not see what his arm has to do with it,' Cressida said robustly. 'I would love you however many limbs you had lost.' She caught at his left hand and kissed the damaged finger. 'Mr Graham is an honest, hard-working gentleman. I think he is kind and more intelligent than his modesty sometimes allows. Do you pay him enough to support a wife?'

Guy sat down again beside her, drew up his knees and rested his elbows on them, gazing out over the park below them. 'He deserves more, I believe. I thought at first he would not settle, but he has and we have found a way of working together that allows for a very free exchange of opinions.' He grinned at her. 'If I had wanted someone who would agree with everything I said, I made the wrong choice. But there is the old steward's house in the grounds and if that was renovated it would make a very respectable home for a married man. I will increase his salary, offer him the house, then he will feel that is all secure if he does wish to offer for Miss Hobhouse.'

'I am so pleased.' Cressida lay back on the rug and closed her eyes against the sunlight slanting through the leaves. 'I want everyone to be as happy as I am.'

'As we are,' Guy corrected. 'Although I believe that may be impossible.' His eyes had that heavy-lidded, thoughtful look that made her feel hot inside. 'You look deliciously wanton, lying there in that robe.'

She smiled against his lips as his mouth found hers, then gave herself up to discovering the joys of love-making in the open air. There was a fleeting moment when she wondered about passing woodsmen, but it was soon gone, lost in the pleasures Guy was show-ing her.

The sun was sinking low when they finally roused themselves to dress. The opportunities presented by that activity almost delayed them another hour, while Guy demonstrated his expertise at lacing stays up, un-lacing them again...

'Tomorrow,' he said as they arrived back at Church Hill. 'Tomorrow we will discuss practical matters, my love. Not today. Today was a day out of time, a day away from the real world. Dream of me tonight, Cres-sida.'

'I will,' she said, sitting demurely beside him in the gig, parasol held by neatly gloved hand at just the right angle, bonnet firmly tied. No one looking at her would think she had spent a day of pure, joyous hedonism. Of sin, no doubt most would say. But love was no sin, of that she was convinced.

Guy helped her down in front of the house. 'Come to luncheon tomorrow,' he said. 'Bring Miss Pomfret. I will show you all of the house that will be your home.'

'You are going to tell people about us?'

'Not until we are ready. This will seem just an ordinary visit between neighbours, never fear. Good day to you, Miss Williams,' he added, holding out his hand as the door opened to reveal Jane on the threshold.

'Good day, Lord Easton.' Cressida shook hands politely, smiled and went inside as though nothing of the slightest importance had happened.

It was not until after supper that the glow of the day wore off. Marjorie was dozing—resting her eyes, as she would say—over her embroidery and Cressida left her to wander through her garden, enjoying the perfume of the night-scented stocks and the ghostly white tobacco plants.

Perhaps it was the effect of a rather stodgy pie or simply that the effect of Guy's lovemaking had finally worn off, but Cressida was conscious of a nagging anxiety at the back of her mind that grew until she could no longer ignore it.

She had been going to tell Guy the truth about who she was. She had tried to, but he had brushed it aside to speak of later and then, lost in a haze of love and sensuality, she had simply forgotten. Forgotten that it mattered that she was the Viola FitzWalden who had jilted him in Stowe Easton church five years ago.

I must tell him the very first thing tomorrow morning. I cannot wait and have that conversation with

*other people there. Immediately after breakfast I will
walk over to the Court.*

'*Whatever you do has such honesty about it,*' Guy
had said. That was important to him. It was to her,
too—truth and honesty and trust. She had been a pris-
oner of her secrets for five long years and it was time
to be free.

Herring came in and cleared his throat meaning-
fully. Guy, who was eating a leisurely, late and very
substantial breakfast, looked up and raised one eyebrow.

'Is something amiss, Herring?' It was very difficult to believe that anything was, just at the moment.

'A William Brent has just arrived, My Lord. He
is somewhat travel-stained and he is asking to speak
with you. I have left him waiting in the hall as I was
not aware he was expected.'

'Put him in my study and see if he needs breakfast,
Herring. He will have come some distance.'

The cold sensation in the pit of his stomach was
making itself felt again. The truth about Viola Fitz-
Walden was about to be revealed and, perhaps, Cressida's secret, too. Guy found that he was not at all
certain he wanted to know either tale now.

Viola's story it was his duty to discover, he told himself. He had to be certain she was well and he should
have done that five years ago. But Cressida... No, he
would tell Brent that he should keep that to himself.
Cressida would tell him in her own good time, he had
absolute faith in that. It was none of his business, in
fact, except that, if there was any avenging or protect-

ing to be done for the woman he loved, then he needed the facts to do it.

His coffee was cold, but Guy made himself finish it. He exchanged a sentence or two with Arthur about his steward's plans for the morning and twitted Penny on the new style she was trying for her hair.

Miss Hobhouse sat quietly at her end of the table, slowly turning the pages of yesterday's newspaper and occasionally glancing towards Arthur, whose slightly pink ears betrayed the fact he was well aware of it. Yes, that was a budding romance and he should see what he could do to ease Arthur's path. If anyone had told him the week before that he would be acting Cupid for his own steward, he would have laughed in their face.

Brent was making good inroads into a plate of ham and eggs, but got to his feet as Guy walked in.

'Finish your breakfast,' he said. 'You look as though you have had a long journey of it.'

'Thank you, My Lord. I'll confess, the mail coach is not the best place for a comfortable night's sleep. At least I managed a wash and a shave at the inn in Stowe Easton. They hired me a horse so I did not have to walk here and present myself in even more of a state of disorder.'

He pushed the plate away empty, wiped his mouth and took the chair so he could sit the other side of the desk from Guy. 'I did not feel I should commit my findings to the post, My Lord.'

'Very well. Tell me. At the moment I do not wish to hear any of the information about Miss Williams.'

It seemed to him that the agent winced as he shifted in his seat, but the man was doubtless sore and cramped after an uncomfortable journey. 'As I reported, My Lord, Miss FitzWalden lived with her great-uncle in Devon until July eighteen hundred and thirteen.'

'A year ago.'

'As you say. I located the livery stables from which she hired a chaise to convey her to her new home after her great-uncle died—' He broke off, stared down at his notes.

'Which was where?'

'Stowe Easton, My Lord.'

'What?'

'My Lord, despite what you said just now, I fear it is impossible to report on one young lady without the other. Do you recall the full name of Miss FitzWalden? No? It is Viola Louise Cressida FitzWalden. Her maternal grandmother's maiden name was Williams. Her cousin, a Miss Pomfret, not only attended the funeral of Mr Rufus FitzWalden in Devon, but was also a guest at the wedding ceremony in Stowe Easton which was so regrettably cut short.

'Miss Pomfret moved to the town having seen it at that time when she apparently took a liking to it. A Miss Cressida Williams joined her in July last year at the same time that I lost all trace of Miss FitzWalden. Although I understand that her brother the Viscount shows no sign of concern about her and, according to servants' gossip, continues in correspondence with her, his staff never see the address to which he writes.' Brent folded his hands over his notebook and gazed out of the window over Guy's left shoulder.

'You are telling me that Cressida Williams is Viola FitzWalden?'

'In my opinion it is beyond any doubt that they are one and the same lady, My Lord.'

It was a blow in the gut, one that left him unable to find any appropriate emotion beyond blank shock. Guy swallowed and managed an amused drawl. 'Most interesting, Brent. I congratulate you on tying the loose ends together in so concise a manner.'

'Thank you, My Lord.'

'That will be all for now. If you find Herring, my butler, he will provide you with a room for tonight, have a bath drawn for you and so forth. Perhaps you would be so good as to present your reckoning to my steward, Mr Graham. I would be obliged if you would hand me all your notes before you leave this house.'

'Certainly, My Lord. I will have them ordered and enclosed in a sealed package. Thank you, My Lord.' Brent bowed and left.

Guy sat staring at his own hands clenched on the blotter, still trying to understand what he was feeling.

Cressida was Viola FitzWalden. She had known him from the moment she saw him and she had not betrayed by as much as a whisper who she was. Or perhaps she had. He recalled her agitation in the church when they had first met. That had not been discomfort at finding herself alone with a strange man, that had been alarm at finding herself on the altar steps again with the man she had jilted standing almost within arm's reach.

Anger. That was it, that was what was churning in his stomach, clouding his vision. He had trusted her, had fallen in love with her, damn it. And all the time she had been…deceiving him. Lying to him by omission, if not by actual words. Laughing at his obtuseness?

As he strode out of the house, round to the stables, his mind was churning with questions. How had that shy little debutante, scarcely out of the schoolroom, changed her life so totally? And how had she become the woman that Cressida—he could not think of her as Viola—was now?

Guy raked his memory for images of the girl he had almost married. Shorter than Cressida, surely? Certainly plumper and dressed in the kind of unflattering fussy pastel gowns that matrons thought suitable for debutantes. Very much shyer. She had hardly ever met his eyes, taking refuge beneath thick brows and frazzled curls. But if she had grown to her full height, tamed those brows, lost the curling tongs, allowed her own good taste to guide her choice of wardrobe then, yes, he could believe that Viola and Cressida were the same woman.

But why the hell hadn't she told him, trusted him? Did she think he would turn on her, expose her publicly, ruin her new life? And what was he going to do when he came face to face with her now? Guy realised he had no idea.

He had a saddle on Blackjack and was leading the horse out before Bates came running.

'My Lord? Do you need me?'

Blackjack snorted and backed, made uneasy by his rider's dark mood.

'Do you think I am incapable of saddling a horse by myself?' Guy snarled as he swung into the saddle

and sent the big black out of the stable yard at a canter, making the groom leap backwards.

Guy put the gelding at the gate into the park. It
soared over with a foot to spare and the canter became
a gallop the moment they landed. The gelding was an
intelligent animal and, given his head, avoided rabbit
holes, took fences in his stride and refused to be startled by deer bursting out of thickets in panic. He gave
Guy very little to do except set a direction and allow
his imagination to run riot.

He was thinking so hard about Cressida that her
appearance on the far side of the little stream where
he had first seen her felt almost like a mirage. But
she was real enough, he saw as she stopped. She had
been running and she was panting, her colour high as
she watched Blackjack take the stream in his stride.
Guy reined in hard and the gelding skidded to a halt
to stand, tossing his head and fidgeting.

'Still,' Guy snapped as he threw his leg over the
pommel and dropped to the ground. He stalked towards Cressida, took her by the shoulders and, somehow, managed not to give her a hard shake. 'Well?
What have you got to say for yourself, Miss Fitz-
Walden?'

Chapter Eighteen

'You know who I am?'

'How long did you think you could carry on lying to me?' Guy demanded. She had never seen him like this, so tight with anger that his face seemed sculpted, his hands hard and unforgiving on her shoulders.

'I tried to tell you yesterday, when you told me you loved me,' she stammered. 'I was determined to. Then you said there were more important things to do... and I forgot.'

'You forgot,' he said flatly. 'You forgot that you have been deceiving me for weeks. Forgot that I might be interested to know that I almost married you five years ago.'

She tried to tell herself that was not hate she saw in his face, but it was hard not to. Hard not to blame him if it was, she thought bleakly.

'You forgot to tell me that I had just proposed marriage to the woman who had already jilted me? Left me on the altar steps and made a fool of me?'

'I meant to tell you, but I was swept away when

we made love and it was magical. Guy, it was another world, wasn't it? You felt it, too, I know you did. I did not come back to reality until that evening and then I knew I must come at once today to tell you. I am here now.'

'It is rather late, don't you think?' But his grip on her shoulders eased. 'Did it amuse you to deceive me? The Honourable Miss Viola FitzWalden playing at being Miss Cressida Williams, modest spinster of this parish with an eye for landscape gardening.'

'It was hellish,' Cressida threw back at him, suddenly finding the blessed release of anger. 'Hellish. Do you think that I *wanted* to exile myself from my family, ruin myself, embarrass you on my wedding day? When I saw you again in the church that day I almost fainted. I thought… I do not know what I thought, except that at first I was afraid. Afraid that you would recognise me, expose me for who I really was and make it impossible for me to continue living in Stowe Easton.

'But then I realised that you did not recognise me and I hoped you would never discover who I was, that no harm would be done.'

'You saw no harm in working closely with me. No harm in being my friend. No harm as I was falling in love with you.'

'As I was falling for you,' she said miserably and twisted out of his slackened grasp, walked away to the edge of the lake. 'I knew I had to tell you eventually.'

The soft grass absorbed the sound of his footfall, but she would have known Guy was near her if she was blindfolded, deafened. He stopped so close she could feel the heat of his body, hear the ragged breathing that he was making no attempt to control.

'Tell me the truth about what happened,' he said. 'Why did you jilt me? A simple *No* when I proposed to you would have been more than adequate to end it all with no bones broken.'

'*You* did not *propose* to me,' she said, the anger flickering into life again as she turned to face him. 'You and your father made a match with my brother and it was agreed between the three of you. I was informed that I was marrying you… No, that is incorrect. I was told I was marrying the Earl of Easton, the heir to the Marquess of Thornborough, that it was a brilliant match and that I should be very grateful.'

'And you were not grateful,' Guy said, his voice flat. 'I thought you merely shy.'

'I was presented to a man who was fresh from the battlefield with a bandage still on his hand. He was all scarlet uniform and swagger, a man who did not appear to be interested in me in the slightest, only in my bloodlines, my family's connections, the fact that I was healthy breeding stock.'

Guy made a gesture of denial, then grimaced and shook his head.

'You see? You cannot deny it. Why should you have been interested? I was hardly away from my governess. I was shy and gauche with no experience whatsoever and no conversation. I still had to grow into myself and my eyebrows were a disaster that my aunts would not allow me to pluck because that was something married women did. They insisted on trussing me up in hideous gowns that were all frills and fuss which made me look hideous. I had a mirror—I knew perfectly well you were not attracted to my looks and, as you hardly said a word to me, you were most certainly not interested in me as a person.'

'I am so sorry,' Guy said. The anger had drained from his face, leaving him pale and, somehow, empty. 'I was resenting it, too, although that is no excuse for the way I treated you. I had no expectation of falling in love with my bride, you see. I thought it was my duty to marry as my father advised. And everyone was telling me how delighted you would be, how honoured, how relieved to have made such a good match. I had every intention of treating you well, of being kind to you. I thought we would get to know each other after we were married. I was very full of good resolutions,' he said with a snort of bitter amusement, presumably at his own youthful folly.

'Yes?' Cressida said bitterly. She walked away from him and sat down on a fallen log close to the lake edge. After a moment she shifted along to make room for him, too, although she did not feel the slightest inclination to lose her anger. It was all that was keeping her from tears. Or worse, pleading with Guy to forgive her, to keep loving her.

'How were you going to do that?' she asked when he sat down at what she guessed he thought a safe distance. 'I assume you would have *got to know me* by attempting to get me with child before you went off to war again. Then you would leave me to try to discover for myself how to be a countess, how to deal with your frankly terrifying father and a household of servants, how to go on in society. Meanwhile you would return to your old life and your mistresses and never give me a thought.'

'I had every intention of forswearing other women once I was married,' Guy said stiffly. 'I am sorry you were frightened of me. I confess, I had very little experience of women.'

Cressida snorted.

'Of respectable young ladies,' he retorted. 'For all I knew then, you'd have been delighted to be a married woman in London with considerable freedom and a large dress allowance.'

She swallowed down a number of possible retorts to that. 'I was not *scared* of you. I just didn't like you. But I was quite resigned to marrying you.' From the silence beside her she thought that had not been the most tactful way of putting it. 'I had been brought up to assume I would make that kind of marriage, although not such a good one.'

'Then what changed your mind?' Guy asked after they had sat side by side staring at the swans in silence for what seemed to her like at least ten minutes. 'Why did you run at the very last minute?'

'I fully intended to marry you, but the man who told me he was my father came to me just before the carriage set out for the church. He told me that he and my mother had been… That my father was not…capable and so she'd turned to him. He was very smug about it. He never threatened me in so many words, but it was clear that he would expect you to pay him to keep silent—and pay him enough for him to live very well indeed.'

'It did not occur to you that my family was quite powerful enough to deal with threats like that?'

'No, it did not. I didn't know what to do. I was *seventeen*, Guy. All I knew was that I could not marry you, not when I was not who you thought I was, not when I would be laying you open to scandal and threats of extortion. I was desperate, the carriage was at the door, I was expected in church in ten minutes' time. I thought I would have to faint, perhaps, cause a delay, but that would still solve nothing. Then I remembered that the priest asks if anyone has cause why the marriage cannot take place. I could stop it all then. So I did.'

There was silence except for the sound of Guy's breathing, the sharp alarm call of a coot in the rushes, the distant splashing of the weir.

'I was sorry, because it must have been very embarrassing for you,' she said, ploughing painfully on when he did not speak. 'But I thought that was better than finding you had married someone who wasn't the person she thought she was and whose father would try to extract large sums of money from you for years.'

When he was still silent, she added, 'And you were so eligible, I didn't think you would have any difficulty finding someone else to marry.'

Cressida had the strong impression that Guy was counting to at least ten in his head and braced herself for what was coming.

'You ran away to your great-uncle in Devon. How the devil did you get there?'

'John, our coachman, didn't know what to do, but I told him I had to get back to the house, that it was an emergency. I think he assumed I was ill,' she explained.

'When I got there I ran in and called one of the maids—it was a rented house, just for the occasion, you see. And my things were all packed for after the wedding. So I snatched up my dressing case with my jewellery, and some money I had been given, and the valise with my things for that night and ran out of the back of the house. I was only just in time, because my brother, Cedric, and Dorinda, his wife, arrived at the front door.

'I ran to the inn and hired a chaise to Cheltenham. Once I got there I paid it off and went to another inn and hired a chaise to go to Great-Uncle Rufus. One of the maids at the inn agreed to come with me.'

'And your great-uncle took you in with no questions asked?' Guy sounded incredulous.

'He was somewhat eccentric and he was my godfather as well, so he felt responsible for me. I told him I could not bear to marry you—I am sorry, Guy—and that Cedric was trying to force me, so he said I could stay. He was becoming frail and I think he was lonely because my great-aunt had died two years before.'

'And what did your brother have to say about this?' To her relief Guy sounded less angry, more curious now.

'I think Dorinda, my sister-in-law, had been telling him that I was ruined and a disgrace and that they should pretend they knew nothing about me. She is rather…demanding. And so Cedric sent me an allowance every quarter and I settled down at Kentiscombe.'

'Where you grew into a beauty in rural seclusion,' Guy said sardonically.

Her cheeks heated, but she managed to keep her voice steady. 'I could walk and ride wherever I wanted. The food was wonderful and the air clean and I grew taller and…grew up, I suppose. There was a Mrs Thornton in the village, the widow of the local squire, and she took me under her wing. She showed me how to pluck my dreadful eyebrows, found me a dressmaker, taught me how to go on in local society. Then she took me to assemblies at the local market town.'

'It was those eyebrows that were what I kept remembering, when your elegant arches became ruffled,' Guy said. 'That and your scent. I kept getting flashes of recollection, but not enough to make me think, *Viola FitzWalden.*'

'Do you understand why I did it?' Cressida asked, twisting around to face him at last. 'Can you understand why I kept my identity a secret when we met again and I realised that you did not know who I was?' She swallowed hard. 'Can you forgive me?'

'For running away at the church?' Guy looked down at his clasped hands, then back up at her. 'Yes. I forgave you almost at once. I thought that if the thought of marrying me was so dreadful that you had no option but to ruin yourself, then it was hardly up to me to bear a grudge.'

His smile was rueful. 'I can't say I liked it, but it probably did me a lot of good to discover that I could not have what I wanted for the snap of my fingers. Of course, the sensible thing for you to have done would have been to tell your brother you were feeling unwell.

We could have delayed the ceremony while you told me about that man and I would have dealt with it, but you were very young, completely inexperienced and you had no reason to trust me. I understand that now.'

'And this time? For not telling you when we met again?'

'I confess I am finding that harder to understand,' Guy said slowly. When he met her gaze his own was dark, troubled. 'I want to say that it does not matter, that we can put it behind us, but I find I need to know why you could not tell me.'

'I thought you would tell people who I was, that it would be impossible for me to carry on living here in Stowe Easton. I thought the safe, happy world I had built for myself would be entirely in ruins.'

'So you were still frightened of me?'

'Of your reaction, not of you. I told you—I was never frightened of you.' She put out a hand to touch his, then snatched it back, uncertain how Guy would react. 'I had jilted you at the altar in front of a packed church full of members of the *haut ton*. You are a proud man now and you were then, too. I can imagine how you felt. And you had done nothing to deserve it, it was all my fault. You told me you were coming here to live. Can't you see how impossible it was?'

'And yet every time we met we became closer and closer.'

'And *still* you did not recognise me. I thought perhaps we could be neighbours. Friends, even, and you would never need to know.'

'That you were, in fact, lying to me?' Guy stood up

and took a step closer to the water's edge. 'I told you how much trusting you meant to me.'

'When we were in love!' Cressida found she was on her feet, too. 'Why should I have trusted you with my secrets—with my whole life and happiness— before then? You are unreasonable, Guy.'

They stared at each other, the few feet between them suddenly a chasm. Then his words as he dis- mounted came back to her and, now that she was no longer preoccupied with her confession, she realised their meaning.

'How did you know who I was?' she demanded. 'After all these weeks, after what has passed between us, you suddenly remember me? It wasn't just a suspi- cion, was it? You were galloping to confront me, cer- tain of who I was.'

'While I have been living here I came to realise that I had been negligent in not finding out what had hap- pened to Viola—to you. I should have done so imme- diately. And, as I was setting my confidential agent to work on that I asked him to—' He broke off. 'You had told me you would never marry, that there was a secret preventing you. I wanted to discover what was wrong because I thought perhaps I could help you.'

For a stunned moment she stared at him. 'You… You pried into my life, into my secrets. You set some- one to investigate me behind my back—and yet you are hurt because *I* failed to trust *you*? If I had wanted to tell you, I would have done. The clue,' she said bit- terly, 'is in the word. *Secret.* But you had the arrogance to assume you knew better than I did, that you could solve my problems whether I wanted you to or not. You set a complete stranger to spy on me. When were you going to tell me what you had done?'

Guy was white around the mouth. 'When I discovered what the problem was.'

'I see. So your spy has told you all about that, has he?'

'He discovered, early on, that he was investigating one woman, not two. He assured me that Viola Fitz-Walden was safe and living in Stowe Easton under the name of Cressida Williams. That is the only secret of yours that he has discovered.'

'Really?' she said in disbelief.

'Upon my word of honour. And he will look no further. He has given me all his notes, his researches. He is a man of integrity the family has known and used for years.'

'Well, I am glad to hear that there is *someone* in all of this whom I may trust,' she flashed at him and turned in a swirl of skirts to stalk off up the meadow.

'Cressida? Where are you going?'

'Somewhere private, somewhere you and your… your *minions* cannot intrude. I am going home to Church Hill where, I can assure you, My Lord, I will not be at home to you.'

'Don't be ridiculous.' He overtook her easily, stood in front, barring her way.

'Ridiculous?'

'I apologise, that was not the right word. Impetuous, I should have said. I love you, Cressida. You love me. We cannot simply give that up at the first hurdle.'

'Trusting the person you love seems fundamental to me,' she said slowly. 'You are finding it hard to forgive me and I am finding it difficult to accept that you have acted out of concern and not arrogance. Both those things require trust and without it we will fail at every obstacle that life throws at us together. I want to pretend this never happened, but it feels as though something has broken.' She found she was pushing the heel of her hand into her breastbone where the deep ache was growing.

'Oh, Cressida.' Guy reached for her, would have pulled her into his embrace, but she held him away, her outstretched arms stiff.

'No. No, if you kiss me then I will give in and we will never settle this, not as it should be settled. I need time to think and you do, too. When did you discover who I am?'

'Less than an hour ago,' he admitted.

'We have had shocks, unpleasant shocks, both of us. This, what is between us, is too important to make mistakes over. Isn't it?' she appealed to him.

'Yes.' Her heart lifted at the instant response. 'How much time do you need, Cressida?'

'A week,' she said, suddenly decisive. 'A week when we do not meet, do not write. A week apart to think and to feel and to be certain.'

'A week's separation is a hard sentence,' Guy said. 'But you are right to impose it. I will leave you now and meet you... Where, in a week?'

'The Temple of the Moon, at this time,' she said. 'We can be sure of being alone there.'

'Very well. But send for me if you need me, Cressida,' Guy said and lifted his hand to brush the back of his fingers fleetingly across her cheek. 'Or should I call you Viola now?'

'Cressida,' she said, certain of that at least. 'She is who I am now.'

She walked away from him, the touch of his fingers still warm on her face. *I will not look back, I will not.* But, halfway up the slope she stopped and turned to find him standing beside the big gelding, watching her.

Guy raised his hand.

If he beckons to me...if he starts to walk towards me...

But he did neither and after a moment she turned again and walked steadily on to the crest of the hill, on until she knew the break of slope hid her from him. Then she sank down under the nearest tree and tried to breathe.

Chapter Nineteen

Guy stood and watched Cressida go. She stopped and his heart missed a beat. She turned and looked at him.

If she raises her hand...if she speaks...

But Cressida did neither. She turned away from him, her face blurred by distance, and walked steadily on until she vanished from his sight over the crest of the hill.

Cressida... Viola. Have I lost you?

Guy mounted and turned Blackjack's head for home, keeping the horse to a walk. Not that he needed time to think; he had that. An entire week. One hundred and sixty-eight hours. Over ten thousand minutes.

Blackjack tossed his head, gave his piercing whinny, and Guy saw another rider coming towards him. Even if Arthur's one-handed riding style was not instantly recognisable, his ugly roan horse was. Guy composed his face into pleasant neutrality and reined in.

'I was just off to see how they are getting on with the repairs to the dam,' Arthur said. 'Unless you have just come from there?'

'No. Arthur, consider your salary increased by half again as of now. And the old steward's house—have that put into order and then you can move into it.'

'Guy? My Lord, I… What have I done to deserve that?'

'I was underpaying you from the start and I have no desire to share a house with a pair of newlyweds. I presume you will now ask Miss Hobhouse to marry you?'

'What? You mean…'

'Arthur, stop dithering and go and ask the woman. Unless your excellent imitation of a mooncalf over the past week is due to some other cause?'

'Yes. I mean, no. Good lord. Yes, I will.' He turned his horse as he spoke and sent it thundering off at a flat gallop.

'Let us hope that somebody has better luck with their courtship than I do, Blackjack. Come on, I suppose I had better investigate what the labourers at the dam are doing.'

Guy returned to the Court at one o'clock having discovered more about the construction of dams than he ever wanted to know and more than a little muddy.

'Luncheon has just been served, My Lord. I will send Bates to your bedchamber immediately.' Herring gestured to the footman to take Guy's hat, whip and gloves and managed not to shudder at the trail of footprints on the marble floor.

'I had best get these off here, Herring.' Guy sat on one of the shield-backed hall chairs and extended a foot to the footman.

He was climbing the stairs in stockinged feet when

Penelope appeared at the top. 'You darling, darling man!' She ran down and hurled herself into his arms. 'Your wonderful father has written to Papa and told him that Nicholas is a perfect match with an ancestry to make a duke jealous and a perfectly adequate income to support me and, as head of the family, he expects no barriers to be put in our way.'

'If you do not untangle your arms from around my neck this moment the question of your marriage will be moot because we will both be at the bottom of the stairs in a broken heap,' Guy observed mildly. 'But I am glad for you, brat.'

Penny released him and sat down on the stairs, beaming up at him. 'And you'll never guess what else has happened.'

'Miss Hobhouse is to marry Mr Graham,' Guy said.

'You knew!'

'I have eyes in my head, Cuz. I will see you, and presumably the doting couple, at luncheon.'

It seemed his career as Cupid was a success. A pity he could not work the same magic for himself.

'Stowe Easton is a very pleasant little town,' Miss Thurlow announced two days later as she and Cressida emerged from the Ladies' Quilting and Embroidery Circle meeting. Neither of them had any fine work of their own to bring along—Cressida because she frankly acknowledged an inability to thread a needle, let alone sew a seam, and Penny because she had forgotten to bring her sewing basket on her flight from home. They had, however, enjoyed the gossip and had made themselves useful by cutting out patchwork pieces and tacking them to the paper patterns for Marjorie.

'Yes,' Cressida agreed. She was working hard to appear cheerful and it seemed to be successful. Guy must be doing so too, because Penelope had said nothing about him being out of temper or cast down, which was discouraging.

'But the shops are not very interesting, are they? Once one has looked at the village shop and its ribbons and stockings, that is,' Penelope went on.

'Wellingbourn is our nearest town with a range of interesting shops,' Cressida said. 'That is the place to go if you want to browse the milliners and haberdashers.'

'Then we can go now? I have the gig and a groom to drive us and I am quite stuffed with all the coffee and cake Mrs Trimingham gave us, so I do not need luncheon. Do you?'

As the answer to that was clearly expected to be, *No*, Cressida shook her head. It would be pleasant to window-shop. In fact, she might even buy a dress length if she saw something she really liked. Mrs Grainger and her maids had worked miracles on the sprig muslin, but it was never going to be the dress it once had been and, somehow, she did not think she was ever going to wear it again. Either it would be put away as a treasured memory of a wonderful day or burned, for the same reason.

'Should we ask if Miss Hobhouse would like to join us?'

Penny's companion had pleaded a lack of interest in sewing and was still at the Court.

'She is helping Mr Graham to copy those old plans on to large sheets of canvas,' Penny said. 'Or that is her excuse.'

'Ah.'

'It is lovely, but rather wearing, the way they just sit and gaze at each other. But he does appear to be a worthy man,' Penny said dubiously.

'I believe you are right. We will not disturb them then,' Cressida said. 'Ask Bates to drive to my house first. Then I can take some money with me. We do not have accounts at the Wellingbourn shops.'

A private parlour in the Rose and Crown on Wellingbourn's main street was the perfect place to rest weary feet after a thorough exploration of the shops. The filling effect of Mrs Trimingham's cakes had worn off, so Penny insisted on ordering an array of little sweetmeats to accompany their tea.

After the first cup they both sat back and viewed with satisfaction the pile of brown paper parcels and the hat box containing Penny's new bonnet. 'That is a very smart hat,' she said smugly. 'And your dress length is exceedingly pretty. I wish I could wear that shade of aquamarine, but I looked washed-out in it. But with your brown hair and blue eyes it is perfect.'

'Have you heard anything from your parents?' Cressida asked.

'A letter from Mama. They are very disappointed in me, from which I guess that Uncle Henry—the Marquess, you know—gave them a rare trimming about rejecting a perfectly suitable suitor. They had hoped that my foolish impetuosity was a thing of the past, she says. And she was disturbed that Uncle Henry felt it necessary to investigate Nicholas's circumstances.'

'Why? Wouldn't they hope he would discover something to his discredit?'

'She knew, in her heart of hearts, that there is nothing to find and now knows that she and Papa are shown up as scheming and prejudiced. But they are resigned to the match, she says, and can only hope that their worst fears for my future will not be realised.'

'They must have been deeply worried by the incident you started to tell me about when we first met,' Cressida probed gently. 'I mean, if they were so desperate to stop you making a mistake again...'

'It wasn't that I was mistaken in a lover,' Penny said before sinking pretty white teeth into a scone. 'It wasn't a romance at all—I thought he was just a friend. I mean, honestly, Cressida, Charles was old enough to be my father.'

Cressida felt an unpleasant sensation in her stomach and told herself that it was too much cake. Charles was a very common name. 'Go on.'

'He used to flirt, just a little—nothing over the line, of course—and that was flattering because he was very much in the mode and handsome. He would drive me in the park in his curricle, which Mama liked because she thought it showed me off to eligible gentlemen. And he listened when I complained about Mama and Papa and their ambitions to marry me off well, how Papa kept reminding me what a good dowry I had and how I only needed to catch the eye of an earl to make a really excellent match.'

'You told this Charles about the dowry?'

Penny wrinkled her nose. 'Yes. So silly of me, I see that now. But I was only seventeen. Anyway, he called one morning and asked me to drive in Hyde Park. It was quite early, but he said it was going to rain later, so I went. And he drove right into a grove of trees and there was a chaise waiting and he wanted me to get into it. I saw luggage strapped on behind and guessed what he was about, all of a sudden. It was such a shock.'

'A mercy that you did realise,' Cressida said. 'Many innocent seventeen-year-olds would not have done so until it was too late.'

'I wouldn't get down from the curricle,' Penny said. 'I hung on to the rail next to the seat and I kicked out at him. And then I took the whip out of its holder and started hitting him and screaming, but he caught hold of my wrists so hard that the pain almost made me faint. I dropped the whip and he had almost dragged me down when Guy rode up. He'd called on Mama and Papa and they told him I was in Hyde Park, so he came to meet me and heard the screams.

'He was *wonderful*. He hit Charles in the chin and knocked him down and then he hauled him up again and hit him some more, even though he had a wounded hand—Guy, I mean. And then he lifted me down and saw my wrists which had blood on them and asked if I wanted to hit Charles, too, so I did, which felt…helpful. And Guy said he was going to call Charles out and put a bullet in him, but he turned away for a moment to make sure I was all right and Charles managed to get into the chaise and drive away, so he couldn't, because he didn't want to just leave me there.'

'But what was Guy doing in London? I thought he was in the Peninsula. This was five or six years ago, surely?'

'He was home on leave recovering from that wound on his arm when he lost part of his finger. He said it wasn't so very bad, but he hadn't had leave for ages and his father wanted him to get married, so he came back to England. He almost got married a month or so later, but the girl ran away, which was horrible for him. Can you imagine anyone running away from Guy?'

'I thought you did not want to marry him,' Cressida said as the knot in her stomach turned into something like a lump of ice.

'I don't, but that's because he is like a brother to me. I can't think why any other woman wouldn't want to.' She studied the half-empty plate. 'Do you think I will be sick if I have the last scone?'

'Yes, I do. What is the surname of this Charles of yours?'

'Not mine. Never mine,' Penny said with a shudder. 'It is Charles FitzWalden and the awful thing was, he was the uncle of the girl Guy was going to marry.'

'Excuse me.' Cressida got unsteadily to her feet. 'I feel rather faint. In fact I…'

She did not have a very clear recollection of what happened next, although she had the vague impression that Miss Thurlow became exceedingly efficient, called a maid, paid their reckoning and summoned Bates with the gig.

'You will feel better in the fresh air,' Penny said. 'Are all the parcels loaded, Bates? Good. Drive steadily, we don't want to jolt Miss Williams. You just lean back and rest, Cressida, we will soon have you home.'

Cressida sat, eyes closed, and let herself be driven away, while all the time her stomach churned and her head spun.

No wonder Guy had been so adamant that her Uncle Charles must never cross their threshold. It had never occurred to her at the time to wonder how Guy had discovered so much to the man's discredit when he had been out of the country fighting.

I should have asked.

The family was used to Charles's bad character and none of them ever acknowledged him, let alone invited him into their homes, but generally the worst was hushed up. She had known from the beginning that Guy wanted nothing to do with Charles FitzWalden, but she had thought that had simply been because the man was a rake and a gambler, a black sheep. Now she realised that Guy had experienced his infamy first-hand, had discovered that the uncle of his bride-to-be had attempted to abduct his own cousin, the girl he loved like a sister, had left her bruised, shocked and bleeding.

Presumably, she reasoned, Guy had decided to go ahead with the marriage to her because Charles was only an uncle, someone who could be effectively barred from the house. But he *wasn't* only an uncle. If she had married Guy, then Charles FitzWalden would have been his father-in-law, perfectly positioned to extort money in exchange for keeping the secret of her birth quiet. If Guy hadn't shot him the first time he caught up with him.

He certainly had not been invited to the wedding and Cressida had believed he was in Ireland. He must have come back, or, knowing Charles, it had suddenly occurred to him that there was money to be made from her marriage and that had overcome the wisdom of getting himself as far away from Guy Thurlow as physically possible.

Everything was becoming clear, but reason and understanding were no help now. She had fallen in love with a man who had every reason to be disgusted by her origins and to despise her for keeping them secret from him. She had thought that the fact that she was the child of adultery was the important thing; the identity of her true father had seemed secondary. Now she knew that Guy would have accepted the truth about her birth, but that the identity of her true father was something he, surely, could never accept.

Cressida opened her eyes, blinked at the sudden light, the dusty green hedgerows bowling past. She could not pretend this was not real, she knew that now. There had been that ridiculous, fairy-tale dream at the back of her mind, that somehow this might come right. That Guy would declare his love was steadfast, deal, somehow, with Charles FitzWalden and marry her regardless. She would be Miss FitzWalden again, then the Countess of Easton and, one day, even Marchioness of Thornborough. And throughout it she would be with Guy, loving him, being loved, raising a family at Easton Court.

A fairy tale, indeed, and about as realistic as elves in the woods, talking foxes and pots of gold at the end of rainbows. The taste of salt filled her mouth and she swallowed hard. She would not cry, not again. Look where that had got her last time—into Guy's arms. And, besides, what explanation could she give Penelope for tears?

By the time they had arrived back in the market square she was outwardly calm and, apparently, looked sufficiently recovered for Penny not to argue when she asked to be set down there and not delivered to her own door.

'A little stroll will do me good,' she said. 'It is all downhill.'

It was not until she had waved Penny goodbye that she remembered the parcel of dress fabric in the gig. She rather thought that she had left all her future happiness there, too.

Chapter Twenty

A sleepless night left Cressida certain of one thing: she had to tell Guy her father's identity at once. There were still four days left of the week they had agreed, but it was pointless to abide by that if, when they met again, she had to confess to the truth about Charles FitzWalden. Best to do it now. And she had to face the fact that once she had told him, she could no longer remain at Stowe Easton. Matters between them had gone too far for that.

Cressida got up as soon as she heard Jane moving about in the kitchen. Then she wrote to her brother, informing him that she would be grateful if she could stay with him and Dorinda while she made plans for her future. She apologised for the short notice, but she would be with him shortly after he received her letter.

Over breakfast she told Marjorie that she was leaving. It was harder than she had feared. Her cousin was in tears, demanding to know how she had failed Cressida, sobbing that she would miss her terribly.

In the end Cressida was forced to tell her the whole truth, although she did not admit to having lost her virginity to Guy and she did not tell her the name of the close relative of his who had almost been abducted. The news about Charles stopped her tears in mid-breath.

'The swine! Oh, the beast, to have hurt that poor girl and to have committed adultery with his own brother's wife. And then to turn on you—why, if I could get my hands on him, I would geld him with the butter knife!'

When Cressida tried to say how sorry she was to have let Marjorie down after she had given her a home, had made her so welcome, her cousin stopped her in mid-flow.

'*None* of this is your fault. You fell in love with a man who is perfect for you and I could have wished for nothing more for you. It is all the fault of that lecherous, conscienceless rakehell. Of course you have to tell the Earl the truth and of course, after that, you cannot stay here. I have loved having you here, but I had a happy life before you came and I will again, however much I miss you. But you, Cressida dear— what will you do?'

'I cannot stay with Cedric and Dorinda for long because she would drive me to distraction, however fond I am of the children and my brother. But I am not without resources. With Cedric's help I will be able to find a pleasant home somewhere, far from here. I will employ a congenial companion and hope to be as happy in that community as you are here, Marjorie. And you will visit me, I hope?'

She managed an encouraging smile and her cousin,

who, despite giving way easily to her emotions, had a great deal of common sense and resolution, mopped her eyes and nodded firmly. 'Of course. I will put it about that your sister-in-law needs you urgently to help with the children. You need have no fear that anyone will think we have quarrelled, let alone that you are having to avoid the Earl.'

She put away her handkerchief and poured them both more tea. 'You will write to him?'

'No. I will tell Guy to his face. I owe him that,' Cressida said. He would think himself fortunate to have escaped such a match, she thought sadly. She was the product of adultery, the child of a man whose behaviour was infamous. Her inheritance was scandal, her breeding that which no gentleman would tolerate.

Once she was certain that Marjorie was recovered enough from the shock for her to leave, Cressida walked up the hill into the town. She paid for her letter at the receiving office, then went to the livery stables to order a chaise and pair for ten o'clock the next morning, and a pony and trap for a few hours that morning. Somehow she did not think she would be able to face the long walk back from the confrontation with Guy.

He was walking across the sweep of gravel in front of the Court when she saw him and reined in. Better to have this conversation here in the open, away from listening ears.

'Cressida!' He came striding towards her, his expression holding surprise and pleasure and—*Oh, my heart*—love. 'You have forgiven me? Believe me, I

knew I had been wrong to behave as I did the moment
you had gone.' He took the pony's bridle and began
to turn it. 'We will take this around to the stables and
then we can talk.'

'No. No, Guy, please. We must speak here, because
there is something I must tell you.'

She saw the happiness drain away from him as she
watched and a wary look come into his eyes. 'What
is wrong, my love?'

'I went with Miss Thurlow to Wellingbourn yes-
terday. She told me about the attempt to abduct her.
She told me the name of the man responsible. Charles
FitzWalden.'

'Oh, hell,' Guy said. He sounded weary. 'Of course.
Your uncle. Cressida, there is no need to be anxious
about that. Penny knew I was going to marry his niece
and she understood, was happy for me. She knew she
could not blame the entire family for one rotten apple
and that I would never allow him anywhere near her
again—or near my wife. She has grown very fond of
you and I know she would never hold it against you
when we tell her your true identity.'

It had to be now, before her courage failed her entirely. 'But you do not know my true identity,' she said
clearly, chin up, hands tight on the reins. 'I am not his
niece, I am his daughter. Charles FitzWalden's bas-
tard daughter.'

'What?'

'So, you see it is impossible,' Cressida said rapidly
into the silence that seemed to echo around them. 'You
might say you could overlook my irregular birth, that
you could deal with my true father if he tried to make

trouble for us, but I know what would happen if you encounter Charles. You will call him out, kill him, and then you will have to leave the country and there will be a terrible scandal. Or he will kill you. And even if you never meet him again, how can you ever forget who I am?'

'I never could forget who you are,' Guy echoed. He had gone very pale, his gaze fastened on her face as though he had never seen her before. 'What do you intend to do now?'

'Leave. This is impossible, I cannot live in the shadow of this house, your home. I should have gone long ago, when I first saw you that day in the church. I should have packed my bags and left and none of this would have happened.'

'That would have saved a great deal of pain,' Guy said, his voice cool. He looked like a man who had been shot and had not yet realised it, she thought as she fought the instinct to reach out and touch him.

What good would that do? It would not bring either of them comfort, that was certain. Cressida gathered the reins more firmly into her hands and clicked her tongue at the pony. 'Goodbye, Guy.'

Guy stood and watched as the little vehicle bowled across the carriage sweep. The pony was trotting briskly, but he could catch it if he ran… Then the moment passed and he stood there unmoving until the sound of hooves faded away. There was a glimpse of movement, a flash of blue through the trees, and then the little vehicle was gone.

'Guy? Was that Cressida?' Penny ran down the steps and came towards him, ringlets flying, skirts swishing.

She always seemed to be in motion, he thought blankly.

And she is happy, so she bounces with joy. Cressida is still, the calm centre of everything.

'Yes. That was Cressida.'

'But she has gone again.' Penny looked up at him, head tipped to one side. 'Guy, what is wrong?'

'She came to tell me who her father is,' he said.

'What?' Penny demanded inelegantly. 'Don't be silly, Guy. He was the late Viscount FitzWalden. Who is dead,' she added, as though he needed 'late' explaining.

'No. He is not.' There was a bench on the far side of the carriage sweep and he walked over to it, Penny pattering along beside him in her thin indoor shoes.

'Ouch. That was a stone. And this bench is all mossy.'

'It is dry,' he said indifferently and sat down.

'You are very strange today,' she complained. 'Give me a handkerchief.' When he found one she spread it out and sat beside him. 'Now, tell me.'

'The reason Cressida fled at the wedding was because someone came to her just before and informed her that he was her father.'

'Oh, no…' Penny breathed. 'And she has just told you about it?'

'No. She had told me that her father was not the man her mother was married to when we began to… When we became close. I told her I did not care, that I could deal with any gossip, with any attempt by the man to extort money, which was clearly his intent.'

'You didn't care?' She gave a little disbelieving snort. 'That is not like a Thurlow! So who was he?'

'I did not ask. She would tell me sooner or later—in fact, I stopped her once when she began to because there were other things more important.'

'You *must* be in love. Uncle Henry would have an apoplexy. And today she came and told you?'

'Yes. She had only just realised how very difficult—no, impossible—the man's identity made things.'

Penny tugged at his arm until he twisted around to look at her. 'Yesterday I told her my story,' she said. 'I told her how Charles FitzWalden tried to abduct me, and she fainted. Is *he* her father?'

No fool, my cousin, he thought and did not try to soften his answer. 'Yes, that is what he told her.'

'Charles FitzWalden had an affair with her mother—his own brother's wife?'

'When she told me that she was not the Viscount's daughter she said she did not know whether it was an affair, or whether her mother was forced.'

'How horrible. Oh, poor Cressida,' Penny said, her voice full of pity. 'Bad enough if it was an affair of the heart, but if it had been—' She broke off with a gulp, then recovered herself. 'And such a man. She must know better than anyone what sort of person he is.'

'She knows. And I had told her before the wedding, before he had spoken to her, that he was never to be admitted to our home, that she must have nothing to do with him. It was clear from her response that the family were all too well aware of his behaviour and that they all shunned him.'

'But until she realised how close he had come to us she must have thought that you would deal with him as you would any other person who tried to extort money from you,' Penny said, as though working it all out aloud. 'But I told her that when you rescued me you were going to call him out, that you said you would kill him.' Her grip on his arm tightened. 'Oh, Guy, I am so sorry.'

'How could you have known? And it is nothing but the truth. Cressida certainly believes that I meant it.'

'She wants to protect him? Surely not?'

'She wants to protect me from scandal, from having to go abroad to escape the consequences of a fatal duel, or of dying in that same duel,' he said, feeling sick now as reaction set in.

'I can imagine what Uncle Henry would say about the daughter of such a man marrying his heir,' Penny said with a visible shudder. 'Bad blood.'

'Bad blood,' Guy echoed. 'Do you know, a few weeks ago I would have agreed with that. Now, I do not know.' He shook his head, as though that might clear it. 'Or, yes. I do know and I should stop trying to deceive myself that this is something that can be remedied. When she first told me of her birth I should not have put my feelings above the family name, our honour.' They were both things that felt very hollow all of a sudden.

'But you *know* Cressida,' Penny protested, switching with mercurial swiftness from doubts to defence of Cressida. 'She is our friend. Have you ever seen, for

one instant, any sign that her character is anything but
honest and honourable? And Miss Pomfret is very respectable,' she added, her tone more thoughtful. 'And
all the ladies of the town like Cressida—I have never
heard the slightest word against her, never saw a dubious look in her direction.'

'Is character bred in the bone or the result of upbringing?' Guy wondered aloud. 'Her brother is a dull
stick, but a man of principle. There has never been any
slight on the rest of the family, just that one man and
he, by all accounts, was a scoundrel from his early
years.'

'You mean that upbringing trumps breeding, but
that neither upbringing nor breeding can prevent an
occasional rotten apple?' she asked, frowning over it.

'Yes, I think I do,' Guy said. 'I love her,' he added,
almost to himself. 'But I do not think I am blinded
by it.'

'Mr Graham says you are the best judge of character he knows,' Penny said, startling him.

'Arthur said that? When were you discussing me,
Penelope?'

'I was asking him how he came to be your steward
and he said that at first he didn't think he should accept, that he wasn't capable of it, but then he recalled
that he had always found your judgement was very
sound, so if you thought he could do it, then he probably could.' A smile that was almost cheeky lit up her
face. 'Don't you think you could trust your judgement
on something far more important than the appoint-
ment of a steward?'

When he did not answer the smile faded. 'Or is what

you think you owe to your ancestry and your bloodline more important? That is what your upbringing is
telling you, is it not?'

'Yes,' Guy said. He could hear his father's voice in
his head now; he could feel the surge of pride he had
always felt when he walked through the Long Gallery
with its rows of portraits or studied the family tree all
the way back to Alberic de Turloe, that Norman knight.

One rotten apple could ruin an entire barrel, but a
careful gardener could find it, remove it before it did
any damage to the whole. Applying horticultural wisdom to matters of marriage felt somewhat trite, he told
himself uneasily. Was he still blinded by his emotions
to the duty he owed to his name and flailing around to
find justification for doing what he wanted?

'I must think,' he said abruptly and stood up.

'I have heard Uncle Henry say, listen to your gut,'
Penelope said, standing, too, and linking her arm
through his. 'Disgusting expression.'

Guy nodded. He couldn't recall feeling any worse
inside, even when he had surveyed the bloody after-
math of battle. He was not going to listen to anything
his insides told him, not yet, he thought, consciously
settling his expression into the one of calm resolve he
had learned to adopt when leading men into danger.
He almost smiled when he realised he had straightened
his back, squared his shoulders. Almost.

'My cousin left an hour ago,' Marjorie Pomfret said
when she received him in her drawing room the next
morning. She was tight-lipped and her normally warm

and enthusiastic manner had been replaced by something closely resembling a block of ice.

Guy almost protested that leaving had been Cressida's decision, but he knew she had only done it to protect him and his family name. The least he could do was to absorb some of Miss Pomfret's displeasure.

'Might I ask her direction?'

'If Miss Williams wishes you to have it, then she will no doubt write to inform you of it.'

Yes, enough ice to freeze Gunter's famous ice creams for a month.

'In that case I will wish you good day, Miss Pomfret,' he said, answering chill with chill.

She tugged at the bell pull. 'Jane, show Lord Easton out. Good day, My Lord.'

He bowed and left, strode away up the hill. He was not going to stand uncertain on her doorstep and he could think as he walked. Cressida and Miss Pomfret did not possess a carriage and she could not have summoned one from her brother in the time available, he concluded.

The head groom at the stables was all too ready to oblige His Lordship. 'That's right, My Lord. A chaise and two for Northamptonshire this morning. I sent a very respectable postilion with her, seeing as how it was Miss Williams. Thank you, My Lord.' The man slipped the coin into his pocket and hurried off to fetch Blackjack.

Unless she was deliberately trying to put him off the scent, then Cressida had gone home to her brother, Guy thought as he pulled on his gloves. That was a relief; she would be safe there.

With that anxiety lifted he realised that now he was uncertain what to do next, or even what he wanted to do. Guy let his hands drop and Blackjack slowed to an amble, apparently in no mood for speed on a hot day.

Honour decreed that he had taken a lady's virginity and must therefore offer her marriage. He had done so and been refused. As a gentleman he should accept that, if it were not for the fact he knew perfectly well that her refusal was driven by her own sense of honour.

Family duty was another matter. It insisted that he marry a lady of virtue and excellent breeding and would dictate that he forgot Cressida. He knew what he wanted and he was certain in his heart that he knew what Cressida wanted, too. What he had to decide was whether he was justified in putting those emotions before family, tradition and what the head of the family— his proud, irascible, much-loved father—would expect of his heir.

The next morning Guy sat at his desk, drew a sheet of paper towards him and wrote,

Dear Miss FitzWalden,
I trust that you had a safe and easy journey.
I believe you will know the emotions of your friends in Stowe Easton on the occasion of your departure from their society.
I remain, yours to command,
Guy Thurlow

He took his time sanding it, folding it precisely and sealing it. He addressed it to *The Hon Miss V. C. Fitz-*

Walden at her brother's house, Walden Park, and set it to one side. Then he took another sheet and sat tapping the end of his quill against his lips while he thought.

After a few minutes Guy found his unfocused gaze had been resting on the family portrait over the fireplace. His father stood beside his mother's chair where she held John, a pouting toddler, on her knee. Guy stood beside her, his father's hand resting on his shoulder.

He must have been seven when it was painted. For the first time he really noticed how his father's eyes were fixed on him: not on his wife, not on his second son, but on his heir. The great ruby on his hand glowed with a life of its own, resting close to Guy's neck as though to brand him with the family crest. It was not a comfortable picture, for all its ordered domesticity, and he wondered why he had never noticed that before.

The *Peerage* lay beside him on the desk and he opened it, running his finger down the interminable lists of names and titles, waiting for them to speak to him. Then he closed the thick book, pushed it aside and began to write.

Twenty minutes later Arthur tapped on the door and came in. 'I just wanted to say, they have finished the dam and the cascade looks very fine.' He put some papers on the desk, glancing at the sheets covered in lists and diagrams in front of Guy. 'It looks as though you are drawing up battle plans and sketching strategic targets!'

Guy looked up and found the first genuine smile in what seemed like days was curving his mouth. 'I rather think that I am doing just that.'

Chapter Twenty-One

'I am going into Northampton this afternoon to visit Miss Henderson, my dressmaker,' Dorinda announced at breakfast, three days after Cressida's arrival at Walden Park. 'You won't mind looking after the children, will you, Viola dear? Only it is Nanny's half-day.'

Cressida put down her knife and fork and prepared to do battle with a smile. 'I'm afraid the nursery maids will have to manage, Dorinda. I intend riding over to the Vicarage to visit Prudence and Elizabeth after luncheon.'

'Riding?' her sister-in-law said sharply. 'Upon what, might I ask? I greatly dislike anyone mounting my own Maybelle and there may not be anything else suitable, given that you have been out of practice for so long, dear.'

'The stables are amply supplied with suitable mounts for Viola,' Cedric said, looking up from his scrutiny of *The Times* and, as usual, completely failing to notice the false smiles and acid sweetness of his female companions. 'She rides so well that a few months out of the saddle will hardly be a problem for her, I'm sure.'

As his wife was a reluctant and nervous rider this was not received by her with any signs of pleasure.

'The mail, My Lord.' The butler laid the salver at Cedric's right hand and waited while he sorted through it.

'Those for Her Ladyship, that for Miss FitzWalden,' he said eventually. 'Who is writing to you, Viola?'

Viola looked at the familiar bold black writing and then up at her brother. It had been years since anyone had thought fit to monitor her correspondence. 'A friend from Stowe Easton,' she said.

'No doubt you are sadly missed there,' Cedric said vaguely, his attention once more on the columns of political news.

'I still do not understand why you have left.' Dorinda was fretful. 'Have you quarrelled with Marjorie?'

'Certainly not.' Cressida laid her napkin over the letter to stop herself staring at Guy's writing. What did he want? 'I felt it was time for a change and I thought Yorkshire sounded pleasant. A small town like Richmond, perhaps.'

'Yorkshire?' said her sister-in-law, in much the same way as she would have responded if Cressida had said *Japan.*

'Yes. Or Kent, perhaps,' Cressida said composedly. 'I shall advertise for a companion and take a small house. Do excuse me, I must respond to this letter. The Vicar's wife at Stowe Easton is such a delightful

woman,' she added. If they chose to take that as referring to her correspondent, that was up to them.

She went to her room and looked thoughtfully at
the door key—Dorinda was quite capable of waltzing
in with barely a tap on the panels. On the other hand
a locked door would arouse her curiosity. As a pre-
caution she set out writing paper and took the stopper
from the ink bottle, then broke the seal on Guy's letter.

Yours to command?

She read the letter three times and was still puzzled
by the final words.

*What does that mean? That I will know his emo-
tions? I know what he says, I know how he looks when
he says it and I believe it hurts him for us to part, but
what am I to take from this?*

Guy was a gentleman, so of course he would write
to enquire about her journey, wish her well. But surely,
after the way they had parted, after what he had discovered about her parentage, that was all it could be?

Cressida folded the page, flattened the creases back
into place and slid it beneath the false bottom of her
writing case. If that note had meant to be helpful, it
had failed. If it had been intended to draw a line under
their relationship, then it had failed at that, too. Bother
the man! Wasn't it enough for him to have made her
fall in love with him? He could at least have had the
decency to behave badly and help her fall out again.

Feeling thoroughly miserable, and irrationally cross
with Guy, Dorinda, and the entire universe, Cressida
wrote to the employment agency, sealed it with a wafer
and went downstairs to find the *Northampton Mercury*,
which, she thought, should have the address among

its advertisements. Then she would find Cedric in his study and have a discussion about money. He was her trustee and, if she was to finance an entire house, a companion and a maid, then she would need rather more advanced from her investments than she had required living under Marjorie's roof.

I will manage alone, she told herself as she opened the newspaper. *I will. And some day it will begin to hurt less, surely?*

A month passed without any noticeable reduction in her heartache and no very great progress on her search for a new home. Cedric, while reluctantly agreeing that she was of age and entitled to the release of funds, and finally realising that his sister and his wife did not make for an easy household, still fussed and dithered over the question of a house. He insisted on taking over the search himself and could be found in his study muttering over house agents' reports, advertisements and solicitors' letters.

Dorinda assisted by securing recommendations for companions she considered suitable from all her friends and relations. She failed to understand why devout spinsters twice Cressida's age would not make congenial companions and tutted over Cressida's intention to find a lively young widow.

Cressida resorted to riding about the countryside, visiting old childhood friends and annoying Cedric's head gardener with what he referred to as, 'Miss Viola's crackpot modern ideas.'

There were no further letters from Guy, for which small mercy she told herself to be grateful, but long newsy ones came from Marjorie full of gossip that made her homesick for the little house on Church Hill. Marjorie carefully refrained from any mention of Easton Court and its inhabitants.

And then, six weeks after her flight, she came in from the stables to hear Dorinda talking to someone in the drawing room, her voice high-pitched with nerves.

'Er... My goodness, such a long time since we met, is it not? Not that one thinks about the circumstances— I mean, that is, would you care for another cup of tea?'

What on earth?

Cressida moved closer to the door, treading quietly in her boots and holding up the skirts of her riding habit so they did not swish on the wide boards.

'Thank you, no,' said a deep voice that seemed to resonate at the base of her spine.

Without stopping to think, she pushed open the door and walked in.

Guy stood up and executed a polite bow while still holding a teacup. 'Miss FitzWalden.'

Out of the corner of her eye she saw movement that must be her brother likewise rising. Dorinda gave a faint squeak and fell silent, the teapot in one hand.

'Lord Easton.' Cressida dropped a slight curtsy. 'What on earth—I mean, what a pleasant surprise. Are you passing though the district?' But nobody ever 'passed through' this quiet little corner of the county.

'No. I came to discuss a matter of business with you, Miss FitzWalden.'

'Business? Oh, you mean something to do with the designs for the park. There was no need for you to come so far—I would have been happy to advise by letter if you explained the problem.'

'Ah, but you see the scope of the problem is such that I need to discuss it with you face to face. Perhaps we could find somewhere else? I hesitate to keep your brother and Lady FitzWalden from their activities with my unannounced visit.'

'Yes, shall we go outside?' Cressida said, suddenly all too aware of Dorinda's avid expression. 'Such a lovely afternoon.' She turned to the door and Guy put down his cup.

'I will accompany you, Viola dear,' her sister-in-law said. 'Or ring for your maid.'

'Dorinda,' Cedric said sharply, in a tone that Cressida had never heard him use to his wife before. 'There is no need for that.'

Cressida dropped her whip and gloves on the hall table, drew out the long hatpin that secured her tricorne and veil and put them beside the gloves. 'The summer house, I think,' she said and, without looking at him, led the way through the flower room and out of the garden door. 'We can speak in privacy while sitting outside in full view of Dorinda, thus giving her no excuse to come and attempt to chaperon me.'

When they were seated facing each other on the miniature terrace in front of the ornate little building she put up her chin and braced herself. 'Well? This is not…helpful, Guy.'

'You have lost weight,' he said. 'It does not suit you.'

'Nor is that helpful either.'

'I have been worried about you.' When she did not answer, did not look at him, he said, 'What you told

me when we parted was a shock. I did not know what
to think, how to feel. I knew that most people would
say that in proposing to marry a lady of irregular birth
I was doing something shocking for a Thurlow, but I
had come to terms with that, I thought.'

'Guy—'

'Hear me out, please, Cressida. I had told myself I
could...*contain* the situation. Then when you told me
the name of the man who had claimed paternity I was
shaken out of all those ideas I had formed because I
was so in love with you that I had to have you, come
what may. I found I was facing marrying the daughter
of a man I had sworn to kill, someone who had tried
to ruin the life of someone very dear to me. Penny
still has the scars from his fingernails on her wrists,
you know.'

Cressida felt sick, but she found her voice and the
courage to look at him. 'There is no need to explain.
I knew that was the final straw, I knew you could not
possibly marry Charles FitzWalden's daughter.'

'So I thought,' Guy said, smiling at her as though
they had agreed amicably on some minor matter. 'But
then I began to think, which was difficult at first, because I was hurting a great deal. I expect you can understand that.'

'Yes,' she agreed.

'I had many things to get straight in my mind—the
duty to my name and family and the standards that
had been inculcated in me since childhood. The fact
that Charles FitzWalden is the scum of the earth. The
knowledge that there was no one else I could imagine
being the mother of my children, other than you.' He

broke off when she made a little choking sound and smiled again, this time with a tenderness that brought the tears to her eyes.

'In fact, I could see no one else being mistress of Easton Court, being Lady Easton, one day the Marchioness of Thornborough. I love you and I know your character, your intelligence, your quality. I also knew that Charles FitzWalden was a liar, an opportunist with neither scruple nor conscience. It seemed to me entirely possible that he lied to you that day.'

'How can we ever know?' It had never occurred to her that Charles had not spoken the truth; the idea of such a foul thing was, even now, impossible to grasp.

'It seemed to me that his assertion had never been tested and it was high time it was. Do you love me still?' He waited, patient and unmoving with that faint half-smile on his lips. The man she had given her heart to.

'You know I do and I believe you love me. But what I do *not* believe is that love conquers all, that if we only have love then everything will be possible.' Surely he understood? 'It is *not* possible and pretending that is not the case is cruel, Guy.' When he did not reply she tried again. 'If we marry, then we hurt too many people.'

'Did you really believe that I would stand by and allow Charles FitzWalden to ruin our lives, Cressida?'

'What have you done?' She stared at him in horror. 'A duel?' Guy shook his head. 'Guy, you haven't had him…' Her voice trailed away, the word *murdered* too frightful to speak. What couldn't the heir to a marquess pay to have done if he so wished it?

'Disposed of?' The smile was wry now. 'No, I am not an assassin. I can employ agents, specialists, when I have to. But not killers, Cressida.'

Guy leant forward and caught her hands in his. 'You once told me that you were a healthy baby, quite a weight, the proud boast of your grandmamas.'

'Yes?'

'A full-term child in other words. The first specialists I consulted were midwives and *accoucheurs*. For you to have been born full-term on August the twenty-eighth, in the year 1791, then you were conceived somewhere between the thirteenth and the twenty-eighth of November 1790.'

She supposed he was correct if he had asked experts in childbirth. 'Yes?'

'Given normal human reproduction, the father is required to be present at conception, you will agree? Therefore, I have set my best agent to discovering just where Charles was between those dates. I have his report here.' He drew a fat wrapper of papers from his breast pocket and dropped it on the table beside them.

'What… What did he discover?'

'I have no idea,' Guy said. 'I have not opened it.' He flipped the packet over with one finger and she stared down at the large red seal, quite unbroken. 'Because you see, I have come to realise that I do not care what that report tells us. Oh, of course I hope that Charles FitzWalden is not your father. Who would want him? And you could stop worrying about your mother's part in this.'

'You do not care?' She stared at him. 'You mean you want to marry me regardless of this?'

'Yes. I weighed up the fact of our happiness, of the future of my family, against rigid rules and prejudices. I discovered I did not believe in bad blood, only in bad character. If it turns out that Charles is the grandfather of our children they will not turn out like him, because you will be their mother and we will raise them to be decent human beings.'

'My father and Charles were raised together,' she said, stubbornly refusing to believe what she was hearing. The pain when Guy realised the impossibility of them ever being together was too great to contemplate.

'Every family has occasional black sheep—it just happens, one of life's tragedies. But Charles did not inherit his behaviour, did he? From all I hear your grandparents were pillars of society—and their parents, too.'

'Your father will be furious. What if he disowns you, Guy?' Despite her best efforts a faint whisper of hope began to stir like a warm summer breeze on her chilled hopes.

'He cannot. I am his heir,' he said simply and took her hands in his. 'I would be very sorry to displease him, but he will come around. If Charles is your father, then we will deal with it and I promise you I will neither kill him, nor set anyone to do so. I'll not have the blood of our children's grandfather on my hands. I cannot promise that I will not make life decidedly unpleasant for him, though.'

Cressida drew a deep breath, found she was unable to speak and simply raised her hands, bringing his with them to her lips.

'You will marry me, Cressida? Whatever is in that report?' And now it was Guy's voice that broke.

'Yes,' she said with the sensation of hurling herself from a high place into space. 'Yes. I love you.'

Then she was in his arms and they were kissing. Guy stood, pulling her with him, sending the chairs toppling, but still he did not let her go and her arms were so tight around his neck it would have been impossible anyway, she thought. She had leapt into the void and a whirlwind had caught her, swept her up, would hold her safe for the rest of her days.

How long they kissed she never knew but, finally, Guy lifted his head and stood with her still tight against him, his cheek on the crown of her head as he murmured sweet nonsense into her hair.

They might have stood there until dusk fell if it were not for the shriek from the terrace. Cressida twisted around to look and saw Dorinda sweeping down the steps to the lawn. Her brother appeared behind his wife, running down after her.

'Oh, Lord,' Guy said. 'Now we're for it. I don't suppose the news we are going to be married will quieten Lady FitzWalden, will it?'

'I doubt it,' Cressida said.

But even as she spoke, Cedric caught up with Dorinda, took her by the arm and marched her back into the house.

'Well,' Guy said. 'It appears I have no need to ask your brother's permission to address you.'

'I rather think it is too late for that, my love.'

Chapter Twenty-Two

'**S**hould we open that report?' Cressida said when they had set the chairs upright, themselves in order, and had managed to stop kissing.

'Are you sure?'

'We can't deal with him until we know the truth, can we?'

'Wise woman.' Guy broke the seal and flattened out the pages. 'William Brent is writing from Scotland. I sent him there because, when I investigated myself, I found that Charles has a quite substantial Scottish estate left to him by his godfather, but none of the scandals I had heard about him were from Scotland. It seemed that he was avoiding the country, which seemed significant.

'The social life in Edinburgh is sophisticated and full, an attraction to a man who likes the good life as much as your uncle. And he has a fine property to boast of to enhance his chances of acceptance into local society. It is exactly the city to offer a refuge when life in London got too hot for comfort, as it frequently does for Charles FitzWalden, and yet he avoided it. That merited investigation.'

He read on, turned the page, gave an exclamation and turned back.

'Tell me!'

'Charles FitzWalden was languishing in Edinburgh's Tollbooth, its debtors' prison, from mid-November until almost Christmas of the year seventeen ninety. He had been living the high life in the city for the past several months, on credit, Brent writes. That might have gone on for longer if it were not for the fact that he made insulting remarks about the Provost's daughter, implying that she was less than modest in her behaviour. Not a prudent thing to do if the Provost, a powerful man, is also a merchant to whom you owe considerable sums of money.'

'Your man is certain? Until Christmas? Then Charles cannot have been my father.' Cressida could hardly take that in. 'It is impossible. It must be. Oh, my goodness.'

It was hard to comprehend that the dark secret she had held like a poisonous spider close to her heart for all this time was a lie. 'But why? Why tell me such a spiteful lie on my wedding morning?' She still could not quite believe that she was free.

Guy read through to the end, then folded the report. 'There is nothing further, just notes on his sources. Why did Charles FitzWalden do it? Extortion, pure and simple, I imagine. He must have been searching for a way to take advantage of the match you were about to make and, possibly, to take some revenge on me for foiling his attempt on Penny.

'You were young and he put you in a position where you could tell no one—your parents were dead, your brother had no way of knowing the truth and to confide outside the family risked scandal and ruin. He expected to have years of extracting money from you.'

When she shuddered he broke off and caught her into his arms again. 'His mistake was in his timing and in his misreading of your character. If he had waited until the knot was tied, then he had you in his trap. But you were too honourable for him. You fled, unmarried, ruining yourself, but protecting everybody else—your brother and the rest of the family from scandal, me from an unseen leech.'

'But my father,' she said, blushing. There really were things one didn't want to even think about in connection with one's parents. 'He said my father couldn't...wasn't...'

'Ah. That was one part of the investigation I could carry out myself without proving or disproving the central allegation. You know Lady Clevedon?'

'I think so. Vaguely. Improbable blonde wigs and an, um, lavish figure?'

'Twenty-odd years ago Deborah Clevedon was a formidable beauty. She was also your father's mistress. And she assured me—with one hand firmly on my thigh, I might add—that your father was as virile a lover as a naughty widow might desire.'

Despite everything, Cressida could not hold back the giggle. 'That was so brave of you! Did you escape with your virtue intact?'

'I did. I leapt to my feet, apparently so excited by the news that I could not sit still. I did not tell her the real reason why I was asking, of course. I confided that there was a question of whether a young man might be a by-blow of your father's, but that I had heard it was highly unlikely because of his, er, incapacity.'

'Oh, Guy, *thank* you.' She was on her feet and so was he, the chair thrown impatiently aside again so he could kiss her properly. 'How can I ever thank you enough? It was a nightmare.'

'I acted out of pure selfishness,' he said, looking down into her upturned face.

For a moment she could not breathe for pure happiness, then, like a douche of cold water his own words came back to her. 'But how can I marry you? You said it yourself just now—I ran away and ruined myself.'

'That is easily dealt with. We can demonstrate that you were living in the utmost respectability the entire time with firstly your great-uncle and then your cousin, and the reason that you fled was entirely my fault.'

'It was?'

'You had heard highly coloured rumours about a certain Spanish lady of great beauty and easy morals. On being charged with the matter I had refused to discuss it, but you had been left with the strong impression that the liaison would continue the moment I returned to the Peninsula. Naturally, being a young lady of unimpeachable virtue yourself, you could not tolerate such infidelity.'

'Guy, that is truly noble of you!' She caught the faintest trace of a smug look. 'Was there a Spanish beauty?' she demanded.

'Er, yes. But we had parted before I came home to be married, I promise you.'

'Indeed? And when you returned to Spain, very much unmarried?' Guy's eyes narrowed and she laughed. 'No, do not tell me. I do not wish to know. I could hardly expect you to live like a monk because I had shunned you, could I? As long as there is nobody else now.'

'Upon my honour. Only you. Now and for ever, Cressida.'

Chapter Twenty-Three

The chapel of Easton Court, Stowe Easton, Hampshire—October 1814

The bride was late.

Unmoved, Captain Guy Thurlow, Earl of Easton, continued his study of the newly repaired stonework behind the altar, pale against the old grey blocks. Brides were always late; at least, that had been his experience of this one.

At his side Arthur stirred uneasily. In two weeks it would be his turn to stand here and he was suffering a severe case of pre-nuptial nerves and would probably have found this easier if they had both still been in uniform—that, at least, helped stiffen the spine.

Behind him there was a low murmur from the wedding guests. There were not even half as many as had filled Stowe Easton's parish church five years ago, but this was more than enough in Guy's opinion. He did not need more than his bride and two witnesses. And the Vicar, of course.

The FitzWalden clan was there in force with one exception. Charles was in Dublin where William Brent had tracked him down to deliver a letter from Guy explaining how, if Charles was expecting a long life with all parts of his anatomy in place, he would do well to remain out of England. It had been accompanied by one from Lord FitzWalden in which Cedric detailed the steps he had taken to ensure not a penny of family funds ever reached his uncle again. The only reply had been, Brent reported, too offensive to repeat.

The organist changed his vague twiddling into something considerably more definite and the murmurs became a hum of anticipation. The bride was coming.

Guy counted the footsteps striking the flagstones as Cedric FitzWalden escorted his sister up the short aisle. Guy had paced it himself only that morning and he knew when to turn.

Cressida wore a gown of primrose silk that was fashionable, elegant and which showed off her supple figure to perfection. Guy's mouth went dry.

The drifting veil of ivory gauze was modest, but gave glimpses of dark brown hair, the pale oval of her face, the glimmer of pearls and the sparkle of blue eyes.

She reached his side and Cedric placed her hand in his and stepped aside. The slender fingers resting on his palm were cool and steady.

A waft of perfume rose to his nostrils, the scent of the roses mingling with something warmer and more herbal from his bride's skin, the scent that had teased his memory on every occasion he had been close to

Cressida. His fingers tightened on hers and she glanced up at his face. He thought she smiled.

The Vicar cleared his throat. 'Dearly beloved, we are gathered together...'

'...can show any just cause why they may not be lawfully joined together let him now speak, or else hereafter for ever hold his peace.'

Mr Truscott did not have the same thespian instincts as the previous Vicar. He spoke the words, then glanced swiftly around. Cressida gave a soft laugh and Guy felt the flutter of her pulse against his.

In the silence the Vicar fixed his gaze on Guy. 'Guy Francis Almeric de Lisle Thurlow, wilt thou have this woman...'

The organ pealed out as the Earl and Countess of Easton walked down the aisle, Lord FitzWalden behind them with Miss Penelope Thurlow, bridesmaid, on his arm, followed by Mr Graham with Miss Hobhouse, the other attendant and his betrothed, on his.

Guy was conscious of their presence, of the smiling faces turned to watch their progress, but only as a blurred background. All he could see, in focus, was Cressida at his side.

They stepped out into the sunshine and a blizzard of rice and rose petals thrown by staff and tenants gathered at the door. He caught Cressida's hand more tightly. 'Run!'

'Again?' she said with a laugh and, gathering up her long skirts, ran with him, as fast as she had done that day she had fled from him, veil flying.

The chapel stood in a grove of oaks to one side of the front carriage drive. They reached the foot of the steps and he scooped her up in his arms, took the curving flight two at a time and arrived at the great double doors as they swung open.

'Welcome home, My Lord, My Lady,' Herring said as he stepped aside.

'Guy?' Cressida said breathlessly, then, 'Guy!' as he went straight up the stairs. 'Guy, there is no *time*.' But she was laughing now as he shouldered open the door to his bedchamber and carried her in.

'There is always time to kiss my wife,' he said as he set her on her feet, 'Even if there is none just now for what I really want to do, which is show you just how much I love you.'

Cressida had turned a very pretty pink and was gazing fixedly at the sapphire pin in his neckcloth. 'No?' she murmured.

'No,' he said firmly, willing his unruly body to behave. 'I don't say I couldn't… But I need time to show you properly. I intend to worship every inch of your body. I plan to turn you into quicksilver in my arms. I—'

'Kiss me,' she ordered, looking up, still pink-cheeked, but confident now. 'Or this dress comes off this minute and I defy you to resist what I will do then.'

Guy swallowed, severely tempted by the thought of being ravished by his almost-innocent wife. Then the hum of voices from the hallway rose up to remind him of their guests, of the dignity he owed his new Countess when he presented her to them.

'One kiss,' he said as his lips met hers and Cressida rose on tiptoe to twine her arms around his neck.

Reluctantly he lifted his head, the taste of her tingling on his lips like vintage champagne.

'One is enough,' Cressida said and he saw her eyes were swimming with tears. 'Your vow, your kiss, your love—everything follows from those three things and I will build the rest of my life on them.'

For one perilous moment his own vision blurred and he had to swallow hard before he could speak steadily. 'We will build a family and a future and, although it does not seem possible that I can love you more than I do now, I think that, too, will grow, day after day.'

'I am glad I ran away all those years ago,' Cressida said as she settled her veil back tidily and slipped her hand into the crook of his arm. 'We were too young for each other, we didn't know who we were.'

'And you do now?' Guy asked as they reached the head of the stairs and looked down at the smiling faces below them.

'Oh, yes. I am Cressida Easton and the happiest woman in England,' said his Countess. 'Shall we begin?'

* * * * *

*If you enjoyed this story, why not check out
Louise Allen's Liberated Ladies miniseries?*